W9-BRD-945

POISON

AN 87TH PRECINCT NOVEL

Ed McBain

AVON BOOKS ◢ NEW YORK

The city in these pages is imaginary.
The people, the places are all fictitious.
Only the police routine is based on
established investigatory technique.

AVON BOOKS
A division of
The Hearst Corporation
105 Madison Avenue
New York, New York 10016

Copyright © 1987 by HUI Corporation
Published by arrangement with Arbor House Publishing Company
Library of Congress Catalog Card Number: 86-17342
ISBN: 0-380-70030-1

First Avon Books Printing: January 1988

AVON TRADEMARK REG. U.S. PAT. OFF. AND IN OTHER COUNTRIES, MARCA
REGISTRADA, HECHO EN U.S.A.

Printed in the U.S.A.

K-R   10 9 8   7   6   5   4

This is for
STANLEY MACHENBERG

1

"THIS IS SOME MESS IN HERE," MONOGHAN said.

"This is some stink in here," Monroe said.

The two Homicide detectives peered cautiously at the dead body on the carpet, and then circled around Hal Willis, who was also looking down at the corpse, hands on his hips. It was pretty easy to maneuver around Willis, as small as he was. Monoghan and Monroe, built like mastodons themselves, were both thinking they would not like to be partnered with any detective as small as Willis, a thin, wiry squirt who barely would have passed the five-foot-eight height requirement back in the old days, although nowadays you could be the size of a fire hydrant and you couldn't be discriminated against because of fair-hiring practices. You got some cops in this city, you could fit them in your vest pocket.

Monoghan and Monroe were both wearing dark suits with vests. They were wearing dark overcoats and dark fedoras. Their faces were ruddy from the bitter March cold outside. They were both holding handkerchiefs to their noses because of the stench of vomit and fecal matter in the apartment. It was difficult to take a step in here without putting your foot in a pile of vomit or shit. It was difficult to keep from vomiting yourself, in fact. Monoghan and Monroe hated sloppy cases. They preferred good old-fashioned stabbings or shootings. The place also stank of stale cigar smoke. There were butts in all the ashtrays, the victim must've smoked like a chimney.

The victim was lying alongside the bed, on his back, in his own vomit and shit. He was wearing only undershorts. The phone receiver was off the hook. Probably been trying to call somebody when he cashed in, Monroe figured. Either that, or he knocked the receiver off the hook when he collapsed. His blue eyes were wide open, the pupils dilated. His face was extremely pale. The assistant medical examiner was kneeling over him, feeling his hands for body warmth. He didn't seem any happier than anyone else in the room. Maybe even *more* unhappy in that he was closest to the body and its various excreted and re-gurgitated fluids. Two techs from the Photo Unit were busy taking their polaroids of the crime scene. Monoghan and Monroe, like a couple of softshoe dancers, took several steps backward, away from the corpse. They still had the handkerchiefs to their noses.

"Last time I saw something like this," Monoghan said, "this mess here, we had an old lady fell in the bathtub, starved to death there in the bathtub. There was shit all over the bathtub, the 911 boys had to scoop her out with a shovel."

"That was a disgusting case," Monroe said.

The assistant M.E. said nothing. He was thinking this one was pretty disgusting, too. He was wondering why he hadn't stayed in private practice out on Sands Spit. Frank O'Neill, M.D. He could still see the shingle in his mind, the neat white clapboard building behind it. Instead, this. Early Monday morning and a dead man lying in his own filth.

"So what do you think?" Willis asked.

"Poisoning?" O'Neill said, shrugging.

"Or maybe a heart attack," Monroe said.

"They drag us out the crack of dawn, some guy had a heart attack," Monoghan said.

"No, it wasn't a heart attack," O'Neill said.

It wasn't the crack of dawn, either. It was 9:20 A.M. by the victim's bedside clock. This was the first squeal Willis and Carella had caught today, an excellent way to start the week. Carella hadn't said much since he'd got here with Willis. The victim's cleaning lady had called the police when she came into the apartment to find her employer lying beside the bed in his own mess. The responding blues had phoned back to the Eight-Seven with a corpse. Carella and Willis had informed Homicide because at first glance and smell it didn't look like death from natural causes. In this city, homicides and suicides were investigated in exactly the same manner, and the appearance of

Homicide detectives at the scene was mandatory, even though the case officially belonged to the precinct detectives. Carella still wasn't saying anything.

He was a tall man with dark hair and brown eyes slanted slightly downward, giving his face a somewhat Oriental cast. Monroe guessed Carella had played high school baseball; he looked like a ballplayer, moved like one, too. Monroe liked him somewhat better—but not much—than most of the cops at the Eight-Seven. The bulls up here took things too serious. Carella had a very serious look on his face now, an almost pained expression, as he stared down at the dead man on the carpet.

"So what do we say under cause?" Monoghan asked. "Poisoning?"

"Cause unknown," O'Neill said. "Until we do the autopsy."

"Cause is throwing up and shitting his pants," Monroe said, laughing.

"Cause is lack of toilet training," Monoghan said, laughing with him.

"Any idea when he died?" Willis asked.

"Not until autopsy," O'Neill said, and snapped his satchel shut. "Enjoy yourselves, lads," he said pleasantly, and started out of the room.

The black woman who'd discovered the body was clearly frightened. She had never had trouble with the police in her entire life, and she believed she had plenty of trouble now. None of it her doing, neither. She sat in a chair across the room watching the huddle of law enforcement officers around the body. Flashbulbs were popping everywhere. People with all kinds of equipment were going all over the room doing things. As the doctor—she guessed he was a doctor, he had a satchel—went out of the room, somebody said, "You through here?" and he nodded and waved his hand in dismissal. Somebody else began sprinkling some kind of powder around the body, outlining it.

"Try not to step in the shit," Monoghan said. "It may be evidence."

It was, in fact, evidence. The techs would be scooping it up, together with the vomit, for delivery to the lab on High Street. It was a messy case all around.

"You don't need us anymore, we'll be breezing along," Monroe said.

"You could maybe open some windows when the techs get through dusting," Monoghan offered.

Both men shrugged, put away their handkerchiefs and started for the door, passing a pair of 911 cops who came in with a stretcher, a rubber sheet, and a body bag.

"You got your work cut out for you," Monoghan said, and walked out.

They were through interrogating the cleaning lady in five minutes flat, convinced that her role in this was entirely innocent and in fact praiseworthy; she had discovered a dead body and had immediately called the police. During the course of the interview, she had identified her employer as Jerome McKennon; now as the tech boys went around the room dusting for latent fingerprints, vacuuming for hairs and fibers, collecting the noisome body fluids on the rug, Willis and Carella began searching for evidence to corroborate the identification.

On the dresser opposite the bed, they found a wallet, a key ring, a comb and a handful of change. The wallet contained two fifty-dollar bills, a twenty, a five, and three singles. It also contained several credit cards and a driver's license which indeed identified the dead man as Jerome Edward McKennon. They searched the pockets of all the clothing hanging in the closet and found only a small penknife in the righthand pocket of one of the sports jackets. They searched all the dresser drawers. There were no empty medicine bottles anywhere in the bedroom.

In the several drawers of a desk in a small study off the master bedroom, they found checkbooks imprinted with the name JEROME EDWARD McKENNON and the address here on Silvermine Oval, plus stationery with the name, address and telephone number. There seemed no doubt that the man who'd been carried out of the apartment in a body bag was Jerome Edward McKennon. They also found, in the top drawer of the desk, a personal telephone directory which they leafed through cursorily and then pocketed for further study back at the precinct.

In the bathroom cabinet, they found several bottles with

prescription drugs in them, none of which—judging from the descriptions on the labels—appeared deadly; they nonetheless bagged them for transfer to the lab.

They searched every drawer in the house and found no other medicines or drugs. They searched the kitchen cabinets for any insecticides or other household products that might contain poison. They found only a cockroach aerosol spray, but the plastic ring-seal on the can was unbroken.

"If he poisoned himself," Willis said, "what'd he use?"

In the bedroom, the techs were still busy.

"You finished with this phone here?" Carella asked.

"Yeah" one of the techs said, and Carella picked up the receiver.

"Who you calling, Steve?" Willis asked.

"M.E.'s Office. I want a fast comeback on this one." He hesitated a moment, looking at the base of the phone. "Redial feature on it," he said.

"Try it," Willis said.

Carella pressed the redial button. A dial tone, and then the phone began dialing out. One ring, two, three . . .

"Hi, this . . ."

"Hello . . ."

". . . is Marilyn, I'm out just now . . ."

"Answering machine," he said to Willis.

". . . but if you'll leave your name and number and the time you called, I'll get back to you as soon as I can. Please wait for the beep."

Carella waited for the beep, identified himself as a police detective, and asked her to call 377-8024, the number at the squadroom.

"Any name?" Willis said.

"Just Marilyn."

"Did she give the number there?"

"No."

"Any batteries in that thing?"

Carella turned over the phone and opened the battery compartment.

"Yes," he said.

"Then we better unplug it and take it with us," Willis said.

* * *

Before they left the building, they knocked on every door. This was boring, an essential part of investigative routine that numbed the brain. Half of the tenants they questioned didn't even know McKennon, which was not surprising for this city. None of them knew what line of work he was in. None of them had seen anyone entering his apartment either last night or this morning. The super told them that McKennon had been living there for almost a year now, an ideal tenant, never any complaints about him. They got back to the squadroom at a little before three, carrying with them McKennon's telephone and his personal directory. There was no one named Marilyn in that directory. Either he'd known her number by heart or hadn't thought she was important enough to list.

Most women in this city listed only their surnames and initials in the phone company's directory, hoping this would discourage obscene callers. This was no guarantee that the heavy breathers would be fooled; some of them looked specifically for surnames with initials. But Marilyn Who*ever* had positively identified herself as a woman living alone by saying *"I'll* get back to you." And to make matters worse, she had said, "I'm out just now," which for any enterprising burglar was a signal to run on over there and loot the joint.

In this city, she'd have been better off saying, "Hi, you've reached 846-0318. If you'll leave a message when you hear the beep . . ." and so on. A no-frills recording, unreadable for clues by obscene caller or burglar. No name. Just the phone number, which the caller would have known anyway, even if he was just running his finger down a page in the directory. No explanation for not coming to the phone. Leave the potential burglar to dope out whether the apartment's occupant or occupants were in the bathtub or asleep; the one thing any burglar dreaded was walking into an occupied apartment.

The detectives wished Marilyn had recorded her phone number, but she hadn't. As it was, all they had now was an unknown number buried in the phone they had taken from McKennon's apartment. If the call had been made to a local number, the phone company would have no record of it. On the off chance that it might have been a long-distance call, Carella spoke to a phone-company supervisor and discovered they had no record of any long-distance calls made from Jerome McKennon's apartment since March 13, eleven days ago. It seemed unlikely that this had been the last phone call McKennon had made—or tried to make. They tried the number, anyway, and reached a mail-order menswear company in California.

Willis had asked at once if there were any batteries in the unit because he thought taking the phone off the Jack might automatically cancel whatever was in its memory; some of these new-fangled phones were very finicky and the batteries were preservation insurance.

They were dealing here with semi-sophisticated machines. McKennon's phone would automatically redial the last number called when you pushed the little REDIAL button on its base. Marilyn's telephone had an answering machine attachment, which meant that anyone calling got a prerecorded message when the machine was in its AN-SWER mode.

The detectives had no doubt that the wizards at the lab downtown could retrieve Marilyn's number from the memory bank of McKennon's phone—but lab responses sometimes took weeks. Instead, they opted for an approach that was the equivalent of good old-fashioned legwork.

In the Clerical Office, they plugged in McKennon's phone and asked for a twenty-four-hour redial surveillance. The instructions to the clerk were to keep hitting the redial button until Marilyn herself, and not her machine, picked up. Under no circumstances was anyone to use that phone for any other calls that would wipe out the memory of the last call made by McKennon. The clerk wasn't too happy to inherit this job. Alf Miscolo, who ran the Clerical Office, wasn't too happy, either.

He was not normally a testy person. But he was trying to catch up on two weeks of filing, and there was an angry scowl on his face now. Wearing a sleeveless blue sweater over his uniform shirt and trousers, dark-eyed with a massive nose and bushy eyebrows, thick neck giving the impression of sitting directly on his shoulders, he looked almost menacing.

"We got plenty to keep us busy in here without having to do *your* work besides," he muttered, and glared malevolently at the telephone intruder.

"In here" was a small cluttered room on the second floor of the old building on Grover Avenue. The aroma of percolating coffee permeated the room. None of the detectives enjoyed Miscolo's experimental brews, but he kept the pot going day and night anyway, mixing Colombian with Viennese, decaff with regular. The detectives always asked him if he was a mad scientist searching for a potion that would keep him eternally young. Miscolo told them to go fuck themselves.

The coffee aroma drifted out of the open door, following the detectives down the corridor to the squadroom, where Carella immediately placed a call to the Medical Examiner's Office. When he hung up, he said, "They'll do their best."

"Which means by next Christmas," Willis said sourly.

He was wrong.

At twenty to four that afternoon, just as the shift was about to change, Paul Blaney called.

"How's this for service?" he said.

"What've you got?" Carella asked.

"And it wasn't easy, believe me," Blaney said.

Carella said nothing. Better to let Blaney do it in his own sweet time.

"Tough poison to recover," Blaney said.

Carella waited.

"The tobacco odor was the tip-off," Blaney said. "Though you don't always get that."

From where he sat at his desk, Willis raised his eyebrows questioningly. Carella shrugged. Across the room, Meyer was pushing his way through the gate in the slatted rail divider. He was wearing a short coat with a fake fur collar, a woolen watch cap pulled down over his bald head. "This is March?" he asked, blowing on his hands. "This is a week before Easter?"

On the phone, Blaney said, "Congestion and acute inflammation of the stomach and intestines. Indicates the poison was taken by mouth. *All* the organs congested, blood very dark, very fluid. I ran tests on the stomach contents, viscera and brain. Color reactions on the recovered samples were positive. Yellow with slight orange cast for the nitrosylsulfuric acid. Yellow with brown cast for the concentrated sulfuric acid, no change on the Erdmann's or the Mecke's, pale orange with a brown cast on the Marquis' reagent. Wine-red on the Janovksy, magenta on the paradimethyl . . . well, you don't need to know all the color tests. I also got huge yellow crystals with the platinum chloride reagent, and an amorphous precipitation with the gold chloride. I'm pretty certain I've nailed it down.''

''What was the poison?'' Carella asked.

''Nicotine,'' Blaney said.

Across the room, Meyer was lighting a cigarette even before he took off his hat and coat.

''Nicotine?'' Carella said.

''Yeah,'' Blaney said. He sounded pleased. Carella could visualize him smiling. ''Deadly poison,'' he said. ''Couldn't have been a very pleasant death, either. Hot burning sensation in the upper digestive tract from the mouth to the stomach. Salivation, nausea, vomiting, diarrhea, pain in the abdomen. Faintness, prostration, falling blood pressure, convulsions and then respiratory paralysis. Makes you want to quit smoking, doesn't it?''

''I don't smoke,'' Carella said, and looked across the room to where Meyer was puffing like a locomotive. ''What's the fatal dose?''

''Depends on your source. Forty milligrams is usually cited as the minimum.''

''How fast does it work?''

''The only thing faster is hydrocyanic acid.''

''And how fast is that?''

''Cyanide can kill you in minutes. Seconds sometimes.''

''And nicotine?''

''Convulsions within seconds, death within minutes. You looking for a post-mortem interval?''

''It would help.''

''Everything else considered—body heat, lividity, stomach contents and so on—I'd say you have a relatively fresh corpse here.''

"How fresh?"

"Sometime early this morning."

"How early?"

"He died at seven-twenty-four A.M.," Blaney said. "Actually, seven-twenty-four and thirty-six seconds."

For a moment, Carella thought he was serious.

"Give me a break, willya?" Blaney said. "Sometime early this morning is as far as I'll go."

"And it was taken by mouth, huh?"

"No question."

"At least forty milligrams."

"Forty would do it. Sixty would do it even better. Ninety would be better yet."

"What's forty milligrams?" Carella asked. "Like a tea-spoonful?"

"Are you kidding? We're talking about a *taste.*"

"That powerful, huh?"

"It's a class-6 drug. Supertoxic."

"Well, thanks," Carella said, "I appreciate this. When will I have the paperwork?"

"Will you need a dental chart on this one? I understand you already have a positive ID."

"It wouldn't hurt."

"Give me a couple of days, okay? You're not desperate for the paper, are you?"

"Not if I can go with nicotine."

"You've got my word," Blaney said.

"Okay, thanks again."

"Talk to you," Blaney said.

Carella put the receiver back on the cradle. Cotton Hawes was just coming into the squadroom. His face was red from the cold outside. Together with his red hair, it gave him a fiery appearance rescued only by the white streak of hair over his right temple. He glanced immediately at the clock and mumbled, "Sorry I'm late."

Willis came over to Carella's desk.

"What've we got?" he asked.

"Nicotine," Carella said.

"Don't *you* start on me, okay?" Meyer said, walking over. "That's all I hear from Sarah day and night. Nicotine, nicotine, nicotine."

"We caught a homicide this morning," Carella said. "Guy was poisoned with nicotine."

"Lay off, willya?" Meyer said.

"You ought to quit," Hawes said.

"I *did* quit. Five times already."

"We've got a twenty-four-hour watch on a phone in the Clerical Office," Carella said. "Don't anybody use it."

"What do you mean?" Hawes asked.

"Just don't use the phone in there," Willis said.

"What'd the guy do?" Meyer asked. "Eat some cigar butts?"

From the slatted rail divider, Miscolo said, "We got a lady on your phone."

2

BY THE TIME THEY GOT DOWN THE HALL TO THE
Clerical Office, she was gone.

"I told her to hold on," Miscolo said. "I told her this
was the police and she should hold on."

"Try it again," Willis said.

Carella hit the redial button The phone rang once, twice,
again, again, again . . .

"Hello?"

A woman's voice. The same as the one on the tape.

"This is Detective Steve Carella, Eighty-seventh
Squad," Carella said. "Is this Marilyn?"

"Listen, what the hell . . . ?"

"I'm investigating . . ."

"Get lost," the woman said, and hung up.

Carella looked at the receiver.

"Hung up again," he said, and immediately hit the redial button.

The moment the woman answered the phone, she said,
"Stop bothering me, will you?"

"Marilyn," Carella said, "I'm a police detective, my
shield number is 714-5632 . . ."

"What'd you do, creep, get my name off the machine?"

"Yes, I did," Carella said. "I work out of the Eighty-
seventh Precinct, and this is a legitimate call. I'm using a
redial button . . ."

"A *what?*"

"Do you know a man named Jerome Edward McKennon?"

There was a silence on the line.

"Miss?"

"What'd you say your name was?"

"Detective Stephen Louis Carella."

Another silence.

"Has Jerry done something?"

"Do you know him?" Carella said.

"Yes. What happened, did he . . . ?"

"Can you tell me your full name, please?"

"Marilyn Hollis."

"May I have your address, please?"

"Why?"

"We'd like to talk to you, Miss Hollis."

"What about?"

"Are you at home now?"

"Yes, I am. Listen, what . . . ?"

"And the address there?"

"1211 Harborside. Can you tell me what the hell . . . ?"

"We'll be there in ten minutes," Carella said. "Wait for us."

Harborside Lane was within the confines of the 87th Precinct, not quite as desirable as Silvermine Oval, but a very good neighborhood anyway—at least when one considered the *rest* of the precinct territory. The Oval, as it was familiarly called, lay in the center of the Silvermine Road complex like an egg in a nest, close to Silvermine Park and the luxurious apartments facing the River Harb and the next state. Striking south from there, it was all downhill, literally and figuratively.

The Stem was a gaudy stretch of real estate brimming with retail stores and restaurants, movie theaters and, of late, massage parlors. South of that was Ainsley Avenue and then Culver, both seeming evidence of the success of the Melting Pot theory in that the population on these two wide thoroughfares was composed of old-line Jews, Irish and Italians who refused to budge under the onslaught of blacks and Puerto Ricans. The precinct territory became increasingly more seedy as it sprawled southward into the short stretch of Mason Avenue where the hookers plied their trade, indignant over the fact that massage parlors were sprouting to the north, thereby encroaching on their exclusive right to the world's oldest profession.

Harborside Lane was much farther uptown than Silvermine Road, but adjacent to the River Harb nonetheless and affording an equally splendid view of the high-rise buildings springing up along the shore in the next state. A lane it wasn't. It was, instead, as wide as any other city street (as opposed to its avenues) and lined with what had once been luxurious brownstones, now covered with graffiti and occupied by upward-striving yuppies.

In this city, the graffiti looked as if it were scrawled in Cyrillic letters. One might have been in Russia—except that in Russia no one wrote on the walls of buildings unless he wanted a vacation in Siberia. The purveyors of graffiti called themselves "writers." What they wrote was a mystery in that it was illegible and therefore unintelligible. A recent law made it mandatory for any retail merchant to keep under lock and key his spray cans of paint. To date, there had been no surveys made as to the law's efficacy. In the meantime, the writers continued writing, and no one understood what they wrote, but perhaps they were hoping to be considered by the Nobel Prize Committee.

1211 Harborside Lane was in a row of brownstones adorned with inaccessible scribblings. A wrought iron gate to the right of the building guarded the entrance to a driveway that led to a garage set some fifty feet back from the pavement; the gate was padlocked. There were wrought iron grilles on the ground-floor and first-floor windows, and razor wire on the roof overhanging the third floor. There was only one name in the directory set beside the bell buttons: M. Hollis. Apparently she occupied all three floors of the building. Willis rang the bell.

No answering buzz.

"Think she ran?" he asked, and rang the bell again. A small loudspeaker above the directory erupted with sound.

"Yes?" a woman's voice said.

"Miss Hollis?" Willis said.

"Yes?"

"Police," he said. "We called you a little while . . ."

"Yes, come in," she said.

A long, loud buzz unlocked the street-level door. The buzzer continued nagging long after they had let themselves in. They were facing a wood-paneled inner door, a brass escutcheon set in the doorframe at eye level, the name MARILYN HOLLIS engraved on it, a bell-button under it. Willis hit this button, too. The door was a thick one; they could not hear the bell ringing inside the apartment.

The woman who answered the door was somewhere in her mid-to-late twenties, Willis guessed, some five feet eight inches tall, with long blonde hair, angry blue eyes, and a complexion as flawlessly pale as a dipper of milk. She was wearing a bulky blue, man's cardigan sweater over blue jeans and a white T-shirt. Pale horse, pale rider, Willis thought, pale good looks.

"Identification," she said flatly.

A native, Willis thought.

Carella showed her his shield and his ID card.

"I'm on my way out," she said, handing the leather case back to him. "This better not take long."

She made her annoyance even more clear with an exaggerated curtsy that ushered them into the apartment. The entry foyer and the living room beyond were paneled in mahogany. Old thick wooden beams crossed the ceiling. The furnishings were Victorian and fussy. For an instant, Carella was transported back to a time when the city was young and people lived in luxury in buildings not covered with graffiti.

"Miss Hollis," he said, "can you tell us whether you spoke to Mr. McKennon at any time last night?"

"No, I didn't," she said. "And I really would appreciate knowing what this is all about. You call while I'm dressing, you tell me *nothing* at all on the phone . . ."

"He's dead," Carella said.

The blue eyes opened wide.

"What?" she said.

"I'm sorry, but . . ."

"God, what the hell are you saying? Jerry? Dead? What?"

"I'm sorry."

"God, what . . . ?"

The blue eyes even wider now. Shock apparent in them. Or perhaps only apparent shock in them.

"How?" she said.

"We don't know yet," he said.

He was lying, but nowhere was it written that a cop had to play fair with a person he was questioning.

"Well, was he *murdered?*" Marilyn said. "You're policemen, this is police business, you're not here 'cause he died in his sleep."

"No, he didn't die in his sleep."

"Well, was he shot, was he stabbed, did he get hit by a car?"

"We won't know the cause of death till we have an autopsy report," Carella said.

Sometimes you told them everything you knew, sometimes you told them nothing, and sometimes—like now—you told them just enough to start them running down the field with the ball. She seemed to be turning over possibilities now, her mind working rapidly, playing amateur detective for them, doing it all out loud, helpful little Miss Hollis, though not so little at five eight. But they weren't forgetting that the last phone call Jerome McKennon had made was to this apartment.

"When did this happen?" she asked.

"Sometime this morning."

"Where?"

"His apartment."

"You found him dead in his apartment?"

"His cleaning lady found him."

"What time?"

"Around nine," Carella said.

"How well did you know him?" Willis asked.

"Then it *was* murder, huh?" she said.

"Nobody said . . ."

"No? Then why do you want to know how well I knew him?"

"Because the call to your apartment was the last one he made."

"Why is that important if he wasn't killed?"

"It could've been suicide," Willis said.

Giving her a little more rope. Testing her. Maybe she'd jump on it, expand on the theory. Instead, she contradicted it.

"Jerry a suicide? That's ridiculous."

"How so, Miss Hollis?" Carella said.

"He had everything going for him. Good looks, a new job . . ."

"Doing what?" Willis said.

"Vice president in charge of marketing for Eastec Systems."

"What do they do?" Carella asked.

"Security."

"A burglar-alarm company?"

"Well, radio telemetry and digital monitoring. For burglary, yes, but also fire, freeze . . . well, total security systems."

"Here in the city?"

"Yes. On Avenue J."

"And you say this was a new job?"

"Relatively new. He started shortly after we met."

Now they were getting there.

"And when was that, Miss Hollis?"

"Just before Christmas."

Willis started counting in his head. This was close to the end of March. Three months, give or take. "Been seeing him ever since?" he asked.

"Yes."

"Can you tell us how well you knew him?"

"Is that a euphemism?"

"I don't know. Is it?"

"I mean, are you trying to ask if we were sleeping together?"

"Were you?"

"Yes. Which in itself is a euphemism."

Willis was thinking he'd have to look up "euphemism" when he got home, make sure it meant what he thought it meant.

"Would you say it was a serious relationship?" he asked.

Marilyn shrugged. "What do you consider serious?"

"What do you consider serious?"

She shrugged again. "We had some good times together," she said.

"Was he the only man in your life?"

"No."

"Then it wasn't serious."

"If serious means Jerry making undying declarations of love and modest proposals of marriage, then it wasn't serious, no. That may be *your* definition of serious, but it isn't mine." She paused. Then she said, "I liked him a lot. We had some good times together. I'm sorry he's dead."

"Miss Hollis," Carella said, "when's the last time you spoke to Mr. McKennon on the telephone?"

"Last week sometime."

"Would you remember the day?"

"Thursday, I think it was."

"Did he call you? Or did you call him?"

"He called me."

"And he didn't call here anytime after last Thursday?"

"No, he didn't."

"Were you home last night?"

"No. I've been away for the weekend."

"Oh? Where?"

"I don't think that's any of your business."

"Can you tell us what time you left the apartment here?"

"Why?"

"It might help us pinpoint the time of Mr. McKennon's death. We're certain that the last call he made from the apartment on Silvermine Oval was to your phone here. If we can . . ."

"How do you know that?"

"His phone has a redial feature. The number here was stored in the unit's memory as the last number dialed. It's possible, but not probable, that the last call he made was the one to you on Thursday. It's more likely that he tried to reach you after that. Possibly last night. Or early this . . ."

"I've been away since Friday afternoon."

"What time Friday?"

"About five-thirty."

"And you got home when?" Willis asked.

"Half an hour ago. Just before the phone started ringing."

"Around four o'clock or so?"

"Aren't you going to ask me who I went away with?"

"If you'd like to tell me, sure."

"A man named Nelson Riley."

"Thank you," Willis said.

She was beginning to irritate him. Maybe because her attitude was so damn antagonistic. No one had accused her of anything—not yet. But her stance was defiant, as if she was certain she'd be railroaded to the penitentiary if she didn't watch her step. Sometimes the innocent behaved that way. Sometimes the guilty did, too.

"And you say you got home here around four this afternoon, is that right?" Carella asked.

"Around then," Marilyn said.

"You mentioned earlier that you're seeing other men," Willis said.

"Yes."

"How many?"

"What's that got to do with Jerry's murder?"

"Or suicide, as the case may be," Willis said. "How many?

"Oh, please, none of my friends killed Jerry."

"How do you know that?"

"Because none of them even *knew* him."

"You're sure of that?" Willis said.

"Positive. I don't make a habit of telling Tom and Dick about Harry."

"How many Toms, Dicks and Harrys are there?" Willis persisted.

Marilyn sighed. "At present," she said, "I'm seeing three or four men."

"Which is it?" Willis said. "Three or four?"

"Four, counting Jerry."

"Then that makes it three."

"Yes."

"On a regular basis?"

"If that means am I sleeping with all of them, the answer is occasionally."

"May we have their names and addresses, please?" Carella said.

"Why? Are you going to drag *them* into this?"

"A man is dead . . ."

"I realize that. But neither I nor any of my friends . . ."

"We would appreciate their names and addresses."

Marilyn sighed again and went to a dropleaf desk in one corner of the room. She took her address book from it and started copying names and addresses onto a sheet of her stationery. When she handed it to Carella, he glanced at it briefly, put it into his notebook, and then asked, "Have you turned on your answering machine since you got home?"

"I was about to," Marilyn said. "But then the *police* started phoning every three minutes."

"Would you mind turning it on now?" Carella said. She went to the equipment on her desk and pushed a button.

Willis opened his notebook.

"Hi, Marilyn," a woman's voice said, "this is Didi. Call me when you get a chance, will you?"

In his notebook, Willis wrote *Didi.*

A click, a buzz, another voice.

"Miss Hollis, this is Hadley Fields at Merrill Lynch. Would you call me, please?"

Wills wrote *Hadley Fields, Merrill Lynch.*

A click, a buzz, and then . . .

"Marilyn, it's Baz. I have tickets for the Philharmonic on Wednesday night. Can you let me know if you're free? By Monday latest, okay?"

Willis kept writing as the tape unreeled.

"I *hate* your machine, Marilyn. This is Chip, call me, okay?"

A click, a buzz . . . and someone hung up.

"I hate when they do that," Marilyn said.

Another click, another buzz.

"Marilyn, this is Didi again. Where the hell *are* you?"

The parade of calls went on. A very busy lady, Willis thought.

And then, buried in the midst of the recorded messages . . .

"Marilyn . . . I need you . . . I'm . . ."

And a gasp . . .

And the sound of the telephone clattering onto a hard surface . . .

And the sound of someone retching . . .

A click, another buzz, and the recorded messages continued.

"Marilyn, this is Didi, I've been calling you *all* weekend. Will you *please* get back to me?"

Marilyn, this is Alice, this is Chip (and I *still* hate your machine), this is Baz (about the Philharmonic again), this is Sam, this is Jane, this is Andy . . .

Not a Tom, Dick or Harry among the male callers.

But a few more men than the three she'd listed for them.

Carella opened his notebook, unfolded the sheet of stationery on which she'd jotted down the names, addresses and telephone numbers, and said, "Are you sure these are all the men you're dating?"

"At the moment," Marilyn said.

"And the others?" Willis said.

"What others?"

"On the phone."

"Acquaintances."

"But not men you're dating."

"No."

"Was that Mr. McKennon's voice?" Carella asked.

She was silent for a moment. Then she said, "Yes," and lowered her eyes.

Carella closed his notebook.

"We may need to reach you at work," he said. "Is there a number you can let us . . . ?"

"I'm unemployed," she said.

Willis thought his face registered blank, but she must have caught something on it.

"It's *not* what you're thinking," she said at once.

"What am I thinking?" he said.

"You're thinking expensive, well-furnished townhouse, you're thinking she's got a sugar daddy. You're wrong. I've got a *real* daddy, and he's an oilman in Texas, and he doesn't want his only daughter starving in the big, bad city."

"I see."

"Well, we're sorry to have taken so much of your time,"

Carella said. "You've been very helpful, though, and we . . ."

"How?" she asked, and showed them to the door.

Outside, the air was cold and the wind was sharp.

3

IN THE CITY, THEY CALLED IT A 24-24.

It applied to homicides and it referred to the importance of the twenty-four hours preceding a person's death and the twenty-four hours following it.

The pre-mortem twenty-four hours were important because what a victim did, where he went, whom he saw, all might have bearing on his death. Officially Jerome McKennon was a victim, even if he'd swallowed the nicotine of his own volition. The post-mortem twenty-four hours were important only if someone had murdered McKennon because then the investigating detectives would be working against the clock, and as more and more time elapsed, the trail could get colder and colder, giving the killer an edge. It was a dictum in police work that if a case went beyond a week without a solid lead, you might as well throw it in the Open File. The Open File was the graveyard of investigation.

There were only two detectives working the McKennon case. This wasn't a big-deal front-page murder. Nobody important had been slain, no exotic setting had been involved, this was just another garden-variety murder in a city that sprouted them like weeds. The poison was unusual, true, but even that wasn't something an aboriginal tribe might dip its arrows into. The media had more than enough sensational murders to shout about every day, and since this case lacked what the cops referred to as the Roman Arena Appeal, it got less than passing notice in the newspapers and on television. Only one of the Tuesday morning commentators—a man who'd been touting the evils of cigarette-smoking for the past six months now, ever since he himself had quit, there's nothing like a reformed whore—found the case an opportunity for mentioning how strong a poison nicotine actually was, but he was a voice in the wilderness.

23

The case was important only to Willis and Carella, and then only because they'd happened to be ''up''—on duty and catching—when the call came in. Neither of them enjoyed poisons that acted within minutes. Such a poison automatically started them thinking suicide. They were not paid to think suicide. The only reason a suicide was investigated as a homicide was that it might in *fact* be a homicide. But nicotine *did* work in minutes, sometimes seconds, and Jerome McKennon *had* died of nicotine poisoning and it was important now to get to work on the 24-24 and to do it fast because if someone had dropped that poison in his beer or forced it down his throat, the edge was widening with every ticking second of the clock.

There were only two of them.

The pre-24 was going to be difficult; they had found no appointment calendar in McKennon's apartment. But Marilyn Hollis had told them he was vice president in charge of marketing at Eastec Systems on Avenue J, so Carella started there.

Willis, working from the list of three names Marilyn had given them, set about trying to find the other men in her life. He was, in effect, working the post-24. She had told them that none of those other men even knew McKennon—''I don't make a habit of telling Tom about Dick or Harry.'' But a goodly number of the murders committed in this city were motivated by jealousy. Husband slays wife's lover. Woman slays *own* lover. Boyfriend kills girlfriend or girlfriend's boyfriend, or, generously, both. Boyfriend kills boyfriend or boyfriend's mother. The possibilities were limitless, the green-eyed monster exploding into violence at the slightest provocation.

If Marilyn had three boyfriends in addition to McKennon, the possibility existed that one of them hadn't appreciated the relationship she shared with McKennon and had decided to put an end to it. The possibility was a slim one, and Willis knew it. But in the post-24, all you were looking for was a place to hang your hat.

The first name on the list was Nelson Riley, Marilyn's weekend playmate. But if Riley had been away with Marilyn, he couldn't have been here in the city poisoning McKennon; nicotine worked within minutes. The detectives had only Marilyn's word for her—*and* Riley's—whereabouts on the two days preceding McKennon's death. Willis called Riley, identified himself, and told him he'd be there in half an hour.

Nelson Riley was a man in his late thirties, Willis guessed, six feet two or three inches tall, with a shock of red hair, a red handlebar mustache, green eyes, massive shoulders, a barrel chest, and the big-knuckled hands of a street fighter. He was not a street fighter—at least not by chosen profession. He was an artist, and his studio was in a loft on Carlson Street downtown in the Quarter. Huge canvases lined the wall of the loft, illuminated by a skylight that poured a cold wintry light into the room. A shoulder-height divider-wall separated Riley's workspace from his living quarters. Beyond the edge of the wall, Willis could see an unmade waterbed.

The paintings against the walls were all representational. Cityscapes, nudes, still lifes. One of the nudes looked remarkably like Marilyn Hollis. The painting on the easel depicted a watermelon. The colors on Riley's palette, resting on a high table alongside the easel, were predominantly red and green. Riley's jeans and his faded blue T-shirt were covered with paint, as were his enormous hands. Willis kept thinking he would not ever like to run into Riley in a dark alley on a moonless night. Even if he had the soul of an artist.

"So what's this about?" Riley asked.

"We're investigating an apparent suicide," Willis said, "a man named Jerry McKennon."

He watched the eyes. The eyes told a lot. Not a flicker of recognition there.

"Do you know him?"

"Never heard of him," Riley said. "You want some coffee?"

"Thanks," Willis said.

He followed Riley to behind the divider-wall, where the waterbed shared an eighteen-by-twenty space with a dresser, a sink, a refrigerator, a wall cupboard, a floor lamp, a kitchen table with chairs around it, and a hot plate on another paint-spattered table. The fierce March wind outside rattled a small window near the foot of the bed. Riley filled a kettle with water and put it on the hot plate.

"It's instant," he said, "I hope you don't mind."

"Instant's fine," Willis said.

Riley went to the cupboard and took down two paint-smeared mugs. "You *did* say *apparent*, didn't you?" he asked. "The suicide?"

"Yes."

"Meaning maybe it wasn't suicide?"

"We don't know yet."

"Meaning what? Murder?"

"Maybe."

"So how am *I* in this? What's this got . . . ?"

"Do you know a woman named Marilyn Hollis?"

"Sure. What's *she* got to do with it?"

"Were you away with her this past weekend?"

"Yeah?"

"Where'd you go, Mr. Riley?"

"What's that got to do with somebody's suicide? Or murder."

"Well, this is just routine," Willis said.

"It is, huh?" Riley said, and raised his eyebrows skeptically.

The window rattled with a fresh gust of wind.

"Mr. Riley," Willis said, "I really would appreciate it if you could tell me where you went with Miss Hollis, what time you left the city, and what time you returned. Please understand . . ."

"Sure, sure, this is just routine," Riley said. "We went up to Snowflake to do a little spring skiing. *Some* kind of spring skiing, I'll tell you. The mountain was a solid block of ice."

"Where's that, Snowflake?"

"Vermont. I take it you don't ski."

"No, I don't."

"Sometimes I wish I didn't," Riley said.

"And you left the city when?"

"I picked up Marilyn around five-thirty. I like to get a full day's work in. Lots of people, they think artists just paint when the mood strikes them. That's bullshit. I put in an eight-hour day, nine to five, every day but weekends.

I used to be an art director at an ad agency before I quit to paint full time. I used to paint at night and on weekends. Once I made the break, I promised myself I'd never again work at night or on weekends. So I don't." He shrugged. "Must be different for you, huh?"

"A little," Willis said, and smiled. "So you left the city at five-thirty on Friday . . ."

"Yeah, about then."

"And came back when?"

"Yesterday afternoon. I know what you're thinking. I tell you I work nine to five, five days a week, and here I don't get back to the city till around four yesterday afternoon." He shrugged again. "But I just finished that big mother against the wall, and I figured I was entitled."

The big mother against the wall was a street scene in downtown Isola, one of those crowded little cobblestoned Dutch lanes near the Lower Platform, a narrow canyon admitting feeble wintry light, a dusting of snow underfoot, men in bulky overcoats hurrying past women clutching coat collars to their throats, heads ducked, a lone newspaper flapping on the wind like a lost seagull. You could almost feel the bite of the wind, hear the click of the women's high-heeled boots on the sidewalk, smell the sauerkraut steaming at the hotdog cart on the corner, umbrella tassels dancing in the wind.

"I used to work out of a precinct down there," Willis said.

"Near the Old Seawall?"

"Yeah. Nice precinct. Dead as a doornail at night."

"Where do you work now?" Riley asked.

"The Eight-Seven. Uptown. Near Grover Park."

The kettle whistled. Riley spooned instant coffee into each of the mugs, and then poured hot water into them. "You take cream or sugar?" he asked.

"Black, thanks," Willis said, and picked up one of the mugs. "So you never met this Jerry McKennon, huh?" he asked.

"Never *heard* of him till a few minutes ago."

"Miss Hollis never mentioned him?"

"No. Why? Did she know him?"

"Yes."

"Mmm. Well, I'm sure Marilyn must know a lot of people. She's a very attractive woman."

"How long have *you* known her?"

"Must be six months or so."

"How would you define your relationship, Mr. Riley?"

"How do you mean? On a scale of one to ten?"

Willis smiled again. "No, sir. I meant in terms of involvement . . . commitment . . . whatever you'd want to call it."

"Marilyn doesn't get involved. She doesn't commit, either. Maybe she doesn't have to. Lots of girls in this town, they're looking for a breadwinner. Marilyn's got a rich father in Texas, she doesn't have to worry about money. She sees a man because she has a good time with him. I'm not talking *sack* time now. That's a given. If a man and a woman don't get along in the sack, they don't get along anyplace else, do they? I'm talking about *being* with a person. Talking, sharing things, laughing together."

"That's involvement, isn't it?" Willis said.

"I call it friendship."

"Is that what Marilyn calls it?"

"I like to believe she considers me a very good friend."

"Do you know any of her other friends?"

"Nope."

"Never met any of them."

"Nope."

"Man named Chip Endicott?"

"Nope."

"Basil Hollander?"

"Nope."

"How about her father? Ever meet him?"

"Nope."

"Do you know his name?"

"Jesse, I think. Or Joshua. Maybe Jason. I'm not sure."

"Do you know where he lives in Texas?"

"Houston, I think. Or Dallas. Or San Antone. I'm not sure."

"Mr. Riley, where'd you stay when you went up to Snowflake?"

"A place called the Summit Lodge. I can give you the number if you plan to check."

"I'd appreciate having it," Willis said.

"This wasn't any suicide, was it?" Riley said. "This was murder, plain and simple."

Willis said nothing.

He was thinking it wasn't so plain and it wasn't so simple.

Vice President in Charge of Marketing for Eastec Systems.

You visualized a giant corporation on the order of IBM or General Motors. You visualized an executive with area maps all over the walls of his enormous office, different colored pins marking the hordes of salesmen in each territory.

Sure.

In this city, where a garbage man was a Sanitation Engineer and a prostitute was a Sex Counselor, Jerry McKennon was Vice President in Charge of Marketing for what appeared to be a two-bit operation.

Avenue J was in a part of the city the cops used to call Campbell's City, in reference to the alphabet soup marketed by that company, but which over the years had come to be known as the Soup Kitchen. Tucked into a downtown poverty pocket that rivaled any in Calcutta, the lettered avenues ran east-west for a goodly stretch of Isola, and north-south from A through L where the Soup Kitchen ended at the River Dix. Across the river you could see the smoke stacks of the factories in Calm's Point.

At the turn of the century, the dingy tenements in this area had been inhabited by immigrants flocking to America to mine the promised gold in the streets. They found instead the manure dropped by horses pulling ice wagons, milk wagons, lumber wagons, and streetcars. Upward mobility and a strong will to survive took them farther uptown into ghettos defined by their countries of origin, and finally out of the inner city itself into the relatively suburban areas of Riverhead, Calm's Point, Majesta, and Bethtown.

In the Forties and Fifties, a new wave of immigrants—

who were nonetheless bona fide citizens of the United States—moved into the tenements, and the sound of Spanish replaced that of Yiddish, Italian, Polish, German and Russian. The Puerto Ricans who came seeking the same gold the earlier settlers had sought found not horseshit but instead a withering prejudice that equated anyone Spanish-speaking with criminal activity. There had been prejudice in this city before. Prejudice against the first Irish who came here to escape the potato famine, prejudice against the Italians who were escaping the blight on their precious grape crop, prejudice against Jews escaping religious persecution, prejudice—always and for any number of rationalizing reasons—against the blacks who inhabited the Diamondback slum uptown. But the prejudice now was deeper, perhaps because the Puerto Ricans steadfastly clung to their old traditions and their native tongue.

It was therefore a matter of high irony when the Puerto Ricans themselves turned so vehemently against the flower children who moved into the tenements—many of them abandoned by then—in the mid-Sixties and early Seventies. It was not uncommon back then for pot-smoking kids to look up in astonishment when a band of Soup Kitchen natives (by now they were natives, though scarcely thought of as such by *other* Americans) burst into an apartment to rob—-ah, yes, the old self-fulfilling prophecy—and rape and occasionally to murder. "Peace," the flower children said, "Love," the flower children said while their skulls were being opened. The hippies eventually vanished from the scene. They left behind them, however, a legacy of drug use, and nowadays the alphabet avenues were a happy hunting ground for pushers and junkies of every stripe and persuasion.

Eastec Systems had its offices in a dilapidated building on the southern side of Avenue J. A nail-filing, gum-chewing receptionist looked at Carella's shield and ID card in something close to awe, pressed a button on the base of her phone, and then told him that Mr. Gregorio would see him at once. Carella walked down a corridor to a door with a black plastic name plate on it: RALPH GREGORIO, PRESIDENT. He knocked. A man's voice said, "Come in." He opened the door. Green metal furniture and filing cabinets. Dusty Venetian blinds on the windows fronting the street. Behind the desk, a chubby man in his early forties, shirtsleeves rolled up, cheeks flushed, wide grin on his face, hand extended.

"Hey, *paisan*," he said, "what can I do for you?"

Carella did not enjoy being called *paisan*. Too many Italian-American mobsters had called him *paisan*, usually in conjunction with a plea for a favor premised on a shared ethnic background.

He took the proffered hand.

"Mr. Gregorio," he said, "Detective Carella, Eighty-seventh Squad."

"Sit down, sit down," Gregorio said. "This is about Jerry, right?"

"Yes."

"Terrible shame, terrible," Gregorio said. "I saw it on television, they gave him, what, thirty seconds? Terrible shame. He killed himself, huh?"

"When's the last time you saw him?" Carella asked, ignoring the question.

"Friday. End of the day Friday."

"Did he seem despondent at that time?"

"Despondent? No. What despondent? Jerry? No. I got to tell you, this comes as a complete surprise, him taking his own life."

"He began working here shortly before Christmas, is that right?"

"That's right, who told you that? Well, I guess you have ways of knowing, eh, *paisan?*" Gregorio said, and winked.

"Did he *ever* seem depressed or despondent? During the past three months?"

"No. Always a smile on his face. He used to go around here singing, would you believe it. *We're* the ones supposed to be the singers, am I right, *paisan?* Jerry was, what, Irish, English, who the hell knows? Singing all the time. The Pavarotti of the security business. We sell and install security systems, you know. Make it tougher for the bad guys. Help you guys out a little." He winked again.

"What time did he leave here on Friday?"

"Five-thirty. He was a hard worker, Jerry. Sometimes didn't get out of here till six, seven o'clock. We're a new company, you know, but we got a brilliant future. Jerry realized that. He was giving it all he had. What a shame, huh?"

"Did he mention anything about his weekend plans?"

"No."

"Didn't say where he was going, what he planned to do?"

"No."

"Did he ever mention a woman named Marilyn Hollis?"

"No."

"Mr. Gregorio . . ."

"Hey, *paisan,*" Gregorio said chidingly, and spread his arms and his hands wide. "What's with the formality? Make it Ralph, huh?"

"Thank you," Carella said, and cleared his throat. "Uh . . . Ralph . . . do you think I could have a look at Mr. McKennon's office?"

"Sure, it's right down the hall. What are you looking for?"

"Anything that might help us," Carella said.

He was looking for an appointment calendar, and he found it at once, on McKennon's desk and open to the month of March.

"Mind if I take this with me?" Carella said.

"It's no good to Jerry no more," Gregorio said.

"I'll make out a receipt . . ."

"Come on, *paisan,* you and me need *receipts?*"

"Well, it's required," Carella said, and began writing.

The second name on Marilyn's list was Chip Endicott.

The name on his door was Charles Ingersol Endicott, Jr.

He was the one who hated her answering machine.

He was also an attorney with the firm of Hackett, Rawlings, Pearson, Endicott, Lipstein and Marsh. Willis wondered how the Jew had snuck in.

Endicott was in his late forties, Willis guessed, though it was really somewhat difficult to tell. A man in tanned good health, some five feet ten inches tall, no age wrinkles on his handsome, narrow face, dark brown eyes intelligent and alert, the only clue to his age was his white hair—but that may have been premature. He shook hands firmly with Willis, said, "This has to do with Marilyn, does it?" and then gestured toward a chair opposite his desk.

The law offices of Hackett, Rawlings, Etc., Etc. were on the twelfth floor of a Jefferson Avenue building, than which no real estate in the city came higher. Endicott's office was furnished in cool modern: a teak desk, a blue carpet, a sofa and side chairs upholstered in a darker blue, an abstract painting on the wall over the sofa picking up the predominantly blue color theme and splashing it with red as shocking as a blood stain.

"Miss Hollis gave us your name as one of her friends," Willis said.

"She's not in any trouble, is she?" Endicott said at once.

"No, sir, none at all. But we're investigating a case . . ."

"What case?"

"An apparent suicide."

"Oh. Who?"

"A man named Jerry McKennon."

Again, Willis watched the eyes.

Nothing in them.

And then, sudden recognition.

"Oh. Yes. Uptown someplace, wasn't it? I read a small item about it in the paper this morning."

A puzzled look.

Then: "I'm sorry, but how is Marilyn involved?"

"He was a friend of hers, too."

"Oh?" Endicott said.

"Had you ever met him?"

"No. Did Marilyn say I did?"

"No, no. I was just curious."

"I'm sorry, the name isn't familiar. McKennon? No."

"Did she ever mention him to you?"

"Not to my recollection." Endicott paused, and then said, "Are you investigating a murder, Mr. Willis, is that it?"

"Well, not exactly, sir. But in this city we investigate suicides the same way we do homicides. Well, you're a lawyer, maybe you already know that."

"My specialty is corporate law," Endicott said.

"Well," Willis said, "that's the way we do it."

"And you say this man was one of Marilyn's friends?"

"Yes, sir."

"And she gave you my name as *another* of her friends?"

"Yes, sir."

"Mm," Endicott said.

"You *are* a friend, aren't you?" Willis said.

"Oh, yes."

"How long have you known her?"

"It must be almost a year now. We met shortly after she got here from Texas. Her father's a millionaire down there, oil or cattle, I forget which. He set her up in a townhouse on . . . well, have you been there?"

"Yes, sir."

"Very luxurious, nothing but the best for his darling daughter. From the way she talks about him, he's a bit of a curmudgeon, but generous to a fault where it concerns his only child."

"Where in Texas, would you know, sir?"

"Houston? Yes, I'm sure she said Houston."

"And her father's name? Did she ever mention it to you?"

"If she did, I don't recall it."

"How'd you happen to meet her, Mr. Endicott?"

"I was going through a divorce . . . have you ever gone through a divorce?"

"No, sir."

"Ever been married?"

"No, sir."

"If marriage is purgatory, divorce is hell," Endicott said, and smiled. "Anyway, I went through the whole bit. Bought myself a hand-tailored wardrobe, started using men's cologne, *almost* bought a motorcycle but sanity prevailed, started going to singles bars, took personal ads in *The Saturday Journal*—down there in The Quarter, you know . . ."

"Yes, sir."

". . . *and,* most important for a newly divorced man on the prowl, started going to museums a lot."

"Museums?"

"Yes, Mr. Willis, museums. There are a great many available and generally higher-class women frequenting this city's museums on any given afternoon of the week. Especially the art museums. And especially on rainy days. That's where I met Marilyn. At the Fine Arts Museum uptown, on a rainy Saturday."

"And this was about a year ago."

"April, I think. Almost a year."

"And you've been seeing her ever since."

"Well, yes. We hit it off immediately. She's an extraordinary woman, you know. Well-bred, intelligent, inquisitive, marvelous fun to be with."

"How often do you see her, Mr. Endicott?"

"At least once a week, sometimes more often. Occasionally, we'll get away for a weekend, but that's rare. We're good friends, Mr. Willis. I'm fifty-seven years old . . ."

Willis blinked.

". . . and I was raised at a time when men didn't have women as *friends.* All we were interested in was getting in their pants. Well, times have changed and so have I. I don't wish to discuss our personal relationship, I know Marilyn wouldn't, either. Anyway, that's not the important thing. The important thing is that we're *friends.* We can unburden ourselves to each other, we can totally relax with each other, we're very good *friends,* Mr. Willis. And that means a great deal to me."

"I see," Willis said, and hesitated. "Does it bother you that she may have other good friends?"

"Why would it? If you and I were friends, Mr. Willis, and you had other friends, would it bother me? You're thinking the way I used to think. That somehow it's impossible for a man and a woman to be true friends without all sorts of nonsense intruding on the relationship. Marilyn sees other men, I know that. She's a beautiful and intelligent woman, I wouldn't expect otherwise. And I'm sure she considers some of them to be friends. But does friendship have to be exclusive? And if she goes to bed with

some of them—as well she may, I've never asked—don't I
go to bed with other women? Do you understand what I'm
saying, Mr. Willis?''

He was saying there wasn't a jealous bone in his body.
He was saying he couldn't possibly have killed Jerry Mc-
Kennon, whoever the hell *that* was, because he didn't know
him and he wouldn't have cared if he and Marilyn were
screwing day and night on the sidewalk in front of the
police station.

"I think so," Willis said. "Thanks very much for your
time."

McKennon's Week-at-a-Glance calendar for the better
part of March looked like this:

MONDAY MARCH 3
thru
WEDNESDAY MARCH 5

Monday March 3		
8 *HAIRCUT!!*		1
9	*CHART NEW*	2
10 *ELTRONICS REP*	*ACCOUNTS*	3
11 *RALPH*	↓	4
12		5

evening

Tuesday March 4		
8		1
9	*CHECK*	2
10 *ZANGER*	*ALL* *INSTALLATION*	3
11 *HOPKINS*	*ORDERS*	4
12 *BARNES @ MARIO'S*		5

evening

Wednesday March 5		
8	*BEGIN*	1
9 *ALL CITY REPS HERE*	*SEMINAR*	2
10 *CALL ELTRONICS*	*SPEECH*	3
" *HOTEL RES.*		
11 *CHICAGO*		4
12		5

evening

THURSDAY MARCH 6
thru
SUNDAY MARCH 9

Thursday March 6

8 STEINBERG — COFFEE SHACK	REVIEW NEW 1 ACCOUNTS
9	2
10 INGRAMS	PACKARD 3
11³⁰ OLIVER	KING 4
12 LUNCH HERE - RALPH	5

evening

Friday March 7

8 WORK ON	1
9 SEMINAR	2
10 SPEECH	3
11 ALL	4
12 DAY	5

evening

Saturday March 8	Sunday March 9
ELLSWORTH 11 AM	WORKSHEETS (AM)
CALL MOM	MARILYN (PM)
DINNER @ HAROLD'S 7 PM	

evening

MONDAY MARCH 10
thru
WEDNESDAY MARCH 12

Monday March 10		
8		1
9 DVNOMAT REP	DAVIS	2
10	FEIN	3
11 ANDREWS	AIRLINE TIX	4
	SEMINAR	
12		5

Tuesday March 11		
8		1
9 BANK	CONSULT INSTALLER	2
	re KREUGER JOB	
10	CARTER	3
11	CALL L.A.	4
MCINTYRE @		
12 30 ASCOT HOUSE		5

evening

Wednesday March 12		
8 CALLS: DIANGELO	RALPH ALL	1
9 LANE	(PM)	2
PIERCE ELECTRONICS		
10		3
10 30 HELLER		
11		4
11 30 RIVERHEAD REP		
12		5

MARILYN PICKUP 6°° DINNER @
JACKIE'S 6 30   evening   CHORUS LINE @ 8°°

THURSDAY MARCH 13
thru
SUNDAY MARCH 16

Thursday March 13

8		1
9	SONITROL REP.	2
10	FINISH SEMINAR SPEECH !!	3
11		4
12		5

evening

Friday March 14

8	CALL ANNIE re HOSPITAL	HALEY @ JONESEY'S	1
9	FLOWERS TO FRANK		2
10			3
11	FARREN		4
12			5

evening

Saturday March 15	Sunday March 16
ELLSWORTH @ 11⁰⁰	VISIT FRANK AM
PARTY @ HILLARY'S	CALL MOM
8⁰⁰ PM	CALL MARILYN

evening

MONDAY MARCH 17
thru
WEDNESDAY MARCH 19

	Monday March 17	
8		1
9 _BETHTOWN REP_		2
10	_FIELDS_	3
11	4⁴ _HARKAVY_	4
12 _LANDON @ MALICO_		5
	evening	

	Tuesday March 18	
8 _LEAVE FOR_		1
9 _CHICAGO_		2
10 _FIRE/SMOKE_	_SEMINAR_	3
11		4
12		5
	evening	

	Wednesday March 19	
8		1
9		2
10	_SEMINAR_	3
11		4
12		5
	evening	

THURSDAY MARCH 20
thru
SUNDAY MARCH 23

Thursday March 20	
8	1
9	2
10 SEMINAR	3
11	4
12	5

evening

Friday March 21	
8	1
9	2
10 SEMINAR	LEAVE CHICAGO 3
11	4
12	5

CALL MARILYN evening

Saturday March 22	Sunday March 23
WRITE REPORT	MOM'S @ NOON
ON SEMINAR	

evening

MONDAY MARCH 24
thru
WEDNESDAY MARCH 26

Monday March 24

8	LUNCH w RALPH 1
9 DISCUSS REPORT w RALPH	BETHTOWN REP 2
10	CALL FOR TIX 3
11 4³⁰ UNGER	LA CAGE 4
12	5

evening

Tuesday March 25

8 REPORT ON	1
9 SEMINAR TO ALL	BEGIN INSTALLER 2
10 REPS.	INTERVIEWS 3
11	(GET SKED 4
12 JAGGER @ MARIO'S	FROM MARY*) 5

evening

Wednesday March 26

8 INSTALLER	1
9 INTERVIEWS	2
10	3
11 ALL DAY	4
12	5

evening

THURSDAY MARCH 27
thru
SUNDAY MARCH 30

Thursday March 27

8	CALL re MICROCHIP	1
	DELIVERY	
9 FIELD TRIP—		2
KREUGER HOUSE		
10	CALL L.A.	3
11 PREPARE RIVERHEAD		4
CHART		
12	AXEL @ NIMROD'S	5

CALL MARILYN re evening EASTER

Friday March 28

8		1
9 CHECK ISOLA		2
PAYROLL		
10		3
11 RALPH re	CALL L.A.	4
FINAL DECISION		
12 INSTALLERS		5

evening

Saturday March 29	Sunday March 30
ELLSWORTH 11:00 AM	MOMS @ NOON
LA CAGE @ 8:00 PM	PARTY @ COLLY'S
	7:00 PM

evening

Carella began cross-checking the appointment calendar against the personal telephone directories he had taken from McKennon's apartment and from his office at Eastec.

The frequently mentioned "Ralph," of course, was the president of Eastec and the many meetings with him were perfectly appropriate for a company that had "a brilliant future."

From McKennon's office directory, Carella learned that:

1) Eltronics was not a misspelling of Electronics. There was in fact an Eltronics, Inc. in Calm's Point, and it was a supplier of electronic equipment for digital systems.

2) Pierce Electronics was another supplier, this time in Isola itself.

3) Dynomat was a burglar-alarm company in Riverhead.

4) Karl Zanger, Paul Hopkins, Lawrence Barnes, Max Steinberg, Geoffrey Ingrams, Samuel Oliver, Dale Packard, Louis King, George Andrews, Lloyd Davis, Irwin Fein, Peter McIntyre, Frederick Carter, Joseph Di Angelo, Michael Lane, Richard Heller, Martin Farren, Thomas Haley, Peter Landon, John Fields, Leonard Harkavy, John Unger, Benjamin Jagger and Axel Sanderson were all potential Eastec clients, listed as such in McKennon's directory. Some of the names were already crossed out. Either they had by then become active clients or else they were no longer interested.

From the Isola phone book, Carella learned—as if he hadn't already surmised it—that Mario's, The Coffee Shack, The Ascot House, Jackie's, Jonesey's, L'Italico and Nimrod's were restaurants. He could find no similar listing for Harold's, where McKennon had dinner at 7:00 P.M. on March 8, so he assumed Harold Somebody was a personal friend, as probably were Hillary (the 8:00 P.M. party on March 15) and Colly (the 7:00 P.M. party McKennon would never attend on the thirtieth).

At this point, Meyer Meyer, smoking a cigarette and kibitzing while Carella was preparing his lists, casually mentioned that he shouldn't too easily chalk off the March

8 and March 15 parties as too distant in time from the
poisoning. He reminded Carella that way back in the days
when dinosaurs roamed the earth, they had together investigated a poisoning in which a television comic named
Stan Gifford dropped dead while performing live before
an estimated forty million viewers. After autopsy, the
M.E.—Paul Blaney in that case as well—reported that Gifford had ingested a hundred and thirty times the lethal
dose of a poison named strophanthin, and that death would
have occurred within minutes.

"Turned out the killer built himself a home-made span-
sule, remember?" Meyer said. "So maybe this is the same
thing here."

"Maybe," Carella said.

But he knew that would be too easy.

Cross-checking nonetheless, he found a Harold Sachs
and a Hillary Lawson in the personal directory he had
taken from McKennon's apartment, and made a note to
call them to ask about those parties. He also found a listing for a Nicholas Di Marino, whom he guessed was the
Colly throwing the party this Saturday night, but he
couldn't see much sense in calling him at this point.

The identical eleven o'clock appointments on March
eighth, fifteenth, and twenty-ninth (another appointment
McKennon would never keep) led Carella to suspect
"Ellsworth" was either a doctor or a dentist. In the cross-
check against McKennon's directory, he found a listing for
a Ronald Ellsworth, DDS, with offices at 257 Carrington
Street, here in Isola.

The Kreuger whose job was being installed was a Henry
Kreuger in Calm's Point. Carella learned this from calling
McKennon's boss. But Gregorio did not know either an
Annie or a Frank, and there were no listings in Mc-
Kennon's directory for either of them. Carella surmised
that *Frank* Whoever had been in the hospital—hence the
flowers—and that McKennon had called *Annie* Whoever to
find out *which* hospital.

Carella did not enjoy movies with casts of thousands.
Neither did he enjoy cases where the possibilities multi-
plied geometrically.

Just once in his life, he would love investigating a case

involving two men stranded on a desert island, one the victim, the other the obvious killer.

Just once.

Meanwhile, he was stuck with this one.

4

BY EIGHT O'CLOCK THAT TUESDAY NIGHT, WIL-
lis had talked to all three men on the short list of "friends"
Marilyn Hollis had less than graciously provided, and
he figured it was time he paid the lady herself another
visit.

He did not call first.

Unannounced and uninvited, he drove to 1211 Harborside Lane, and parked his car at the curb adjacent to the
small park across the street from her building. It was still
bitterly cold. March had come in like a lion and was going
out like a lion, so much for the Farmer's Almanac disci-
ples. The wind tossing his hair, his face raw after only a
short walk from his car across the street, he rang the front
doorbell and waited.

Her voice over the speaker said, "Mickey?"

"No," he said, "it's Detective Willis."

There was a long silence.

"What do you want?" she said.

"Few questions I'd like to ask you. If you have a minute."

"I'm sorry, I can't talk to you just now," she said. "I'm
expecting someone."

"When can I come back?" he asked.

"How about never?" she said, and he could swear she
was smiling.

"How about later tonight?" he said.

"No, I'm sorry."

"Miss Hollis, this is a homicide . . ."

"I'm sorry," she said again.

There was a click. And then silence.

He pressed the doorbell button again.

"Listen," she said over the speaker, "I'm truly sorry,
but . . ."

48

"Miss Hollis," he said, "do I have to get a warrant just to *talk* to you?"

Silence.

Then: "All right, come in."

The buzzer sounded. He grabbed for the doorknob and let himself into the entrance foyer. Another buzzer sounded, unlocking the inner door. He opened the door and stepped tentatively into the paneled living room. A fire was going in the fireplace across the room. Incense was burning. Not a sign of her anywhere.

He closed the door behind him.

"Miss Hollis?" he called.

"I'm upstairs. Take off your coat, sit down, I'm on the phone."

He hung his coat on a rack just inside the door, and then sat close to the door in a chair upholstered in red crushed velvet. Mickey, he thought. Mickey who? He waited. He could hear nothing from the upstairs levels of the house. The fire crackled and spit. He waited. Still no sounds from upstairs.

"Miss Hollis?" he called again.

"Be with you in a minute!" she called back.

He'd been waiting for at least ten minutes when finally she came down the walnut-bannistered staircase from above. She was wearing something glacial-blue and clingy, a wide sash at the waist, sapphire earrings, high-heeled pumps to match the dress. Blonde hair pulled back from the pale oval of her face. Blue eye shadow. No lipstick.

"You caught me at a bad time," she said. "I was dressing."

"Who's Mickey?" he asked.

"An acquaintance. I just called to say I'd be running late. I hope this won't take too long. Would you like a drink?"

The offer surprised him. You didn't hand a man his hat and offer him a drink in the same breath.

"Or are you still on duty?" she asked.

"Sort of."

"At eight-fifteen?"

"Long day," he said.

"Name your poison," she said, and for a moment he

thought she was making a deliberate if somewhat grisly joke, but she was heading obliviously for the bar unit across the room.

"Scotch," he said.

"Ah, he's corruptible," she said, and turned to glance over her shoulder, smiling. "Anything with it?"

"Ice, please."

He watched her as she dropped ice cubes into two short glasses, poured scotch for him, gin for herself. He watched her as she carried the drinks to where he was sitting. Pale horse, pale rider, pale good looks.

"Come sit by the fire," she said, "it'll be cozier," and started across the room toward a sofa upholstered in the same red crushed velvet. He rose, moved toward the sofa, waited for her to sit, and then sat beside her. She crossed her legs. There was a quick glimpse of nylon-sleek knees, the suggestion of a thigh, and then she lowered her skirt as demurely as a nun. In an almost subliminal flash, he wondered why she had chosen a word like "cozier."

"Mickey who?" he asked.

"Mouse," she said, and smiled again.

"A *male* acquaintance then."

"No, I was making a joke. Mickey's a girlfriend. We're going out to dinner." A look at her watch. "Provided we're through here before midnight. I said I'd call her back."

"I won't be long," he said.

"So," she said. "What's so urgent?"

"Not urgent," he said.

"Pressing then?"

"Not pressing, either. Just a few things bothering me."

"Like what?"

"Your friends."

"Tom, Dick and Harry?" she asked, and smiled again. She was making reference to their first somewhat irritating meeting, but she was making sport of it now, seemingly trying to put him at ease. He thought at once that he was being conned. And this led to the further thought that she had something to hide.

"I'm talking about the list you gave us," he said. "The men you consider close friends."

"Yes, they are," she said.

"Yes, so they told me." He paused. "That's what's bothering me."

"What is it, exactly, that's bothering you, Mr. Willis?" She shifted her weight on the sofa, adjusted her skirt again.

"Nelson Riley," he said. "Chip Endicott. Basil Hollander."

"Yes, yes, I know the names."

Basil Hollander was the man who'd left a message on her answering machine saying he had tickets for the Philharmonic. His comments to Willis were echoes of what Nelson Riley and Chip Endicott had already told him. He considered Marilyn Hollis one of his very best friends. Terrific girl. Great fun to be with. But Hollander (who'd identified himself as "Baz" on Marilyn's answering machine) was a "Yes-No-Well" respondent, the kind detectives the world over dreaded. Getting him to amplify was like pulling teeth.

"Have you known her a long time?"

"Yes."

"How long?"

"Well . . ."

"A year?"

"No."

"Longer?"

"No."

"Ten months?"

"No."

"Less than ten months?"

"Yes."

"Five months?"

"No."

"Less than ten months but more than five months?"

"Yes."

"Eight months?"

"Yes."

"How well did you know her?"

"Well . . ."

"For example, were you sleeping with her?"

"Yes."

"Regularly?"

"No."
"Frequently?"
'No.'
"Occasionally?"
"Yes."
"Do you know anyone named Jerry McKennon?"
"No."
And like that.

The thing that troubled Willis was that the men had sounded identical.

Taking into allowance their different verbal styles (Hollander, for example, had interrupted the questioning with a surprisingly eloquent and exuberant sidebar on a pianist Willis had never heard of), accepting, too, the differences in their life styles and vocations (Hollander was an accountant, Riley a painter, Endicott a lawyer), and their ages (Endicott was fifty-seven, Riley thirty-eight or -nine, Hollander forty-two), taking all this into account, Willis nonetheless came away with the feeling that he could have tape-recorded his first conversation with Marilyn and saved himself the trouble of talking to the three men on her list.

We're very good friends, the lady had said.

We sleep together occasionally.

We have a lot of fun.

They do not know Jerry McKennon.

They do not know each other.

Yet three different men who did not know each other had defined their relationship with Marilyn Hollis exactly as she had described it. And each of them had come up with substantial alibis for Sunday night and Monday morning—while McKennon was either killing himself or getting himself killed:

Nelson Riley was with the lady in Vermont on Sunday night—or so he'd said. He was still there on Monday morning, taking a few final runs with her on icy slopes before starting the long drive back to the city.

Chip Endicott was at a Bar Association dinner on Sunday night, and at his desk bright and early Monday morning.

On Sunday night, Hollander had been to a chamber music recital at Randall Forbes Hall in the Springfield Center complex downtown. On Monday morning at eight o'clock, while McKennon was presumably gasping his life out to an answering machine, Hollander was on the subway, commuting to his job at the accounting offices of Kiley, Benson, Marx and Rudolph.

All present and accounted for.

But Willis could not shake the feeling that he'd seen the same play three different times, with three different people playing the same character and repeating the playwright's lines in their own individual acting styles.

Had Marilyn Hollis been the playwright?

Had she picked up the phone the moment the detectives left her and told Nelson, Chip, Baz—mustn't forget old taciturn Baz—that the police were just there, and she'd appreciate it if they said they were dear good buddies who never heard of anyone named Jerry McKennon, thanks a lot, catch you in the sack sometime.

But if so—why?

Her alibi was airtight.

But so were the others.

If only they hadn't sounded so very much alike.

Well, look, maybe the relationships *were* identical.

Maybe Marilyn Hollis defined the exact course a "friendship" would take and God help the poor bastard who strayed an inch from that prescribed path.

Maybe.

"Tell me more about them," he said.

"There's nothing more to tell," she said, "they're good friends."

And then, suddenly and unexpectedly: "Have you ever killed anyone?"

He looked at her, surprised.

"Why do you ask?"

"Just curious."

He hesitated a moment, and then said, "Yes."

"How did it feel?"

"I thought *I* was asking the questions," he said.

"Oh, the hell with the questions," she said. "I've already talked to all three of them, I know exactly what you said and exactly what they said, so why go through it all over again? You're here because they all gave you the same story, isn't that right?''

This time he blinked.

"Isn't it?"

"Well . . . yes," he said.

"Now you sound like Baz," she said, and laughed. "I adore him, he's such a sweetheart," she said. "I adore them all, they're *such* good friends.''

"So they said.''

"Yes, I *know* what they said. And you think they were lying, that I rehearsed them, whatever. But why would I have done that? And isn't it entirely possible that we think of each other *exactly* that way? As very good friends? All of us? Separately?''

"I suppose.''

"Do *you* have any good friends, Mr. Willis?''

"Yes.''

"Who?''

"Well . . .''

"Ah, there's Baz again.''

"I have friends," he said, and wondered about it for the first time.

"Who? Cops?''

"Yes.''

"Women cops?''

"Some of them.''

"Who are friends?''

"Well . . . I don't think any of the women cops I know are . . . well . . . what you'd call friends, no.''

"Then what? Lovers?''

"No, none of the women I see are cops.''

"Do you have any women friends at *all?* Women you could actually call friends?''

"Well . . .''

"You do a very good Baz imitation, Mr. Willis. Do I have to keep calling you Mr. Willis? What's your first name?''

"Harold.''

"Is that what your friends call you?''

"They call me Hal.''

"May I call you Hal?''

"Well . . ."

"Oh, come on, I didn't for Christ's sake *murder* him! Relax, will you? Enjoy your scotch, enjoy the fire, call me Marilyn, *relax!*"

"Well . . ."

"Hal?" she said.

"Yes?"

"Relax, Hal."

"I'm relaxed," he said.

"No, you're not relaxed. I know when a man is relaxed, and you're not relaxed. You're very tense. Because you think I murdered Jerry and you're sure that's why I offered you a drink and the comfort of my fire, isn't that right?"

"Well . . ."

"If you want to be my friend, be honest with me, will you please? I hate phonies. Even if they're cops."

He was looking at her in open astonishment now. He took a quick swallow of scotch and then—to reassure himself that he was a working cop with some serious questions to ask—immediately said, "Well, you have to admit it was sort of funny, getting the same playback from three different . . ."

"Not at all," she said. "None of them would know *how* to lie, that's why they're my friends. That's what we enjoy with each other, Hal. Relationships that are entirely free of bullshit. Have you ever had such a relationship in your life?"

"Well . . . no. I guess not."

"You're missing something. Would you like another drink?"

"I know you've got a date . . ."

"She can wait," Marilyn said, and rose from the couch. "Same thing?"

"Please," Willis said, and handed her his glass.

He watched her as she moved toward the bar.

"Are you looking at my ass?" she said.

"Well . . ."

"If you are, then say so."

"Well, I was. Until you mentioned it."

She came back to him with the drink. She handed him

the glass and sat down beside him. "Tell me about the man you killed," she said.

"It wasn't a man," Willis said.

He hadn't talked about this in a long long time. Nor did he want to talk about it now.

"A woman then."

"No."

"What does that leave?"

"Forget it," he said. He swallowed most of the scotch in his glass, rose, and then said, "Miss Hollis, I know you're busy, so maybe it'd be best if I . . ."

"Scared?" she said.

"No, not particularly."

"Then sit down."

"Why?"

"Because I like talking to you. And talking is the way people begin."

He looked at her.

"What is this?" he said.

"What *is* it? What is *what*?"

"I walk in here off the street . . ."

"Yes . . ."

"You spit fire the first time we meet . . ."

"That was the first time."

"So now . . ."

"So now sit down and talk to me."

"Your girlfriend's expecting you to . . ."

"Who'd you kill?" Marilyn said.

He kept looking at her.

"Sit down," she said. "Please."

He said nothing.

"Let me freshen that," she said, and took his nearly empty glass. He did not sit. Instead, he watched her again as she went to the bar, and half-filled two water tumblers, one with scotch, the other with gin.

He did not want to talk about who the hell he'd killed or didn't kill. He looked at her ass instead. He hoped she wouldn't ask again if he was looking at her ass, and was relieved when she didn't. She came back to him, handed him the scotch, and then sat again. Nylon-sleek knees again. No tug at the skirt this time. He did not sit beside her.

"Sit," she said, and patted the sofa. "Who'd you kill, Hal?"

"Why do you want to know?"

"Honesty," she said, and shrugged.

He hesitated.

"Tell me," she said.

The fire crackled and spit. A log shifted on the grate.

"Tell me, Hal," she said.

He took a deep breath.

"A boy," he said.

"What?"

"He was a boy."

"How old?"

"Twelve."

"Jesus," she said softly.

"With a .357 Magnum in his fist."

"When was this?"

"Long ago."

"How long ago?"

"I was a rookie cop."

"Was he white or black?"

"Black."

"Which made it worse."

"Nothing could have made it worse," he said.

"I meant . . ."

"I know what you meant. There was that, yes, but . . . you see, that wasn't what mattered to me . . . I mean, what the newspapers were saying, white cop kills innocent black kid . . . he was coming off a robbery, he'd just killed three people inside a liquor store, but that wasn't . . . I had to shoot him, it would've been me in the next three seconds. But . . . he was twelve years old."

"God," she said.

Almost a whisper.

"Yeah" he said. "That was the thing."

"How awful for you," she said.

"Yeah," he said again.

Silence.

He wondered why he was telling her this.

Well, honesty, he thought.

"His mother . . . his mother came to the police station" he said, his voice very low now. "And she . . . she asked the sergeant where she could find Patrolman Willis . . . they called us patrolmen in those days, now they call the blues police officers . . . and I was just coming in from downtown where I'd been answering questions at Headquarters all morning, and the sergeant said, There he is, lady, not realizing, not knowing she was the boy's mother, and she came up to me and . . . and . . . spit in my face. Didn't say anything. Just spit in my face and walked out. I stood there . . . I . . . there were guys all around . . . a muster room is a busy place . . . and I . . . I guess I . . . I guess I began crying."

He shrugged.

And fell silent again.

She was watching his face.

Two shots in the chest, he thought.

Kept coming.

Another shot in the head.

Caught him between the eyes.

Questions afterward. Two big bulls from Homicide. Confusion and noise. Some guy from one of the local television stations trying to get a camera inside the liquor store there, take some pictures of the carnage. The owner and two women lying dead on the floor, smashed whiskey bottles all around them. The kid outside on the sidewalk with his brains blown out.

Ah, shit, he thought.

This city, he thought, this goddamn fucking city.

"Are you all right?" Marilyn asked.

"Yes," he said.

"You haven't touched your scotch."

"I guess I haven't."

She lifted her own glass. "Here's to golden days and purple nights," she said, and clinked the glass against his.

He nodded, said nothing.

"That was my father's favorite toast," she said. "How old are you, Hal?"

"Thirty-four," he said.

"How old were you when it happened?"

He took a swallow of scotch and then said, "Twenty-two." He shook his head. "He'd just killed three people inside that liquor store. The owner and two ladies."

"I would have done just what you did," Marilyn said.

"Well . . ." Willis said, and shrugged again. "If only he'd put down the gun . . ."

"But he didn't . . ."

"I *told* him to put it down, I warned him . . ." He shook his head again. "He just kept coming at me."

"So you shot him."

"Yes."

"How many times?"

"Three times," Willis said.

"That's a lot of times."

"Yes."

They both fell silent. Willis sipped at the scotch. Marilyn kept watching him.

"You're small for a cop," she said.

"I know. Five eight."

"Most cops are bigger. Detectives especially. Not that I ever *met* a detective before now. I mean in the movies. Most of them are very big."

"Well, the movies," Willis said.

"You never killed anybody before that, huh?"

"No."

"Wow," she said, and fell silent for several moments. At last, she said, "What time is it?"

He looked at his watch. "Almost nine," he said.

"I really have to call Mickey," she said. "I'm sorry, I don't mean to rush you out."

"That's okay," he said, "I've taken enough of your time."

"Well, finish your drink," she said. "And if you want my advice, you'll put the whole thing out of your mind, really. You killed a man, okay, but that's not such a big deal. Really. Do you understand what I'm saying?"

He nodded and said nothing.

He was thinking Not a man, a boy.

He drained the scotch. He was feeling warm and a bit light-headed. He put the empty glass down on the coffee table.

"Thanks for the drink," he said. "Drinks."

"So where do you go now?" she asked.

"Back to the office, type up the reports."

"Will I see you again?"

Still sitting, looking up at him, pale eyes studying his. He hesitated.

"I didn't kill Jerry," she said.

Eyes fastened to his.

"Call me," she said.

He said nothing.

"Will you?"

"If you want me to," he said.

"I want you to."

"Then I will," he said, and shrugged.

"Let me get your coat," she said, and rose, sleek knees flashing.

"I can find my way out," he said, "I know you're in a hurry."

"Don't be silly," she said.

She took his coat from the rack and helped him into it. Just before he went out, she said, "Call me, don't forget."

"I'll call," he said.

The wind hit him the minute he stepped outside, dispelling alcohol and cozy fire, yanking him back to reality. He walked across to where he'd parked the car, struggled with a frozen lock, held a match under the key and finally managed to open the door. He started the car and turned on the heater. He wiped his gloved hand over the frost-rimed windshield.

He did not know why he decided to sit there in the car, watching her building across the street.

Maybe he'd just been a detective for too long a time. Twenty minutes later, a black 560 SL Mercedes-Benz pulled up to the curb in front of Marilyn's building. Willis watched as the door on the curb side opened.

Her girlfriend Mickey, he thought.

Better late than never.

Mickey—if that's who it was—locked the car door, walked the few steps to Marilyn's building, took off a glove, and pressed the bell button.

A moment later, Mickey—if that's who it was—opened the door and went inside.

Mickey—if that's who it was—was a six feet three inch tall, two-hundred-and-twenty-pound male white Caucasian wearing a bulky raccoon coat that made him look even bigger than he was.

Honesty, the lady had said.

Bullshit, Willis thought, and jotted down the license plate number and then drove back to the station house to type up his reports in triplicate.

5

APRIL THAT YEAR CAME IN WITH A SUDDEN-
ness that took the breath away. There had been in the
city a sense of siege, the winds of March blowing like
war trumpets, troop-trampled soot-blackened snow underfoot, a gunpowder sky unrelieved by sunshine. The
citizenry hurried along the streets, bundled inside bulky
garments, faces pinched and tempers short. The cold
was something that attacked incessantly, turning even
more inward a populace never noted for its generosity of
spirit. Willis despised the cold. He felt disembodied in
time and space, the victim of a relentless foe attacking
without provocation, determined to level the city and de-
vour its dead. Relief seemed only a distant dream. The
forecasters kept promising warm fronts from Georgia but
the warm fronts never materialized. Day by day, the
gloomy greyness of March persisted, the cold a penetrating, remorseless, vengeful adversary bent on abject
surrender.

But all at once, it was April.

Balmy breezes wafted in unexpectedly off the Old
Seawall downtown. Heads bowed too long by the en-
emy lifted tentatively toward the clearing sky, numbed
noses sniffed suspiciously of the warming air, watery
eyes blinked in surprise and disbelief. The coats came
off. Strangers in this city of strangers smiled at each
other in the streets. Uptown, along the stone walls bor-
dering Grover Park, forsythia bushes and cornelian
cherry shrubs burst into shy, tentative yellow and pink
bloom against the soiled and melting patches of snow.

It was April at last.

And in April, two days after Easter, a corpse turned
up in the Twelfth Precinct.

The dead man's neighbor, perhaps remembering *Swee-*

ney Todd, complained to the building superintendant that it smelled like somebody was baking human meat pies in apartment 401. The Emergency-911 cops who responded recognized the stench of decomposing flesh at once. They cursed the suddenly balmy weather and unrolled a body bag before they took two steps inside the apartment.

The dead man was identified as Basil Hollander, who was an accountant with the firm of Kiley, Benson, Marx and Rudolph.

The Twelfth Squad detectives investigating the case were named Sam Kaufman and Jimmy (The Lark) Larkin. Neither of them knew that a pair of detectives uptown were investigating a poisoning case. In fact, neither of them knew Carella or Willis at *all.* The two Homicide detectives who put in a mandatory appearance at the scene of the crime were named Mastroiano and Manzini. They worked out of Homicide West and knew Monoghan and Monroe—who worked out of Homicide East—only casually.

Monoghan and Monroe had read most of the 87th Squad D.D. reports on the McKennon case, and presumably knew that among the men questioned was an accountant named Basil Hollander. But they had nothing to do with the case down there in the Twelfth; this was a big city. As a matter of fact, they might not have made the connection even if they'd been called in on the case, which they could not have been, the police department guarding its geographic territories as jealously as it guarded its spotless reputation. Anyway, Monoghan and Monroe were very busy cops with a lot of scatological jokes to tell.

It was therefore not until the next day, April 2, that Willis happened to read about the downtown corpse.

He'd been busy until then trying to get a handle on the black Mercedes-Benz that had driven up to Marilyn Hollis's townhouse on the twenty-seventh of March and deposited a great big raccoon on her doorstep. A check with Motor Vehicles had advised Willis that the license plate on the car he'd seen was affixed to a new model Mercedes Benz registered to the president of a dress firm called Lily Fashions, Inc. with offices on Burke Street downtown. The president's name was Abraham Lilienthal, hence (Motor Vehicles guessed) the Lily Fashions.

A call to Mr. Lilienthal revealed that his car had been stolen on the night of March 23 and to his knowledge had not yet been recovered. Was Willis calling to say it had been found? Willis asked Lilienthal if anyone ever called him Mickey. Lilienthal said, "What? Mickey? You kidding me or something?"

A subsequent call to Auto Theft informed Willis that the car had been snatched outside a homosexual bar in the Quarter, though Lilienthal claimed he had been upstairs in an apartment over the bar, visiting a friend who was as straight as a Methodist minister. At any rate, it was true that the car had not yet been recovered. It was the opinion of the detective at Auto Theft that by now the car had already been inside a chop shop and that its parts were being sold hither and yon across the great length and breadth of these United States.

When Willis informed him that he had spotted the car as recently as last Tuesday night, the Auto Theft detective said, "That was last Tuesday night, pal. This is this Wednesday." Willis nonetheless said the car might have been driven by a man named Mickey who'd been wearing a raccoon coat. The Auto Theft detective said, wryly it seemed to Willis, "Terrific, I'll check our M.O. file for raccoons," and hung up.

So it now appeared that Marilyn's line backer girlfriend was either a car thief or else *knew* someone who stole cars. Willis was ready to call Marilyn again, not so they could become pals but because it now seemed she had a few more questions to answer. But then he spotted the news item on Basil Hollander, and called the Twelfth Detective Squad instead.

Detective/First Grade James Larkin was a burly man in his mid-fifties, red hair going grey, blue eyes on the thin edge of burn-out. He wore a shoulder harness, baggy blue trousers with brown shoes, and a white shirt with the sleeves rolled up. His jacket was on the back of his chair. He seemed relieved that Willis had called him.

"If he's yours, take him," he said into the telephone.

"Well, I don't know if they're related yet," Willis said.

"Even if they *ain't* related you can have him," Larkin said.

"Was he poisoned?" Willis asked.

"Stabbed," Larkin said.

"When?"

"M.E. estimates sometime Sunday night."

"That would make it . . ."

"Easter Sunday. We didn't catch it till yesterday. April Fool's Day. Guy next door notified the superintendant about a stink, the super called 911. The front door was unlocked, they walked right in. Found the body in the living room, fully clothed, throat slit."

"What kind of lock on the front door?"

"Spring latch. Mickey Mouse."

"Any security in the building?"

"Nope. What makes you think he's yours?"

"My guy knew a lady your guy also knew."

"This lady carries a knife?"

"I don't know."

"So what do you want to do, Willis? You're welcome to him, believe me. But if this is gonna go ping-ponging back and forth between precincts, we'll be asking for more headaches than we already got."

"How far along on this are you?"

"I told you, we only caught it yesterday. We done the building and neighborhood canvass, and we got a verbal report from the M.E.'s office, but no paperwork from them yet. Cause was severance of the carotid artery with a very sharp instrument. Post-mortem interval I already gave you."

"Any latents in the apartment?"

"Just the victim's. No wild prints."

"Any sign of forced entry?"

"Like I told you, it's a Mickey Mouse lock. Could've been loided, but who knows? Maybe he knew the killer, just opened the door for him."

"Any signs of socializing?"

"Like what?"

"Glasses on the coffee table . . . peanuts in a bowl . . . whatever."

"You looking for a lady's lipstick stains?"

"I'm looking for a place to hang my hat."

"Ain't we all?" Larkin said. "Looks to me like the guy was reading a book and drinking a cup of coffee when the killer came in. We found the coffee cup on an endtable alongside the couch, the book on the floor."

"Looked like it was dropped, or what?"

"Looked like it was on the floor," Larkin said.

"So you think he was surprised while he was reading?"

"I don't think nothin' yet."

"Where was the body? On the couch or . . . ?"

"On the floor in front of the couch. Decomposing. It was still cold Easter Sunday, the super still had the heat on. Then we got the tropics all of a sudden, so it started going bad fast."

"Anybody in the building see or hear anything?"

"Deaf, dumb and blind," Larkin said wearily. "Like always."

"Have you talked to anyone at his office yet?"

"We were gonna do that today. So where do we go from here, Willis? You want it or not? If so, I gotta talk to the Loot."

"I guess it may be ours," Willis said, and sighed.

"Good," Larkin said.

"Can you send the paperwork up here?"

"I'll have it copied and stick it in the pouch. We get a pickup around eleven."

At ten minutes past eleven that Wednesday morning, April 2, Steve Carella rang the doorbell to apartment 12A in a building on Front Street in midtown Isola. He was expected and the door opened almost at once. The man standing in the doorframe was perhaps five ten, and weighed something like a hundred and sixty pounds. He had pleasant blue eyes behind dark-rimmed eyeglasses, sandy brown hair, a mustache of the same

color, and a welcoming smile on his face. He was
wearing a plaid sports jacket and grey slacks, blue shirt
open at the throat. Carella guessed he was in his early
forties.

"Dr. Ellsworth?" he said.

"Detective Carella? Come in, please."

Carella followed him into a living room eclectically
furnished in an improbable but successful blend of modern with antique. An ornately carved Brittany sideboard
was on the wall opposite an arrangement of leather mod-
ular sofas. A riotously red abstract expressionist painting
hung over the sofas. Something that looked like a Rem-
brandt—but surely wasn't—hung on another wall. There
were two black leather Saarinen chairs. There was a
straightbacked sidechair that looked Victorian, upholstered in a rich green brocade.

"Sorry you had to track me all over town," Ellsworth
said. "Wednesday's my day off."

Carella was thinking that Wednesday was a bad day to
get a toothache. Most dentists in this city took Wednesdays off.

"No trouble at all," he said. "Your home number was
listed right under your office number."

"Still," Ellsworth said, and smiled apologetically.
"Can I get you a cup of coffee?"

"Thanks, no," Carella said.

"So," Ellsworth said. "You're here about Jerry Mc-
Kennon."

"Yes."

"What would you like to know?"

"According to his appointment calendar, he saw you
on March eighth . . ."

"Yes?"

". . . at eleven o'clock . . ."

"Uh-huh."

". . . and again on the fifteenth at the same time . . ."

"Uh-huh."

". . . and he was scheduled to see you again last Saturday, the twenty-ninth . . . but, of course, he never kept
that appointment."

Ellsworth sighed heavily. "No," he said, and shook his head sadly.

"He did keep those other appointments, didn't he?"

"I assume so. I don't have my appointment calendar here, but . . ."

"Did he usually keep appointments he'd made?"

"Oh, yes."

"Had he been a patient of yours for a long time?"

"Since January," Ellsworth said.

"What sort of person was he?"

"I knew him only professionally, of course . . ."

"Of course."

"But he always seemed extremely outgoing and friendly. Many people who come to a dentist's office aren't anticipating a pleasant experience, you know. I'm afraid dentists haven't enjoyed a very good press over the years. When *Marathon Man* was playing—did you see that movie?"

"No, I didn't," Carella said.

"Well, Laurence Olivier plays an ex-Nazi who does these *awful* things to Dustin Hoffman's teeth while he's strapped in a dentist's chair. I thought I'd never see a patient again. And more recently . . . did you see *Compromising Positions?* Or read the book?"

"No, I'm sorry."

"It's about a philandering dentist who gets murdered. You have no idea how many jokes I've suffered since! Even from my own *wife!* Rushing off to the office again, darling? The implication being that once a dentist has a woman's *mouth* open . . . well . . ." He shook his head ruefully. "In any event, not many people think of dentists as . . . friendly types, shall we say? Do you like *your* dentist?"

"Well . . ."

"Of course not. We're the bad guys," Ellsworth said, shaking his head again. "When all we're trying to do . . . well, never mind. I didn't mean to deliver a sermon on The Dentist as Knight in Shining Armor. I was merely trying to explain that Jerry McKennon never felt he was in my office to be *tortured*. In fact, Jerry told me some of the best jokes I've ever heard. None of them *dentist* jokes, by the way.''

''Are there a lot of dentist jokes?'' Carella asked.

''Oh, *please*,'' Ellsworth said.

Carella couldn't think of a single dentist joke.

''The point is . . . until recently, anyway . . . he was always pleasant and jocular and totally at ease in my office.''

''When you say 'until recently' . . .''

''Yes, well, he . . .''

Ellsworth shook his head.

''It may have been the nature of the work, I don't know. Some people hear the words 'root canal,' and they visualize the dentist digging clear across Suez or Panama. Actually, it's a commonplace procedure. We remove the dead nerve, clean and seal the canal, and then cap the tooth.''

''Is that what these last several appointments were about? Root canal work?''

''Yes. What were those dates you gave me? I know I saw him several times in February . . .''

''I only have the dates for March,'' Carella said.

''Sometime early in the month, wasn't it?''

''Yes, one of them was on the eighth.''

''It must've been around then, yes. During the February visits, I removed the nerve, reamed the canal, obtunded it, and so on. In March . . .''

''Obtunded?''

''Sealed it. It must have been on that March eighth visit that I fitted him with a temporary cap. And a week or so later . . .''

''Yes, the fifteenth . . .''

''Is that what you have? Then that's when it was. What I did then was take an impression of the tooth . . . a mold, you know, for the permanent cap . . . and then cemented the temporary cap back on. I expected to have the permanent cap a few weeks later . . .''

''That would have been the twenty-ninth . . .''

''Yes, I would guess so.''

''The appointment he never kept.''

''Yes.''

Ellsworth shook his head again.

"I'll tell you . . . I should have suspected something like this coming."

"How do you mean?"

"People never think of dentists as *medical* men, you know, but we do study the same biological sciences a physician does. Human anatomy, biochemistry, bacteriology, histology, pharmacology, pathology . . . our training includes all that. And when an essentially cheerful man suddenly comes in looking so . . . *hangdog* . . . well, I should have suspected a psychological problem."

"He seemed depressed to you, did he?"

"Enormously so."

"Despondent?"

"That's another definition of depressed, isn't it?"

"Did he mention why?"

"No."

"Never hinted . . ."

"No."

". . . not even obliquely . . ."

"No."

". . . at what might have been troubling him?"

"No."

"I gather you weren't surprised then," Carella said.

"By what?"

"His death. By poisoning."

"Do you mean did I think he was suicidal?"

"Did you?"

"No, I never once suspected he would take his own life. Never. In that respect, I was *enormously* surprised. When I heard about it . . . *God,* what a shock! A patient poisoning himself? And . . . I'll tell you the truth, Detective Carella . . . I felt guilty."

"Guilty?"

"Yes. For *not* having been more alert, for *not* suspecting that his depression was quite so serious, for *not* anticipating . . . yes, his suicide." He shook his head. "We take things so much for granted, you know. We miss the important signs."

"Yes," Carella said, and nodded and looked at his notebook again.

"Did he ever mention any of these names to you?" he asked. "Marilyn Hollis?"

"No."

"Nelson Riley?"

"No, I'm sorry."

"Charles Endicott. Or Chip? Either one?"

"No."

"Basil Hollander?"

"No."

Carella closed his notebook.

"Dr. Ellsworth," he said, "thank you very much for your time, I'm sorry to have bothered you on your day off." He rose, fished out his wallet, and handed Ellsworth a card. "Here's where you can reach me," he said. "If you happen to remember anything Mr. Mc-Kennon said to you, anything that might have some bearing on his death, I'd appreciate your giving me a call."

"I will indeed," Ellsworth said.

"Again, thank you," Carella said. "If I ever need a good dentist . . ."

"Don't go to Laurence Olivier," Ellsworth said, and smiled.

The paperwork from the Twelfth Precinct arrived in the messenger pouch at a little after one o'clock. It told Willis essentially what Larkin had told him on the phone, but it also pinpointed the exact time Hollander had got home on Easter Sunday. A neighbor had seen him going up in the building's elevator at approximately seven-thirty P.M. Hollander had got off on the fourth floor. The M.E.—faced with uncertainties like the changing temperature in the apartment and the fact that the body had been lying on a heat-absorbing carpet—had vaguely estimated the time of his death as sometime late Sunday night or early Monday morning. At any rate, he'd still been alive at seven-thirty, presumably heading for apartment 401 down the hall. Willis wondered what Marilyn

Hollis had been doing after seven-thirty last Sunday
night.

He had not seen Carella since they'd both checked in
this morning. Carella did not yet know they'd inherited
a corpse from the Twelfth Squad. Neither did Lieutenant
Byrnes. Willis went into his office and told him now.

"Are you crazy?" Byrnes said.

His corner windows were wide open to April's balmy
breezes. He was sitting in his shirtsleeves behind a pile
of paperwork on his desk—close-cropped iron-grey hair,
flinty blue eyes opened wide in astonishment. Willis had
the feeling he was going to leap over the pile of papers
and lunge for his throat.

"Why the hell did you . . . ?"

"They've got to be related," Willis said calmly.

"*I'm* related to a third cousin in Pennsylvania . . ."

"This isn't a third cousin, Pete," Willis said. "This
is the second victim with close ties to a woman named
Marilyn Hollis."

"Are you saying she killed them?"

"Come on, Pete, how can I say that?"

"Then what are you saying? We've got a caseload
here'll take us till *next* Easter to . . ."

"So what do you *want* me to do?" Willis said, somewhat testily considering he was talking to the boss. "Give
Larkin *our* case?"

"Who the hell is Larkin?" Byrnes asked.

"The Twelfth," Willis said. "Is that what you want
me to do?"

"I want you to check with *me* next time, before you
go taking on half the goddamn homicide cases in this
city!"

"I should've checked, you're right."

"You damn well should've. Who's handling the transfer papers?"

"Larkin."

"Thank God for that. We dump this on Miscolo's
desk . . ."

"No, the Twelfth is handling it."

"Can you trust Larkin not to screw it up? If I get
departmental flak on this, I'll . . ."

"He's an experienced cop, Pete. He'll take care of it, don't worry. He's happy to get rid of it."

"I'll bet he is," Byrnes said.

Over coffee and sandwiches in a greasy spoon around the corner from the station house, Willis broke the news to Carella.

"A knife huh?" Carella said.

"Well, some kind of sharp instrument," Willis said.

"But not poison."

"Definitely not poison."

"I don't get it, do you? Guy goes to all the trouble of setting up a complicated murder . . ."

"It *had* to be murder, don't you think?" Willis said. "I mean, if there was any doubt earlier, we've got a second victim now, and he's another one of Marilyn Hollis's pals. They've got to be linked."

"Well, sure," Carella said. "But that's the point. Somebody used nicotine, *however* the hell he got it, a deadly poison that acts within minutes. Okay, I have to ask myself *why*. Because he wants us to think suicide, right? Wants us to chalk it off as suicide. But then he turns around and *stabs* somebody. Primitive stuff, Hal, a one-on-one act. No attempt to hide the fact that it's murder. So why a class act the first time around, and then something out of the gutter the next time? That's what I don't get."

"Yeah, that's the bitch of it," Willis said.

Both men were silent for several moments.

"You think the Hollis woman is behind this?" Carella asked.

"Well, maybe. But if she's knocking off her pals one by one . . ."

"Or getting someone else to do it . . ."

"Then why give us a list? That's asking for trouble, isn't it?"

"Yeah," Carella said.

Both men were silent again.

"Does she know Hollander bought it?" Carella said.

"I haven't talked to her yet."

"We'd better. Right away."

"Let me do it," Willis said.

Carella looked at him.

"Alone," Willis said.

Carella was still looking at him.

"She wants to be my friend," Willis said, and smiled.

6

SHE WAS IN TEARS WHEN WILLIS TELEPHONED.

"I just read about poor Baz," she said.

"When can I see you?" he asked.

"Come right over," she said.

She buzzed him in the minute he rang the front door-bell. Didn't even ask who it was. He had no sooner let himself into the entrance foyer when the buzzer on the inner door sounded. He let himself into the living room. Empty.

"Miss Hollis?" he said, and then remembered that she'd asked him to call her Marilyn. "Marilyn?" he said, and felt stupid.

Her voice came from upstairs someplace.

"Come up, please," she said.

A wide stairway led to the upper stories of the house. Carpeted steps, polished walnut bannister, smooth to the touch. On the first level, a mirrored dining room with a table that could seat twelve comfortably, a kitchen with stainless steel ovens, refrigerator and range, and a room—the door slightly ajar—that seemed to be a study of sorts, with a rolltop desk, bookshelves, and an easy chair with a Tiffany lamp behind it.

"Marilyn?" he said again.

"Up here," she said.

Up here was a bedroom. Wood-paneled as was the rest of the house. A canopied bed. Antique dressers on two of the walls. An ornate, brass-framed, full-length mirror opposite the bed. Another Tiffany lamp. Persian rugs on the parqueted floor. A love seat upholstered in royal-blue crushed velvet. On the window wall facing the street, velvet drapes that matched the love seat. On the love seat . . . Marilyn.

Wearing blue jeans and a man's shirt, the sleeves rolled

up on her forearms, the tails hanging out. She was barefoot. Little Girl Lost. Her eyes, testifying to the validity of her telephone tears, were puffy and red.

"I didn't kill him," she said at once.

"Who said you did?"

He realized she had immediately placed him on the defensive. Big, bad police officer coming in making accusations.

"Why else are you here?" she said. "I asked you to call me, and you promised you would. But you didn't. Now Baz is dead . . ."

"That's one of the reasons I'm here, yes," he said.

"What's the other reason?"

"I wanted to see you again," he said, and wondered if he was lying.

She looked up at him. He was standing not four feet from where she sat on the love seat. Her pale blue penetrating gaze searched his face, seemed trying to pierce his skull to search the corners of his mind for the truth. Honesty, she had said. Maybe that's what she really wanted, after all. But then why lie about Mickey in the raccoon coat?

"Let's start with poor Baz, okay?" he said.

Bit of sarcasm in his voice, he'd have to watch that. No sense putting *her* on the defensive.

"The newspaper said he was stabbed," Marilyn said. "Is that true?"

Which, if she was the one who'd stabbed him, was a very smart question.

"Yes," he said.

The appropriate answer, whether she'd stabbed him or not. But somehow, he didn't like playing detective with her. He wondered why.

"With a knife?"

Another smart question. The M.E. had said only "a sharp instrument." Could have been a knife, of course, but it could just as easily have been anything capable of tearing flesh and tissue. Most citizens, as opposed to law enforcement officers, automatically assumed "stabbed" meant with a knife. So why had she asked him if the weapon had been a knife? Had she been the stabber? With something other than a knife?

He decided to get tricky.

"Yes," he said, "a knife," and watched her eyes.

Nothing showed in them.

She nodded.

That was all.

Said nothing.

"Where were you on Easter Sunday?" he asked.

"Here we go again," she said.

"I'm sorry. I have to ask."

"I was with Chip."

"Endicott?"

"Yes."

The lawyer who'd given Willis a lecture on male-female friendship.

"From what time to what time?" he said.

"You *do* think I killed Baz."

"I'm a cop doing his job," Willis said.

"I thought we were about to become friends," she said. "You told me you came here because you wanted to see me again."

"I said that was one of the reasons."

She sighed heavily.

"All right," she said, "fine. He picked me up here at seven."

"Where were you at seven-thirty?"

The time a neighbor had seen Basil Hollander in the elevator of his building on Addison Street.

"Eating," she said.

"Where?"

"A steak house called Fat City."

"Where?"

"On King and Melbourne."

All the way uptown. The Eight-Six? He was pretty sure King and Melbourne was in the Eight-Six, a hell of a long way from the Twelfth.

"What time did you leave the restaurant?"

"About nine."

"And went where?"

"To Chip's apartment."

"What time did you leave the apartment?"

"Around eight Monday morning."

"You spent the night with Mr. Endicott?"

"Yes."

Somehow that annoyed him.

"I'm sure he'll corroborate all this," he said.

"I'm sure he will," Marilyn said.

The M.E. had said Hollander was killed sometime late Sunday night or early Monday morning. According to Marilyn now (and surely according to Endicott when he got around to questioning him) they'd been in his apartment together from nine Sunday night to eight Monday morning. That was very nice. Unless one of them had gone out to skewer poor Baz.

"Is there a doorman at Endicott's apartment building?" he asked.

"Yes," she said.

"He see you go in?"

"I assume so."

"Same doorman at eight in the morning?"

"No."

"A different doorman saw you go out, right?"

"He hailed taxis for us, yes."

"Two taxis?"

"Yes. Chip was going to his office, I was coming back here."

"I'll be talking to both those doormen, you realize."

"I would hope so," she said. "You're a cop doing his job."

"What's your father's name?" he asked abruptly.

"What?" she said.

"Is it *Jesse* Hollis? Joshua? Jason?"

"Jesse. And it's Stewart. He's my stepfather."

"How does he spell it?"

"S-T-E-W. Why? Do you think *he* killed Baz?"

"Somebody did," Willis said. "Where does he live?"

"Houston," she said. "Are we finished with the third degree?"

"Not a third degree," he said. "Just . . ."

"Just a cop doing his job, yes, you told me."

"Yes," he said. "And no, I'm not finished yet."

"Well, hurry up and finish so we can have a drink."

He looked at her.

"Because I like it much better when you're not a cop doing his job."

"Who's Mickey?" Willis asked.

"Mickey? Oh. You have a very good memory. Mickey's a girlfriend."

"What's her last name?"

"Terrill."

"Does she weigh two hundred and twenty pounds and wear a raccoon coat?"

Marilyn's eyes opened wide.

"Does she drive a stolen Mercedes-Benz?"

Marilyn smiled.

"My, my," she said, "we've been very busy, haven't we?"

"Why'd you lie about Mickey?"

"Because I didn't see any sense in adding to your lists of suspects. Which, incidentally, I seem to be at the top of."

"Tell me what you know about him."

"Not much."

"Is he a car thief?"

"I have no idea."

"He *came* here, didn't he? What do you mean, you have no . . ."

"That was the first time I ever saw him. And the last. Look, would you mind very much if I made us some drinks? I really need one. Believe it or not, Baz's death came as quite a shock to me."

"Make yourself at home," he said.

She rose from the love seat and walked to one of the antique dressers. She opened a door. Rows of bottles and glasses inside there. She took out a bottle of gin, opened another door. A small refrigerator.

"Are you still drinking scotch?" she asked.

"Not at three o'clock in the afternoon."

"I hate scotch," she said. "What time are you off duty? I'll set the clock ahead."

"Four. Well, I'm relieved at a quarter to four."

"Break the rules," she said.

"No," he said. "Thanks."

She shrugged, cracked open an ice cube tray, dropped three cubes into a glass, and poured a healthy shot of gin over them.

"Here's to golden days and purple nights," she said, and drank.

"Tell me about Mickey," he said.

Marilyn walked to the bed and sat on the edge of it. "He was in the city for a few days," she said. "My girl-friend Didi asked him to call me. Period."

"Do you always go out with men you don't know? Strangers who may turn out to be car thieves?"

"I didn't know he was a car thief. *If,* in fact, he is. And I didn't go *out* with him. We had a . . ."

"You were dressed to go out. Fancy blue dress, sap-phire earrings, high-heeled shoes . . ."

"You noticed," she said, and sipped at the gin. "How do you know I didn't get all dressed up for *you?*"

"Come on," Willis said.

"You have a very low opinion of yourself, don't you?"

"No, in fact I think I'm the cat's ass. And let's not start the psychotherapy again, okay? If you *didn't* go out with this Mickey Terrill punk . . ."

"We had a few drinks here, and he went his merry way," Marilyn said. "Why does he make you so angry?"

"Thieves make me angry," Willis said. "And let's not get off the track. You told me you were going out with a girlfriend. You said you were going to dinner with her."

"Yes," Marilyn said, and sipped at the gin again. "I guess I lied."

"Why?"

"Because if I told you Mickey was a man, you'd have started asking me the same questions you're asking me now, and I didn't want you to think I was the kind of girl who went out with men I don't even know, which only would have made you angry, the way you're angry now."

"I'm not *angry!*" Willis said.

"Oh boy, listen to who's not angry," Marilyn said, and rolled her eyes.

He didn't say anything for several seconds.

Then he said, "You're a pain in the ass, do you know that?"

"Thank you," she said, and lifted her glass to him in acknowledgment. "It's getting closer to four o'clock, you know."

He looked at his watch.

"Would you like that scotch now?"

"No," he said.

"Or would you like to come here and kiss me?" she said.

He looked at her. His heart was suddenly pounding.

"If you'd like to, then just say so," she said.

"I'd like to," he said.

"Then come do it," she said.

He went to her where she sat on the bed. He sat beside her.

"I didn't kill either of them," she whispered, and kissed him.

Their lips parted, heads tilting, tongues insinuating. He took his mouth from hers and looked into her face.

Her blue eyes flashed in the glow of the Tiffany lamp in the corner near the bed. Wordlessly, she unbuttoned her blouse. No bra beneath it, adequate breasts with good nipples. He touched her, kissed her again. She unzipped the blue jeans and took them off. His hand moved to her panties, cupped her there. She responded with an exhalation of breath that sounded like a serpent's hiss, her back arching as he lowered the panties, her hand finding his zipper, and lowering it, and reaching into his pants to free him, her eyes averted like a nun's.

The clock on one of the antique dressers ticked loudly, urging a hurried coupling, setting a tempo like a metronome, ticking into the silence as he probed her, springs jangling in accompaniment, their bodies finding at last a rhythm faster than the clock's, a bone-rattling, jarring, steady, fierce rhythm that initially forced grunts from her, and then moans, and then a high shrill keening that sounded like an Irish wake, something primitive and animal and frightening.

Their position was absurd, they were locked in intimate embrace, enclosing and enclosed, grinding, gasping,

moaning, writhing—but they didn't even know each other.
Drunk on the gin scent of her breath, dizzied by her wild
keening, lost in a frantic rhythm that outraced time, Willis
passionately acknowledged this ridiculous secret they were
sharing as strangers, and with each animal lunge forgot
more and more completely that he was a cop investigating
a double homicide.

"Give it to me!" she screamed. "Oh, Christ, give it to
me!"

Secrets.

She told Willis later all about her father—her *natural*
father, he of the golden days and purple nights. The man
was a drunk who used to beat her mother black and blue
every time he got loaded. He tried to do the same thing
to Marilyn one night, came home pissed to the gills and
burst into her room while she was getting ready for bed,
standing there putting on her nightgown, came in with his
belt strap in his hand, and began chasing her through the
house, swearing at her. She left home the next day.

"I went to the Coolidge Avenue bus terminal," she said,
"in my school uniform, St. Ignatius, I used to go to St.
Ignatius in Majesta, little plaid skirt and blue blazer with
the school crest embroidered in gold right here," she said,
and touched her left breast. "A beautiful day in May, three
months before my sixteenth birthday, I took a bus clear to
California. He was *one* son of a bitch, I'll tell you. The
Irish are supposed to be the big drinkers, am I right? Well,
my father was the champion booze hound in all Majesta,
and his parents were born in London."

Willis listened intently to every syllable she uttered,
feeling a closeness that transcended the love they'd earlier
made; no woman on earth had ever talked to him this way
before. He held her in his arms and listened.

"I went out there, you know, to California," she said,
"so I could get away from my father, I mean who the hell
wanted to get batted around every time he had a few
drinks? So I got involved out there with this beach boy
who used to be a weight lifter. He had muscles like an
ape, hair all over his back, too, I hate men with hair on
their backs, don't you? And tattoos. You should always

watch out for men who have tattoos, they're the craziest bastards in the world. It's a fact that most armed robbers have tattoos, did you know that?''

"Yes," Willis said.

"Well, sure," she said, "you're a cop. This guy didn't happen to be an armed robber, but he used to beat me up regularly, just the way my father would've if I'd stayed home in Majesta. That's something, don't you think? The irony of it? He told me he used to be a skinny runt till he started lifting weights, and that lifting weights made all the difference in the world, gave him the self-confidence he needed, you know, and the assurance, and made him feel like a whole new individual. This was after he almost sent me to the hospital one night.

"I finally called the cops, they're so polite, the cops out there, not like here, oops, excuse me. They tip their hats, they say, 'Yes, Miss, what's the problem, Miss?' I'm standing there with a black eye and a swollen lip, and Mr. America is flexing his muscles all over the place, and they ask me if I'm sure I want to press charges. I told them forget it. I mean, what was the sense? But the next time he raised his hand to me, I split open his forehead with a wine bottle. I told him this time *you* call the cops, you bum! He didn't call the cops, but he didn't hit me anymore, either. In fact, we broke up the very next week. I guess he couldn't stand being around somebody he couldn't smack from wall to wall. Some guys just like to beat up girls, I guess, don't ask me why. *You* don't, do you?''

"No," Willis said.

"I didn't think so," Marilyn said. "Anyway, I was out there for a bit over a year when my mother found me, a few months before my seventeenth birthday. Told me she'd married this big Texas oil millionaire . . . well, Jesse, my stepfather . . . and I went to live with them in Houston. A happy ending, right? I love happy endings, don't you?''

The afternoon lengthened imperceptibly into the night. And because she'd been so honest with him, had given to him so unreservedly of her body and her mind, he started to tell her about what he'd felt that afternoon long ago when he'd shot the twelve-year-old boy, but her mind was elsewhere now, her mind was where her hand had gone, her mind was on what her hand was doing to him.

"You never know how life is going to turn out, do you," she said, "come on, I want you hard again. This girl I know, she used to pose for Nelson, you met Nelson Riley, the artist, come on, baby, she was a dancer who couldn't get a job but she refused to get discouraged, and finally she had an audition with this choreographer, there we go, that's better, I forget his name, a very important choreographer, and that's how she ended up with the Isola Ballet, uh-uh, not till you're enormous," until finally he rolled onto her and into her again and she screamed again in orgasm that must have shattered every window in the city.

Now she listened.

Now that the urgency had passed, now that their secret had been reaffirmed and lay divulged between them, their bodies covered with perspiration, the sheet tangled at their feet, the nighttime sounds of the city pulsatingly alive beyond the bedroom windows—now she really listened.

They pulled the blanket over them, and she lay in his arms, and he whispered to her in the night, trying to reveal the other secret, the darker secret, told her again about the two dead women and the liquor store owner on the floor, and the gun in the twelve-year-old's hand, the glazed look in his eyes, " 'Put it down,' I said, and he came at me. I fired twice, two to the chest, but he kept coming at me, and I put the last one in his head, between the eyes. I think he was already dead, though, I think his coming at me was a reflex, the body just moving, like a chicken when you cut off his head. The last shot wasn't necessary. I'm sure one of the other shots took him in the heart."

He paused.

"His brains spattered all over me," he said.

There was a long silence. He could hear her breathing heavily beside him.

"You poor thing," she said at last. "But you mustn't let it get to you, really. You were doing your job, the man had already killed three people . . ."

"Yes, but . . ."

"He would've killed you, too, if you'd let him. You were only doing your job."

"You don't understand," he said.

"Sure, I do. You . . ."

"I enjoyed it," Willis said.

She fell silent again. He wondered what she was thinking. Then she said, "Well, don't worry about it," and drifted off to sleep, her legs scissored around his thigh, one arm across his waist. He did not fall asleep for a very long time. He kept thinking of what he'd told her: *I enjoyed it.*

They woke up at eleven in the morning. She yawned and said, "Hi, sweetie, how's the big killer?" and then stretched and sat up, and glanced idly at the clock on the dresser, and jumped out of bed at once.

"Jesus," she said, "I've got a twelve o'clock doctor's appointment!" and started across the room toward the adjoining bathroom. "Put up some coffee, will you?" she said. "Jesus, we should have set the alarm," and ran into the bathroom.

He went downstairs to the kitchen, took a container of orange juice from the refrigerator and set a pot of coffee on the stove. She came downstairs ten minutes later, wearing what looked like a designer suit, blue to match her eyes, white blouse under it, low-heeled walking shoes. Sitting opposite him at the kitchen table, she said, "Do you remember what you said last night? Would you pour me some more coffee, please? About enjoying it, do you remember? Killing him?"

He carried the coffee pot from the stove and began pouring into her cup. Their eyes met. "Well, that's okay, your enjoying it. I mean, there are plenty of things I've done in my life, kind of awful things, and I had to admit to myself later that I enjoyed them. Also, man, this is the *city,* you know what I mean? I mean, all *kinds* of terrible things happen here . . . well, you know that, you're a cop. But you either let them get you down or you put them out of your mind and you survive. What time is it?"

"Half past," he said.

"I think I'll be okay. It's just that he takes a fit if a patient is even a minute late. What I'm saying is you can let this city poison you or you can drink it down like honey from a cup. So you killed a man and you enjoyed it. So what? Forget about it.'' She swallowed what was left in her cup, reached into her handbag, and took out a lipstick and mirror.

Secrets.

Mysteries.

Lips puckered to accept the bright red paint. Tissue pressed between her lips, imprint of her mouth coming away on the tissue. She crumpled the tissue, tossed it into the wastebasket under the sink. Pale horse, pale rider, pale good looks.

''Well, at least I'm not a *total* wreck,'' she said.

''You look beautiful,'' he said.

''Ah, sweet,'' she said, and touched his face. ''I've got to run,'' she said, and put the coffee cup in the sink.

''Will you be back?'' he asked. ''I don't have to be in till four this afternoon.''

''Oooo, I wish I could, sweetie,'' she said, ''but I'm busy all day. Save it for tomorrow, okay? Can you save it for me?''

''I'll save it,'' he said.

''Mmm, yes,'' she said, and glanced at his groin, and smiled. She kissed him on the cheek, gave his cock a friendly little squeeze, backed away from him, and said, ''Tomorrow morning, okay? Ten o'clock.''

''Ten o'clock,'' he said.

''Don't be late,'' she said, and started out of the kitchen, and then stopped and turned to him again. ''Just let yourself out when you're ready to go, okay? I'll set the answering machine, you don't have to answer the phone. Pull the doors shut behind you, the inner one *and* the outer one, they lock automatically.''

''I won't be long,'' he said. ''I just want to shower and . . .''

''Take as long as you like.''

She looked at him tenderly and then came to him again and kissed him fiercely. ''Mmmm,'' she said, ''this is going to be good, isn't it?'' and then released him abruptly and went out.

He heard her going down the stairs. He heard her setting the answering machine in the living room. He heard the front door closing behind her.

He went to the upstairs bathroom, showered, and then dressed.

He left the apartment at a little after twelve.

And although he wasn't due in till a quarter to four, he went immediately to the squadroom.

7

THERE WERE THREE SHIFTS ON THE SQUAD-
room duty-chart, more closely resembling the blues' shifts
than they used to, an innovation initiated by the new Chief
of Detectives, but one honored more in the breach than in
actuality; detectives were used to making their own sched-
ules.

Nonetheless, the day shift officially began at eight in the
morning and ran through to four P.M. The evening shift
started at four and ended at midnight. The night shift (familiarly called the Graveyard Shift) began at midnight and
ended at eight in the morning. The detectives tried to work
the shifts so that they'd be on days for a couple of weeks,
then evenings, then nights—the better to establish sleep
patterns that were seriously threatened, anyway.

The morning shift was midway and a bit more through
its inexorable cycle when Willis got to the squadroom at
a quarter to one. Kling and Brown were sitting at Kling's
desk, eating sandwiches and drinking coffee when Willis
pushed through the slatted rail divider that separated the
squadroom from the corridor outside. Brown looked up in
surprise.

"You bucking for Commissioner?" he said.

Willis ignored this. He had learned over the years that
if a person tried to respond to every quip and jibe bounc-
ing off the squadroom walls, he had to learn how to play
squash.

"Three hours early," Kling said. "The man is dedicated."

Willis sighed.

"There are three kinds of cops," Brown said, and Willis knew he was in for an impromptu standup-comic routine (though in this case, both Brown and Kling were
sitting). "You've got your burned-out cop . . ."

"Burnout occurs after four minutes on the job," Kling said.

". . . who tries to do as little work as possible without calling the Loot's attention to the fact that he is goofing off."

Brown and Kling, the best Mutt and Jeff team on the squad, now doing their world famous comedy shtick. Willis much preferred them as Mutt and Jeff. Big Bad Leroy Brown (though his given name was Arthur and he was familiarly called Art or Artie by every other detective on the squad) as black as midnight, six feet two inches tall, tipping the scales at a hard, muscular two-twenty; and tall, blond, slender Bert Kling, looking like a farmboy from the wheatfields of Indiana (wherever that was), peach fuzz on his jaw and chin, mild hazel eyes reflecting worlds of innocence, a cop willing to listen to any sob story a cheap thief pitched, the perfect Mutt and Jeff team. "Gee, Artie, I really do think we've got the wrong man this time," and Brown looking like a ferocious bear ready to pounce and claw and bite, "Let me at 'im, Bert, I'm goan tear the man apart!" Within minutes, the thief was in Kling's arms, begging for mercy and willing to confess to the murder of a maiden aunt twelve years ago. But now . . .

"And you've got your time-study cop . . ."

"In on the dot . . ."

"Out on the dot . . ."

"Types up everything in triplicate . . ."

"Goes to court uncomplainingly . . ."

"Doesn't mind working on Christmas or New Year's . . ."

"Protector of the innocent . . ."

"Dedicated to the pursuit of justice . . ."

"But who won't give you a nickel's more than the time he's being paid for." Brown grinned like a wolf. "And then you've got your cop like Willis here."

"On the job twenty-four hours a day . . ."

"Takes his pistol to bed with him . . ."

"Do not be afraid, *guapa*, it is only my pistol."

"Breaks up armed robberies when he's off-duty . . ."

"Never calls in a 10-13 . . ."

"Constantly bucking for promotion . . ."

"Comes in three hours early to relieve the shift . . ."

"Your eager-beaver cop . . ."

"Appearing for the first time in America . . ."

"Live and in person . . ."

"Detective/Third Grade . . ."

"Looking for Second . . ."

"Harold O. Willis."

"Take a bow, Oliver," Brown said.

Willis wondered how Brown had tumbled to his middle name. He brought up his hands and clapped hollowly, twice. Then he went to Kling's desk and dropped a quarter onto Brown's paper plate. "Very nice," he said. "Thank you very much, boys."

"Big tipper, too," Brown said, but pocketed the quarter anyway.

"Steve left a note on your desk," Kling said.

"I'll be going now," Brown said, "seeing as I'm relieved and all."

"You're not relieved," Willis said. "Sit down."

He went to his own desk and picked up Carella's note.

It told him to expect a callback from the Food and Drug Administration, which Carella had phoned yesterday (while Willis was in bed with Marilyn, but Carella didn't know that) in an attempt to learn whether nicotine was used in any commercial products. It also advised Willis not to expect him at four on the dot because he was going first to Basil Hollander's building to recanvass the tenants Larkin of the Twelfth had already canvassed. *Since it's ours now,* he'd written, *I want to make sure he got everything.*

Willis wondered in which of Brown's cop-categories Carella would fit.

He also wondered about the honesty—to use Marilyn's word—of what had happened yesterday afternoon *and* last night *and* this morning in her apartment, his cop-mentality considering the possibility that the lady had let him into her pants and into her bed only as a diversionary tactic.

He had told her yesterday that he thought he was the cat's ass, but in the private recesses of his mind, he knew this wasn't the truth. He had never been a ladies' man, somehow always favoring women who were much too tall for him, a penchant that inevitably led to rejection of the

Did-You-Bring-Your-Stepladder sort. He considered himself an average-looking man in a world populated more and more, it seemed, with spectacularly handsome men. He knew he was short. He knew, too, that short men were supposed to carry chips on their shoulders, angry at the world for the genetic unfairness that had robbed them of the inches necessary to compete in a nation of giants. He might have felt more at home in Japan. Or India. But he was stuck with the U.S. of A., where even your average cab driver looked like a linebacker for the Los Angeles Rams. Generation after generation growing taller and broader, the result of good food and good medicine. Unless you lived in a slum.

As a result of that long-ago shootout—Christ, he shouldn't have told her about it, why had he opened up to her that way?—he had developed a severe aversion toward using the gun. Almost immediately after that worst day in his life, he had enrolled in a Judo school, and had since supplemented his education with police-academy lessons in karate. He was now capable of tossing any cheap thief on his ass in ten seconds flat, without having to resort to deadly force. He somehow enjoyed the feeling of secret power this gave him. Kick sand in Shorty's face? Okay, pal, wham, bam, how does it feel to have a broken arm and swollen balls? Drive your extended forefinger and middle finger into the space over the upper lip and the nose, hit the hard ridge there, and you could send bone splinters flying into a man's brain, never mind using the damn gun.

He had told Marilyn, in the hours he'd spent with her, more about himself than he'd ever told any other woman he'd known. There was that about her. An openness—no pun intended—that demanded openness in return. And yet he wondered. An undeniably beautiful woman deliberately encouraging the runt of the litter? Why? He was *not* the cat's ass, and he knew it. He was Harold Oliver Willis— even the name seemed appropriate for a short man—Detective/Third Grade, street-smart, experienced, wise to the ways of the con artist, but perhaps gulled anyway by a lady whose close friends seemed to be departing with amazing rapidity for that great big fraternal order in the sky. Four men on that list, two of them already dead and gone. Were the other two similarly marked for imminent extinction? Was he himself now on that select list, a fifth man who had shared Marilyn's bed and bountiful honesty?

If it *was* indeed honesty.

She had told him her stepfather's name was Jesse Stewart.

Big oil millionaire.

In Houston, Texas.

At the risk of incurring the lieutenant's wrath for making an unnecessary long-distance phone call, he asked the operator for the number of police headquarters in Houston, was informed by her that the main police facility down there was called Houston Central, and then immediately dialed the number and asked for the detective division.

The detective he spoke to was a man named Maynard Thurston. Willis imagined a big, red-faced man in a cowboy hat. He told Thurston he was working a double homicide up here and would appreciate anything the Texas cops could give him on an oil man named Jesse Stewart.

"He break the law?" Thurston asked.

"Well, I don't think so. He's a rich oil man down there."

"All oil men are rich down here," Thurston said. To Willis's northern ear, the words "all" and "oil" sounded identical. "Why you calling a law-enforcement agency if the man hasn't broken no law?"

"I thought you might run a quick check for me," Willis said. "I could call the Chamber of Commerce, I guess . . ."

"Yeah, why don't you do that?" Thurston suggested.

"But it's been my experience," Willis said, doing a quick tap dance for Texas, "that cops get better cooperation from other cops."

There was a long silence on the line.

Then Thurston said, "Mmm."

Willis waited.

"This's a double homicide, huh?" Thurston said.

"Yes," Willis said. "A poisoning and a stabbing."

"I got on my hands just now somebody chopped up seven people with a chainsaw."

Willis continued waiting. He was thinking he was glad he didn't work in Houston Central. Poisonings and stabbings were bad enough.

"I get the time, I'll see I can look into this for you," Thurston said. "May take a coupla days."

"I'd appreciate whatever . . ."

"How you spell that last name? Is it S-T-U, or S-T-E-W?"

"S-T-E-W," Willis said.

"Give me your number there, I'll see what I can do." Willis gave him the number before he changed his mind.

"I really appreciate this," he said.

"I ain't *done* nothin' yet," Thurston said, and hung up.

Willis put the receiver back on its cradle.

He looked at the wall clock.

Two P.M. sharp.

Twenty hours until ten o'clock tomorrow morning, when he would see Marilyn again.

The return call from Houston Central came at eight that night, midway through the evening shift.

By then, Carella had talked to most of the tenants in Hollander's building. As Larkin had reported, all of them—with the exception of the one who'd seen Hollander in the elevator at seven-thirty on Easter Sunday—were deaf, dumb and blind, a not uncommon phenomenon in this city insofar as witnessing a murder was concerned. Better not to get involved. Better to go one's own way. In this indifferent city, where a tenant rarely knew even the name of the person living next door, it was risky to say too much about what one had seen or heard. The fear of reprisal was always present. If someone had killed *one* person, was he not then capable of killing yet another? Why volunteer as the next victim? A policeman's lot was not a happy one.

They were laying out a strategy of sorts when the call came.

Carella was not dismissing the possibility that the homicides were of the Boy-Meets-Girl garden variety. Jealous lover does in the lady's two other lovers. Which made Nelson Riley and Chip Endicott prime suspects in the Eternal Triangle Tragedy, although in this case the triangle was four-sided, a geometric impossibility, but well within the realm of investigative speculation. The possibility also existed, Carella suggested, that the murders were of the classic Smokescreen variety, the lady herself doing in two of her lovers in the hope that suspicion would fall on—

"No, I don't think so," Willis said at once. "I think she's clean, Steve."

"How so? What'd she tell you?"

"She was with Endicott the night Hollander was killed. I checked with Endicott this afternoon, and he confirms . . ."

"That doesn't eliminate a double alibi."

"I don't think she had anything to do with this," Willis insisted. "Endicott may have sneaked out of bed . . ."

"Oh? They were in bed together."

"Well . . . yes," Willis said.

"What's the matter?" Carella said at once.

"Nothing."

"You look."

"You look . . . I don't know . . . funny."

"Funny, I don't feel funny," Willis said, and attempted a smile.

Carella was still studying him. Willis opened his notebook, avoiding his gaze.

"All I'm saying is that it's unlikely Endicott got out of the apartment without her realizing it, and also got past the doorman—*twice*—without being seen . . ."

"You talked to the doorman?"

"Yes. He saw them both go in at a little after nine—which checks with their stories—and he didn't see either one of them go out anytime later."

"When did he go off?"

"At midnight."

"Did you talk to his relief?"

"Same story."

"What time *did* they leave the apartment?"

"Eight the next morning."

"Same doorman?"

"A third one. He corroborates. Got taxis for both of them."

"Any back way out of the building?"

"A door opening onto a courtyard where the garbage

cans are stacked. But both the elevator and the steps are clearly visible from the front door.''

"Is that all the security? Just the doorman?''

"Yes.''

"So you're assuming all of these guys were wide awake all during their shifts, right?''

"They seemed like reliable witnesses,'' Willis said.

"So that would eliminate both Endicott and the Hollis woman.''

"It would seem to,'' Willis said.

"Which leaves only Nelson Riley. On that list she gave us. *If* this was Boy-Meets-Girl.'' He hesitated, and then said, ''But he was off skiing when McKennon caught it.'' He hesitated again. ''Unless he and the Hollis woman are in this together. In which case, their alibi for that weekend . . .''

"No, I think she's clean, Steve.''

"So you said.''

"But let's assume for the moment . . . well, where's the motive, Steve? Why would the two of them, her and the artist—he'd have to be in it if they're lying about that ski weekend . . .''

"He would.''

"So why would they knock off two people who were close friends of hers? I mean, I genuinely believe they were friends, Steve. I think she's telling the truth about that.''

"Maybe she's mentioned in both their wills, who knows?'' Carella said.

"Come on,'' Willis said, ''the girl's independently wealthy. Her stepfather's an oil millionaire in . . .''

"Oh? He's her *step*father?''

"Yes.''

"And he set her up in that swanky place on the Lane?''

"Well, yes, they're very close, from what I could gather. That's not unusual, Steve. Sometimes the relationship between a stepfather and . . .''

"Sure,'' Carella said.

"What I'm saying is . . . even if there *are* these wills you were talking about, which I don't think you really believe . . .''

''We can check with Probate,'' Carella said, and shrugged.

''Well, I just don't think money is the motive here. I really don't.''

''There are only two motives for murder,'' Carella said. ''Love or money. Unless we're dealing with a crazy, in which case we can throw away the manual.''

''Well, I don't think this was money.''

''That leaves love.''

''Or a crazy.''

''So which do you think it is?'' Carella asked.

''I don't know. But I've got a gut feeling the girl is clean.''

''Do you have a gut feeling about Riley, too?''

''Well, if he was up skiing with her that weekend . . . I mean, if *she's* clean and telling the truth . . .''

''Then Riley's clean, too.''

''Yes.''

''Which leaves us with nobody.''

''Or anybody. Anybody connected with McKennon or Hollander. The possibility exists, you know, that these are unrelated. That's not so far-fetched, Steve. A poisoning and a knifing are worlds apart.''

''Tell me all about it,'' Carella said, and sighed.

The telephone rang.

Carella picked up the receiver.

''Eighty-seventh Squad, Carella,'' he said.

''You got a Willis there?'' the voice on the other end said.

''Who's this, please?''

''Detective Colworthy, Houston Central.''

''Just a second,'' Carella said, and covered the mouthpiece. ''You place a call to Houston?'' he asked Willis.

''Yeah,'' Willis said, and took the receiver. ''Detective Thurston?'' he said. ''This is Hal Willis, what'd you . . . ?''

''It's Detective Colworthy here, Thurston passed this on to me. You wanted a check on somebody named Jesse Stewart?''

''That's right,'' Willis said.

''S'posed to be an oil millionaire down here?''

"Yes?"

"We got nobody by that name's an oil millionaire down here," Colworthy said.

"Have you got any Jesse Stewarts at all?" Willis asked.

"We got a shitpot full of 'em," Colworthy said. "Jesse's a common name down here, and so's the last name. That includes two or three dozen assholes doing hard time. But none of them's an oil millionaire."

"What are they then?"

"Buddy, you asked us to check oil millionaires, and what we checked was oil millionaires. You want a census by occupation, you picked the wrong people to call."

On impulse, Willis asked, "Have you got anything on a woman named Marilyn Hollis?"

"What do you mean by 'anything'? We ain't about to go through the phone book again."

"Criminal," he said, and immediately wondered why the word had popped into his head. Not five minutes ago, he'd been telling Carella she was as pure as the driven snow.

"You wanna hold while I punch up the computer?"

"I'll hold," Willis said, and turned to Carella. "Nothing on Jesse Stewart," he said.

"Who's Jesse Stewart?"

"Her stepfather," Willis said. "The oil millionaire who set her up in that townhouse."

"Willis?" Colworthy said. "You there?"

"I'm here."

"Nothing on a Marilyn Hollis."

Good, Willis thought.

"But we got a one-time sheet on a Mary *Ann* Hollis, if that's any help to you. Picked her up on a 43.02 seven years back."

"What's a 43.02?" Willis asked.

"Prostitution," Colworthy said. "Her pimp paid the fine, and she's never been heard from since."

"You got a description there?" Willis asked, and held his breath.

"White Caucasian," Colworthy said, "seventeen years old at the time. Blonde hair, blue eyes, five feet eight inches tall, weight a hun' eighteen, no visible scars or tattoos.''

Willis sighed heavily.

"What was her pimp's name?" he asked.

"Joseph Seward," Colworthy said.

8

NEVER MIND TOMORROW MORNING AT TEN
o'clock, never mind saving it for her till then. This had
to be *now*, he had to talk to her *now* about Mary Ann
Hollis whose description fit her to the toenails. Mary
Ann Hollis who'd been picked up on a 43.02 seven years
back, and whose pimp's name was Joseph Seward, not a
far stretch from Jesse Stewart, why did criminals have
no imagination at all? Talk to her right this goddamn
minute and get a few things straight.

It was a little past nine when he got to the townhouse
on Harborside Lane.

Springtime in the Rockies maybe, but still a wintry chill
on the nighttime air, enough to cause him to raise the
collar on his coat as he walked from the car to the front
door. He rang the doorbell. No answer. He rang it again.
Oooo, I wish I could, sweetie, but I'm busy all day. Busy
all night, too? He kept his forefinger pressed insistently to
the button. Still no answer. Okay, he thought, I've got all
the time in the world. Or maybe not. Maybe time was
running out for him and Marilyn Hollis both, though he
wondered why he should give a damn.

He crossed the street to where he'd parked the car, unlocked it, got in, closed the door behind him, and hun-
kered down behind the wheel, watching the door to 1211
Harborside. At ten minutes to ten by the dashboard clock,
a taxi pulled up to the building. Marilyn got out, wearing
a light topcoat over what she'd been wearing this morning
when she'd left the apartment. She paid the cabbie and
started for the front door searching in her bag for her keys.
Willis came out of the car in a wink, slamming the door
behind him. She turned at once.

As he came across the street toward her, she said, "Hey,
hi, what a surprise."

99

"Yeah," he said.

She kissed him on the cheek. "You're early," she said.

"By almost twelve hours."

"But come in anyway."

"No, let's take a walk," he said.

"Bit chilly for a walk, isn't it?" she said, and smiled.

"We can use a little fresh air," he said. "All around."

She studied his face, tried to read his eyes in the illumination coming from the street lamp.

"Sure," she said, and took his arm.

They walked down toward the river.

This city wasted the river running along its northern edge. Bordered by a highway that made no allowance for a walking path, the Harb could have taken lessons from the Thames or the Seine or the Arno. No river for lovers, this one, though tonight he wasn't here as a yesterday lover, merely as a cop doing his job. *I like it much better when you're not a cop doing his job.* I'll bet, he thought. As they entered the small park across the street from her building, a fresh gust of wind blew up off the river far below, and she tightened her grip on his arm. Lady, you better hang on real tight, he thought.

"Who's Joseph Seward?" he asked.

Straight for the jugular.

No answer for several moments. No tightening of the hand on his arm, no expression on her face, very cool, this one.

"A man I used to know," she said.

"What's his occupation?"

"If you already know, why ask?"

"He's a pimp, isn't he?"

"When I knew him, he was, yes. I haven't seen him in at least six years."

"Make it seven," Willis said. "When he paid a fine for a prostitute named Mary Ann Hollis."

"All right, so what? I *told* you I'd done some awful things in my life."

"You also said you'd enjoyed them."

"Yes, it was marvelous fun, is that what you want to hear? So that's what friends do, is it?" she said, shaking

her head and sounding very, very hurt, poor darling.
"Check up on a person's past?

"That's what *cops* do," he said.

"You weren't such a cop last night," she said.

"I'm a cop tonight. Is that the name you used in Houston? Where you were hooking?"

"That's my real name," she said.

"Mary Ann Hollis."

"Mary Ann Hollis, yes. I started using Marilyn when I came east."

"Why? Are you wanted for something in Houston?"

"Of course not!" she said.

Which was the correct answer. Colworthy had told him the prostitution arrest was the last thing they had on her.

"Does Jesse Stewart exist?"

"No."

"No millionaire stepfather?"

"No."

"Then who paid for that pad across the street?"

"I did."

She was still holding his arm. He was amazed that she was still holding his arm. Together, they strolled the park's winding path like lovers, which technically they were, moving from one pool of lamplight to the next. A casual passerby might have thought they were quietly discussing plans for the future. Instead, they were discussing a past—and a possible end to the present.

"Where'd you get that kind of money?" he asked.

"I *earned* it," she said.

"Hooking?"

"That's *earning* it, believe me."

"That building had to've cost at least a mi . . ."

"Seven-five," she said.

"Even so. You telling me you earned that kind of money on your back?"

"On my knees, usually."

"You must have been a very busy lady."

"I was at it for a long time."

"Seward let you take home that kind of money?"

"I broke with Seward after the bust."

"He let you walk? Who are you kidding?"

"I didn't walk, I ran. All the way to Buenos Aires."

"Where you earned seven-hundred and fifty . . ."

"More than that. There are lots of high rollers in Argentina. I was an independent, I kept every penny for myself."

"Are you wanted for something in Argentina?" he asked suddenly.

"I'm not wanted for anything *anywhere!* What the hell's the matter with you?"

"Then why'd you change your name?"

"Does that make me a wanted desperado? What's that, my only claim to fame? That I changed my name? How about what I've *accomplished?* I broke with the past, I came here and started a new life . . ."

"Are you still hooking?"

"I told you no."

"No, you *didn't* tell me no!"

"I said I started a new life, didn't I? Does that sound like hooking?"

Now they were arguing. Like lovers.

"Was that punk Mickey a john?"

"He was someone a girlfriend asked me to . . ."

"How about the men on your answering machine?"

"Casual acquaintances."

"That means johns!"

"It doesn't fucking mean johns!" she shouted.

"Nice talk on the lady."

"I *am!*" she said.

"If you're not hooking, how do you support yourself?"

"I left Buenos Aires with two million dollars."

"Busier than I thought."

"*Much,*" she said angrily. "I gave great head. I still do." She paused and then said, softly, "You know that."

"But not professionally, right?"

"How many times do I have to say it?"

"As often as I want to hear it."

"I'm not hooking anymore," she said, and sighed heavily. "I invested what was left over after I bought the house. My broker is a man named . . ."

"I know. Hadley Fields at Merrill Lynch."

"Yes."

They walked in silence for several moments.

"Why'd you lie to me?" he asked at last.

"Why'd you have to go snooping?"

"Why the fuck did you *lie* to me?" he said, and shook off the hand on his arm, and stopped dead in the center of the path, and grabbed her by the shoulders. "Why?"

"Because I knew you'd run if I told you the truth. The way you're about to run now."

"Why would that have mattered to you?"

"It mattered. It *still* matters."

"Why?"

"Why do you think?" she said.

He released his grip on her shoulders. His own shoulders slumped. He felt suddenly very short.

"I don't . . . I don't know what to think," he said.

"Do we have to discuss this out here in the cold?"

She took a step closer to him. She stood very close to him.

"Hal?" she said. "Will you come inside now?"

He was trembling. He knew it was not from the wind that blew in off the river.

"Hal? Please. Come inside. Let me love you. Please."

"Don't lie to me ever again," he said.

"I promise," she said.

Her hand came up to touch his face. She kissed him gently on the mouth.

"Now come with me," she said. "Come."

And she took his arm again, and led him out of the park, and across the street, and into the house.

Nelson Riley was working when Carella got there the next morning at nine o'clock. It was a Friday, and Riley was annoyed.

"I wrap for the week on Friday," he said. "Try to get a lot of work done, set my ducks in a row for Monday. You should have called first."

Big redheaded giant, green eyes blazing with anger, paint smears on his big-knuckled hands, paint brush clutched like a saber in one of them.

"I'm sorry," Carella said. "But there are a few more questions I'd like to ask."

"Where's the other cop? The little guy. At least he had the decency to call first. You guys think all an artist does is sit around on his ass waiting for inspiration to strike. I'm a working man, same as you."

"I appreciate that," Carella said. "The only difference is I'm working a murder."

He did not mention that he was now working *two* murders. He was here because he wanted to learn what Riley knew about the *second* one.

"Who cares *what* you're working?" Riley said, still angry. "I'm working a nine-by-twelve canvas that's breaking my balls! You think your murder is tough to solve? Try taking a look at that big mother against the wall."

Carella took a look at the big mother against the wall, which wasn't a mother at all, but was instead a ski slope swarming with skiers in motion.

"You get any sense that it's snowing?" Riley asked.

"No," Carella said.

"Neither do I. I want it to be snowing. But each time I lay on the white, I lose color. Those primaries on the skier's costumes, the brilliant purples and greens on the flags from the base lodge, the rich brown chairs on the lift—you see those brilliant colors? I'm an artist who uses *color.* But I've had to rework all that stuff a dozen times, because the white overlay filters it down to pastels. If I can't make it snow by the end of the day, it'll drive me nuts all weekend. So who gives a shit about your murder? Anyway, I told the other cop everything I knew."

"Mr. Riley," Carella said, "if you don't make it snow, you only go nuts for the weekend. If we don't crack this case, somebody gets away with murder. And that can drive *us* nuts for a long, long time."

"Look, mister, don't come bleeding on *me,* okay?" Riley said. "I really don't *care* if you're overworked and underpaid. Go tell it to the Salvation Army. Nobody forced you to become a cop."

"That's true," Carella said. "But I am one, and I'm here, and it won't kill you to extend a little common courtesy."

"A little common courtesy is picking up a phone before you barge in on a man trying to make it *snow!*"

"Only God can make it snow," Carella said, and Riley unexpectedly burst out laughing. Carella smiled uncertainly. "So can we talk?" he said.

"All right," Riley said, shaking his head, "but let's make it quick, okay? I really do have to get a handle on this."

You and me both, Carella thought.

Out loud, he said, "I just wanted to prod your memory again on the people my partner asked you about."

"What people?"

"Marilyn Hollis's friends."

"Here we go again with Marilyn and her friends," Riley said. "For Christ's sake, she had nothing to *do* with this guy's murder, whatever the hell his name was."

"McKennon," Carella said. "How do you know she had nothing to do with it?"

"Because first of all she was with *me* when he poisoned himself. That painting against the wall is all *about* where we were that weekend. If you look closely, you'll see Marilyn there near the chair lift, kneeling to adjust her bindings. The girl in the yellow parka, though she was wearing a sort of peach-colored thing that weekend. I prefer primary colors. And secondly, Marilyn swore she had nothing to do with the guy's death. And Marilyn never lies."

"Everybody lies," Carella said.

"Not Marilyn."

Saint Marilyn, Carella thought. Newly canonized. The only person in the universe who never lies.

"Everybody," he said again, leaning on the word.

Even me, he thought, if only by omission; he had still not mentioned Basil Hollander's death. But then again, neither had Riley. Maybe *both* of them were lying.

"When did she tell you that?" he asked.

"Tell me what?"

"That she'd had nothing to do with McKennon's death."

"We talked on the phone after the other cop . . ."

"Willis."

"The little guy, yeah. I talked to her after he was here. I told her I knew she was with *me* that weekend, but was it possible she'd hired some goon—for whatever reasons of her own—to drop the poison pellet in the guy's cup?

That's when she swore up and down that she hadn't even *known* he was dead till you guys broke the news to her.''

''Were those her exact words?''

''More or less.''

''And of course *you* knew nothing about it until my partner informed you.''

''Yeah, the little guy.''

''Willis.''

''Yeah.''

''What made you think Miss Hollis—or anyone—might have hired a goon to do the job?''

''I didn't *seriously* think . . .''

''Well, seriously enough to have suggested it to her.''

''Jokingly.''

''Oh, you were *joking* about it.''

''Not about the murder, nobody jokes about murder. About the *goon.*''

''Because you felt it was a far-fetched notion.''

''Well, who hires a *goon* to drop poison in somebody's drink?''

''Is that how you think McKennon got poisoned? Someone dropping the stuff in his drink?''

''I don't know how he got poisoned. I'm only saying. Goons break your arms or shoot you in the kneecaps. They don't do dainty little ladylike pois . . .''

He stopped dead.

''What are you getting me into?'' he asked.

''I'm just listening,'' Carella said.

''Well, I don't like the way you listen,'' Riley said. ''It's very selective listening.''

''Do you think a goon might have *forced* that poison down McKennon's throat?''

''I have no idea how that poison got into McKennon.'' Defensive now, muscular arms crossed over his burly chest, scowl on his craggy face, even the red handlebar mustache seeming to bristle.

''Well, let's talk about these other two men she was seeing,'' Carella said.

''I don't know those other two men, the ones your partner mentioned.''

''Willis.''

"Yeah, the little guy. I don't know them, and I didn't know McKennon and if I don't start making it snow soon, I'm going to get pretty fucking irritable, Mr. Carella."

"Chip Endicott?" Carella persisted. "Never heard of him? That would be Charles Endicott, Jr. He's a lawyer."

"I didn't know him when your partner was here, and I *still* don't know him."

"How about Basil Hollander?"

"I don't know him."

"The name isn't familiar to you?"

"It isn't . . ."

"It wasn't familiar to you when my partner came here on . . ." Carella checked his notebook and then looked up. "March twenty-fifth? The day after McKennon's murder? The name wasn't familiar to you then?"

"It was not."

"And it isn't familiar to you now?"

"It is not."

"Do you read the newspapers, Mr. Riley?"

"I do."

"Do you watch television?"

"I don't own a television set."

"Do you listen to the radio?"

"While I'm painting."

"And the name Basil Hollander still isn't familiar to you?"

"I just told you . . ."

"Do you know that Basil Hollander is dead?"

Watch the eyes.

"Do you know he was murdered?"

Keep watching the eyes.

"He was stabbed to death in his apartment on Addison Street, downtown in the Twelfth Precinct. But you didn't know that, did you?"

"No, I . . ."

"Have you talked to Marilyn Hollis since the beginning of the month?"

"Actually, no, I . . ."

"This is the fourth, Mr. Riley. You haven't spoken to Miss Hollis anytime since the first?"

"No, I haven't."

"I thought you were close friends."

"We are, but . . ."

The cavernous loft went silent. When Riley spoke again, his voice was almost a whisper.

"This is serious, isn't it?" he said.

"Very," Carella said.

"I mean . . . is someone knocking off all her friends?"

"Two so far," Carella said, and kept watching the eyes. He had seen nothing in those eyes when he'd broken the news about Basil Hollander, no quick lie-detector needle jump, no mirroring of a guilty soul, nothing to indicate that Riley had been anything but genuinely surprised. Now he saw in those eyes only something that looked like fear. Big redheaded grizzly bear of a man suddenly realizing that two of Marilyn's friends had been killed, and he was *another* of Marilyn's friends.

"Am I a suspect or a target?" he asked. His face had gone pale against the fiery red hair and the handlebar mustache.

"You tell me," Carella said.

"I want police protection," Riley said.

9

SO DID CHARLES INGERSOL ENDICOTT, JR.

At eleven o'clock on that Friday morning, April 4, after having given considerable thought to the matter, and after having discussed it with his partners at Hackett, Rawlings, Pearson, Endicott, Lipstein and Marsh, he telephoned the squadroom and spoke not to Willis—who at that moment was still in bed with Marilyn Hollis—but instead to Carella, who had just returned from his brief encounter with Nelson Riley. He told Carella that it appeared to him and his colleagues that someone was systematically murdering Marilyn Hollis's friends—what with the second murder on April Fool's Day, did Carella attach any significance to the date?—and that it might be advisable, since he was after all a close friend of Marilyn's, to request some sort of police protection at this juncture. Didn't Carella agree that he might be in line for imminent extinction?

Carella secretly agreed that Endicott might very well be a candidate for termination with extreme prejudice, but he said only that he would take the matter under advisement (his language automatically emulating the lawyer's somewhat curlicued style) with the lieutenant and get back to him as soon as a decision had been made.

Lieutenant Byrnes said, "Where the hell is Willis?"

"He's not due in till four," Carella said.

"So what the hell are *you* doing here?"

"I want your job," Carella said, and smiled.

"You're welcome to it," Byrnes said.

"What do I tell Endicott? And Riley?"

"They're worried, huh?"

"Wouldn't you be?"

Byrnes shrugged. "I've been around too long," he said. "You start worrying about a safe falling out of a

109

ten-story window and hitting you on the head, you go crazy. What are the odds on this guy trying to nail the other two? I'd say one in a million.''

"Which are heavy odds if you happen to be one of the other two.''

"What are they asking for? Round-the-clocks? Three shifts?''

"They didn't specify.''

"That'd mean taking six men away from where they *should* be. I can't spare six detectives, that's for sure. Not with the weather turning nice and all the bedbugs coming out of the woodwork.''

"We can use patrolmen.''

"In plainclothes, if they're going to serve our needs. He spots a blue uniform, he'll run like hell.''

"That's the idea, isn't it?''

"No. The idea is if we're going to divert manpower, it has to serve some purpose other than protecting two guys who are running scared. If we sent policemen around to protect everybody in this city who thinks somebody's gonna kill him, we'd have no cops left to do anything else. I'm in favor of the round-the-clocks only because if our man *does* try another hit, we'll have somebody there to nab him. Let me see if Captain Frick can spare six blues. Put Endicott and Riley on hold till then.''

It was determined within an hour, and over Captain Frick's objections, that six patrolmen could indeed be diverted from their usual posts in order to set into motion the undercover round-the-clocks on Endicott and Riley. Frick (because the bedbugs were coming out of the woodwork not only for detectives but for the uniformed force as well) chose six men he could most afford to lose, a half-dozen fuck-ups who looked upon the surveillance job as a welcome break from the tedium and danger of streetwork—until they were told a murderer might put in an appearance. All at once, the job didn't look like a paid vacation in the country anymore. They began arguing among themselves about who would have the Graveyard Shift, the choice shift in that Endicott and Riley presumably would be asleep during the empty hours of the night and morning, and their protectors might also

get a chance to do a bit of cooping. Frick settled the
quibbling at once by assigning the shifts himself, you for
the day shift, you for the evening shift, you for the night
shift. Period. Reluctantly, at two o'clock that afternoon, two of the six fuck-ups trotted off in opposite directions, one to Nelson Riley's loft downtown on Carlson
Street, the other to Endicott's law office midtown on Jefferson Avenue.

For now, both men were protected.

Sort of.

Willis came to work at a quarter to four that afternoon.
He was whistling.

Carella, who'd been on the job since nine that morning, nonetheless worked through the shift till a quarter
to twelve that night. During the shift, the men caught an
armed robbery in progress, an attempted rape, three as-
saults, and a burglary. Nobody tried to kill either Endicott or Riley, much to the joy of the two fuck-ups who
had been relieved on post at a quarter to four that afternoon. At a quarter to twelve, the third pair of fuck-ups
reported for duty and were respectively told that Endicott
and Riley had been tucked in for the night. Carella and
Willis were relieved at that same time.

Both men had the weekend off.

Carella went directly home to his wife and kids in Riverhead.

Willis went directly to the house on Harborside Lane.

One wing of the house had been closed off—''To save
on the heating bill,'' she told him—and served as a storeroom for a collection of junk she could find no place for
in the rest of the house. A brightly colored, hand-painted
vase, for example, sat on what Willis thought was a low
coffee table covered with a red shawl. Marilyn told him
that the vase was hand-painted by a man who'd been sitting on the sidewalk downtown in the Quarter, with all
these ugly little clay things all around him, except for
this one, which she thought was really beautiful, although she suspected the colors might wear off one day.
The vase used to contain artificial flowers, but she'd
thrown those out when she discovered there was a leak

in the ceiling, after which she'd moved the box with the shawl and the vase on it under the leak because if you had to have something for a leak, the vase was more esthetic than a kitchen pot, wasn't it?

What Willis had thought was a coffee table under the vase and the shawl was instead the "box" to which she'd referred. She had bought the shawl in Buenos Aires, where she'd gone after running out on Joseph Seward. The box was a Sunkist orange crate she'd found behind a grocery store when she first got here to the city. She had planned to soak off the label on the end panel and then have it framed in a little shop she knew on the Stem, where they did absolutely marvelous work and could make even a crumby little pencil sketch look like a Picasso. She'd taken the crate here when she bought the house, but she'd never got around to soaking off the label, and finally she moved it into the storeroom where she'd covered it with the shawl and put the vase with the artificial flowers on it, until the ceiling developed a leak.

There were four dog leashes hanging on the wall in the storeroom.

She'd once had a dog, this was after she'd bought the house, a huge Lab named Iceberg because he was black, but she couldn't take him to the park for the exercise he needed because she was always running here and there to interior decorators and showrooms when she was furnishing the house. So she gave the dog to this man who was a friend of hers—

"A friend or an acquaintance?" Willis asked.

"Well, he was a friend, I thought," she said.

—but the dog got run over by an automobile, which could have been the end of their friendship right then and there, the man being so careless and all. Instead she kept seeing him until she learned that he had a wife and four kids in Las Vegas, at which point she told him she didn't care for either philanderers or liars, especially philandering liars who let a dog run out loose in the street where he could get run over by a Caddy. She kept the leashes because she'd really loved that dog, and also because one day she might decide to buy another dog, although that was only a remote possibility.

The storeroom was packed from floor to ceiling with cartons. Some of the cartons contained letters she'd saved, mostly from friends here in the city when she was living on the Coast and later in Houston when she was in Seward's stable. She didn't want to go into detail about how she'd got in the life—''The usual story, Hal, a guy turned me out, and that was that''—but she did say that she'd drifted to Houston after she walked out on the Malibu beach bum who used to smack her around. No, her mother never contacted her there in California. No, her mother never married an oil millionaire. As he already knew, those were lies. Because if she'd started telling him the truth about what had happened after she left California, she'd have had to go into Houston and all the rest, Buenos Aires, all that, and she might have lost him right there on the spot.

Most of the cartons contained newspaper and magazine clippings.

There were articles on breast cancer . . .

''I worry to death that someday I'll get breast cancer. Or worse, cancer of the uterus. When I was in the life, I used to worry all the time about picking up a dose. I was lucky, but can you imagine what those poor girls have to worry about *nowadays?* I mean, gonorrhea or syphilis you can cure. But herpes is for life, and AIDS is for death. I never worried about cancer, though maybe I should have. I'm scared to death of it now because my mother died of cancer. Jewish women never get cancer of the uterus, you know, or at least not many of them, because Jewish men have their cocks circumsized, it's a shame I'm not Jewish. Uterine cancer is mostly a Gentile disease, it's from rubbing against a man's foreskin. But my mother died of cancer, so you see I could be prone to it. That's why I saved all those articles about breast cancer because who knows what might happen one day? Would you love me if I had only one breast?''

. . . and pictures of fashion models snipped from *Vogue* and *Harper's Bazaar* and *Seventeen* . . .

''When I was in the life, I used to dream of being a fashion model. They only get sixty, seventy dollars an hour, most of them, and I was getting sometimes three *hundred* an hour, but oh, how I used to dream of trading places with them. I used to pose in front of the mirror naked and practice standing the way models do. You have to stand differently, you know, like this sort of, with one foot in front and the hips sort of sideways. I have narrow hips, a plus for a fashion model, and small breasts, too.''

''Your breasts aren't small,'' Willis said.

''Well, I'm not your earth-mother type, that's for sure,'' she said. ''But thank you.''

There was a whole file of material on World War I in the storeroom, including some 1919 copies of a newspaper she'd picked up in an antiques shop on Basington Street . . .

''Because, you know, that's a war that really fascinates me. All those men sitting out there in trenches, just looking across No Man's Land, with rats crawling all over everything, and jerking off and whatnot to while away the time. It wasn't like modern-day warfare at all, where people just drop bombs on each other. I hope they don't drop the big one, don't you? If they do, I hope we're in bed together. Do you know what I'd really like to do some day? Please don't laugh. I'd like to write a book about World War I. That's ridiculous, I know, I haven't got a shred of talent. But who knows?''

Her legacy from the years she'd spent in Buenos Aires was a command of the Spanish language that floored Willis, especially when she turned it loose on an unsuspecting Puerto Rican cab driver who—driving them back to the house after lunch out that Saturday—had the gall to take them a few blocks out of their way. She spoke the language fluently, colloquially, and obscenely as well, peppering her diatribe with directives such as *''Vete el carajo''* (which she told Willis meant ''Go to hell''), and epithets like *''hijo de la gran puta''* and *''cabeza de mierda,''* the latter causing the diminutive cabbie to come out from behind his wheel shouting some choice language of his own, both he and Marilyn squaring off in the middle of the street, nose to nose and toe to toe, screaming at each other like Carmen and an arresting army officer, while crowds gathered on the sidewalk and a uniformed cop looked conveniently the other way. In bed with Willis later that afternoon, she told him she'd only called the cabbie a shithead.

She was not, he discovered that weekend, much of a housekeeper.

A woman came in to clean for a few hours on Mondays, Wednesdays and Fridays, but between visits—as now—Marilyn let the house "return to the jungle," as she put it. The kitchen was total chaos. The sink was cluttered with dirty dishes, pots, and pans because Marilyn found it easier to use her entire supply and leave everything for the housekeeper to clean when she came in. The refrigerator was a brand new model, but the only things in it were several open containers of yogurt, a wilted head of lettuce and a slab of rancid butter. Marilyn explained that she rarely ate at home, or if she planned to it was easier and more healthful to stop in the grocery store on the Stem just two blocks south, to buy fresh produce or milk and eggs or whatever when she needed it, instead of letting it sit in the fridge. There was a pile of dirty clothing on the bedroom floor and even in the living room just inside the entrance door. Marilyn liked to take off her clothes the moment she came into the house, locking the door behind her, dropping blouse and skirt, or jumper and leotard, kicking off her shoes, wandering around in her panties. She explained that the house was very well protected from the street and no one could see in, and besides even if some guy in the park across the way happened to look up and spot her starkers, he wouldn't be seeing anything a hundred thousand other guys hadn't already seen.

"I'm sorry," she said at once. "Does that bother you?"

"Yes," he said.

"I promise I'll never mention the life again, I swear to God. But it's what I did, you know. For a long time."

"I know."

He was thinking lots of cops ended up marrying prostitutes; he wondered why.

He also wondered why marriage had popped into his mind.

On Sunday afternoon, they smoked pot together.

He'd never smoked pot in his life, though he knew other cops who did.

They were lying in bed together when she got up and went naked to one of the antique dressers. When she came back to the bed, she was carrying what appeared at first glance to be a pair of cigarettes.

"I don't smoke," he said.

"These are joints," she said, and of course, now that she extended them on the palm of her hand, he recognized them at once as marijuana.

"*This* is a joint," he said, grasping his erection.

"That's a joint for sure" she said "but these are joints, too. Come on, sweetie, we're going to turn on."

"I'm turned on already," he said. "Witness the joint."

"Put that thing away for now," she said. "This is very good stuff, it'll make the sex even better."

"How can it possibly get better?"

"Well, don't you *know?*" she said, and then looked at him in surprise. "Haven't you ever smoked pot?"

"Never."

"Oh, goodie," she said, "a virgin! Come, let me teach you.

"I'm not sure I want to learn."

"Oh, come on," she said. "I'll bet even the Commissioner smokes pot."

"Maybe so, but . . ."

"It's only a little *pot,* Hal! Nobody's about to stick a needle in your arm."

"Well . . ."

"What you do is you take a very deep drag on it, much deeper than you would on a cigarette, and you swallow the smoke and hold it in for as long as you can."

"I've seen it done," he said drily.

"When you finally let out your breath," she said, "there shouldn't be anything but the tiniest trace of smoke left, okay?"

"Marilyn . . ."

"Just watch me, and stop being such a Goody-Two-Shoes. I'll take the first drag so you can see how it's done, and then I'll pass the toke to you. Please drag on it right away, Hal, because this is Acapulco Gold and not a Winston or a True.''

She inhaled on the joint and handed it immediately to him. He took a deep drag and began coughing violently.

"Oh, my," she said, and clucked her tongue. "Try it again."

He tried it again. This time he didn't cough.

"Good. Now let me have it."

They passed the joint back and forth half a dozen times until it was scarcely more than a glowing little stub. Holding the roach between her thumb and forefinger, Marilyn sucked on it noisily and then dropped the coal in an ashtray on the bedside table.

"Evidence," she said. "In case you're planning a bust."

"I'm off duty," he said.

"Boy oh boy, *are* you!" she said. "How do you feel? Do you feel anything yet?"

"Nothing."

"Give it a few minutes," she said. "Sometimes, with virgins, it doesn't work right away."

"I don't feel anything," he said.

"Isn't everything getting sort of very sharp and clear?"

"No."

"It works differently with different people," she said. "I see everything very sharply and clearly, all the outlines crisp and sharp and clear. All the outlines. Crisp and clear."

"You forgot sharp," he said.

"Yes, crisp and clear and sharp," she said. "For some people, everything gets fuzzy, but not for me. What happens with me is I feel very relaxed and everything just shines with a sharp, clear crispness."

"What happens with me is nothing," Willis said.

"How do you see me?" she asked. "Do I look crisp and sharp?"

"You look naked."

"I know, but am I also crisp and sharp?"

"No, you're soft and round."

"Some people see things soft and round," she said.

"Especially if they *are* soft and round."

"Try to be serious," she said. "Get up and walk across the room, okay? Oh, look," she said, "it's gone. What happened to it?"

"Your Acapulco Gold killed it," he said.

"No, it makes sex better, you'll see. Get up and walk across the room."

"Will that bring my hard-on back?"

"I want you to see how the timing is off. And the distance. With a lot of people, distances get distorted. The wall there'll seem a million miles away, it'll take forever to walk across the room and touch the wall. Go ahead, try it."

"I want my hard-on back," he said.

"Go on over to the wall there."

"Don't I get a blindfold?"

"Does the wall look far away?"

"It looks right there."

"Right where?"

"Right there at the end of the tunnel," he said, and began giggling.

"There was a man I used to see . . ."

"You promised you wouldn't . . ."

"No, no, this was a friend. And he said Hell is the Holland Tunnel. Hell is getting stuck forever in the Holland Tunnel."

"Where's the Holland Tunnel?" Willis asked. "In Amsterdam?"

"No, in New York. He was a New Yorker. He recited a poem to me."

"A Dutch poem?" Willis said, and giggled again.

"English, English. He wrote it himself, would you like to hear it?"

"No," Willis said, and giggled.

" 'Twas brilliant when the slimy toads . . ."

"The *what?*"

"The slimy *toads*. Just listen, okay? 'Twas brilliant when the slimy toads, set fire to Gimbel's underwear. Aunt Mimsy was in Borough Park, and the Nome rats ate her there."

"The *what* rats?"

"The Nome rats."

"From Alaska?"

"I guess. They ate her."

"Who?"

"Aunt Mimsy. Just like the ones in Mexico. Or maybe all over the world, for that matter. The rats, I mean."

"Mexico? What are you talking about?"

"Eating poor Aunt Mimsy. Regular cannonballs."

"Cannibals, you mean."

"Yeah," Marilyn said.

"Do you know you have a hammer here?" Willis said. "Where?"

"Here on this table."

"What table?"

"This table alongside the bed here. With this lamp on it, and this phone, and this hammer."

"Oh, yeah, my hammer," she said.

"Are you perhaps a carpenter?" he said, and giggled.

"That's for protection," she said. "It's the best weapon a woman can own. I saved an article about it."

"Do you have a permit for that hammer?" he asked. He was still giggling. He couldn't seem to stop giggling.

"I'm serious," she said.

"Carry or Premises?" he said, giggling.

"A woman knows how to *use a* hammer. There isn't a woman on earth who hasn't at one time or another had to hammer a nail or something. She knows how to grip it, she knows how to swing it, she knows how to *use* it. I pity any poor bastard who comes in here and tries to mess with me. In Mexico, there were people who used hammers on the rats down there."

"Mexico?"

"Sure, there were rats the size of crocodiles down there. They used to jump on people while they were asleep in their beds, try to chew off their faces. They were regular *cannibals,* those rats."

"Cannibals only eat their own species," Willis said.

"Great idea," she said, grinning. "Come eat me."

They made love tirelessly and endlessly all day Sunday, and late that night as they were lying spent in each other's arms, whispering about their favorite colors and their favorite ice-cream flavors, and their favorite movies and television shows, and their favorite songs—all the favorites new lovers feel obliged to list for eternity—she mentioned that no two lines rhymed in the song "Moonlight in Vermont." He asked her where she'd come across this astonishing piece of information, and she said she'd learned it from a trombone player she used to know.

"You didn't tell me about the trombone player," Willis said.

"Well," she said, "there's no sense telling you about every little thing I've ever done, or everyone I've ever known in my life. Anyway, it's true that no two lines in the song rhyme. Try it," she said.

"I don't know the words," Willis said. "Tell me about the trombone player."

"Why? So you can get mad all over again? The way you got mad in the park Friday?"

"I won't get mad."

"He was just somebody I knew, that's all."

"A john?"

"Yes. A john."

"Where?"

"In Buenos Aires."

"A South American?"

"No. He was from New Orleans."

"That's right, South Americans play guitars, don't they?"

"See?" she said. "You're getting mad again."

"No, I'm not," he said.

"I think we'd better get something straight right now," she said.

"Sure," he said.

"I used to be a hooker, okay? That's something I never told anyone else I know in this city. But if . . ."

"You only told me because I found *out* about it," he said. "From the Houston P.D."

"Why*ever* I told you it happens to be a fact. Let me finish, will you please?"

"Sure."

"What I'm trying to say is that if what I did a long time ago is going to cause problems all the time . . . I mean, I can't watch everything I say or do, Hal, I'm sorry.''

"No one's asking you to do that."

"Yes, I think you are. I used to be a hooker, yes. But I'm not anymore."

"How do I know that?"

"Oh, shit, here we go again," she said, and got out of bed.

"Where are you going?" he asked.

"To get another joint," she said.

"No, let's talk about this. You're the one who wanted to talk about it, so let's . . ."

"Fuck you, I want another joint," she said.

"Marilyn . . ."

"Listen, you," she said, and stamped back to the bed and stood beside it naked, her hands on her hips. "I don't want to hear another word about was he a friend or was he a john or did I fuck him or suck him or let him shove a cucumber up my ass, okay? I did all those things and worse, and if this is going to be the kind of relationship I *want* it to be . . ."

"What kind of reiationship is that?"

"Honest," she said. "Open. And if you make a dumb comment about that word, I'll hit you with the hammer, I swear to God."

"No comment," he said, and smiled. "I'm afraid of hammers."

"Sure, joke about it. I'm being serious here, and you're . . ."

"I'm being serious, too."

"You think I'm still hooking, don't you?"

He didn't answer.

"You think the trombone player was last week instead of five years ago in Buenos Aires, don't you?"

"Was he?"

"I *am* going to hit you with the fucking hammer!" she said, and reached for it.

"Calm down," he said, and grabbed her wrist.

She tried to pull away from him.

"Calm down," he said more gently.

"Let go of me," she said. "I don't like being man-handled."

He released her wrist.

"You want to talk or what?" he said.

"No, I want you to get dressed and get the fuck out of here."

"Okay," he said.

"No, that's not what I want, either," she said.

"What do you want, Marilyn?"

"I want you to move in with me."

He was shocked speechless.

He tried to read her face in the dim light that filtered in under the drapes from the street outside. Was she serious? Did she really . . . ?

"Then you'll know for sure," she said. "You'll know I'm clean. And then . . . maybe . . . you can love me."

He was moved almost to tears. He brought his cupped hand up to his eyes to shield them, fearful that he would begin crying in the next moment, and not wanting her to see his eyes if he began crying.

"Will you?" she said.

"I thought you'd never ask," he said, trying to keep it light, but the tears came anyway, and suddenly he was sobbing uncontrollably.

"Oh, baby," she said, taking him in her arms, "please, there's nothing to cry about, please, baby, don't cry," she said, "oh God, what am I going to do with this man, please, darling, please don't cry," and she kissed his wet cheeks and his eyes and his mouth, and she said, "Oh, God, how I love you, Hal," and he wondered how long it had been since a woman had spoken those words to him, and through his tears he said, "I love you, too," and that was the real beginning.

10

THE ROUND-THE-CLOCKS ON ENDICOTT AND RI-
ley proved advantageous in that no one tried to knock off
either of them. But a week into the protective surveillance.
Lieutenant Byrnes called Carella into his office and asked
how much longer he thought they should keep the six fuck-
ups on the job.

"Because you have to look at this two ways," he said.
"Nobody's tried to kill them, that's true, but maybe that's
because whoever our man is, he's tipped to the plainclothes coverage and is afraid to make a move. On the
other hand, maybe our man's Endicott or Riley, who are
covered day and night, and who aren't about to make a
move, either of them, when they've got cops sticking to
them like a dirty shirt, am I right?"

It was the eleventh day of April, a balmy Friday morning, almost three weeks since Jerome McKennon had been
found lying in his own filth in his apartment on Silvermine
Oval. Two weeks and four days was a long time to be
working a case without any concrete results. That was what
Captain Frick had told Lieutenant Byrnes first crack out
of the box this morning. Frick was in command of the
entire precinct. Byrnes rarely listened to him, but this time
the captain had a point. The captain wanted to pull those
six cops off the surveillance and put them back on post.

"Frick wants his people back," Byrnes said.

"Then let 'em go," Carella said.

"You think so, huh?"

"I think the only possible suspects we've got are Endicott, Riley, and the Hollis woman. If she's our man, she
already knows from both of them that they're covered, and
she'd be crazy to make another move. The other two have
cops with them, you're right, so they can't *possibly* expose
themselves."

"What troubles me is they're the ones who *asked* for the cops."

"Maybe to throw us off."

"How do you see this, Steve? Level with me. You said three suspects . . ."

"Three *possibles*, I said."

"Say it's the woman, okay? Just to noodle it. What's her motive?"

"I don't know. I checked with Probate. McKennon died intestate, and Hollander left what little he had to his sister. The Hollis woman claims the two victims were close friends of hers, and I believe her. So does Hal. And she's got alibis a mile long for where she was when . . ."

"Her alibis are your two *other* suspects."

"Don't I know it," Carella said, and sighed.

"You checked on everybody in McKennon's orbit?"

"I did. I don't see any possibles there."

"How about Hollander?"

"Virtually a loner, except for his relationship with the Hollis woman."

"An accountant, huh?"

"Yeah."

"How'd she meet him?"

"I don't know."

"Was he doing accounting work for her?"

"I don't know."

"Find out. Maybe there's something fishy in her books. Maybe she killed McKennon as a smokescreen. If Hollander was her real target, maybe he knew something she didn't want the IRS to know."

"Maybe," Carella said.

"It's a possibility, isn't it?"

"It is."

"You say she used to be a hooker, huh?"

"Just the one fall, Pete. In Houston, seven years ago."

"I never yet met a hooker with a heart of gold, did you?"

"Never."

"Where'd she come across all this money she's got? Your report says she owns a fancy joint on . . ."

"I don't know. I'll have to check with Willis. He's been doing most of the work with her."

"Check with him. And check with her, too. How'd Hollander spend Easter Sunday? Before he went back to his apartment?"

"He was with his sister. The one named in his will."

"Did you talk to her?"

"Yes."

"What'd he leave her?"

"Peanuts."

"I know people who'd slit your throat for a nickel."

"Not this one, Pete. She's married to a plumber, she's got two kids and another one in the oven. I don't see her . . ."

"Pregnant ladies can stab somebody the same as anybody else."

"She's eight months gone, Pete. Waddles around like an elephant. Besides, she was watching television with her next-door neighbor the night Hollander caught it."

"From what time to what time?"

"Went back home at about eleven."

"Neighbor corroborate?"

"Yes."

"What time did Hollander catch it?"

"M.E. says sometime late Sunday night or early Monday morning."

"Where was she at . . . ?"

"In bed. And then up getting her kids off to school."

Byrnes sighed.

"Call the Hollis woman," he said. "Find out how she met him, was he working for her, and so on."

That was how Carella found out that Willis was living with her.

He called the number he had for Marilyn Hollis and a man answered the phone.

"Hello?"

Carella recognized the voice at once.

"Hal?" he said, surprised.

"I know I'm late," Willis said.

Carella looked up at the wall clock. A quarter past nine. Willis should have been in a half hour ago. But . . . ?

"I must've dialed the wrong number," Carella said, and looked at the open notebook in front of him. Marilyn Hollis's number, no question about it. There was a long silence on the line. Then:

"I've been staying here," Willis said.

"Oh?" Carella said, and then, not really intending a pun, "Doing what? Undercover work?"

"I don't need wisecracks," Willis snapped. "I'll be there in an hour or so."

And hung up.

Carella looked at the receiver.

Well, well, he thought.

He put the receiver back on its cradle.

He kept staring at the phone for a long time.

Walter Johnson of the Food and Drug Administration called back at ten that morning. Carella had called him on the second day of April. Today was the eleventh. He'd almost forgotten he was expecting a callback. Carella had the kind of mentality that assumed people shared his own sense of responsibility. If he asked someone to do something, he put it out of his mind until his tickle file reminded him that the task had not been performed, the request not honored. In this city's bureaucratic morass, Carella normally allowed two weeks before getting on the pipe to holler a little. A call to Johnson was on his calendar for the sixteenth. In that respect, Johnson was early.

"I know I'm late," Johnson said.

Everybody knew he was late this morning. But Willis was not yet in the office.

"What have you got for me?" Carella asked.

"You wanted to know the commercial applications of nicotine."

"That's right."

"Why are you interested?" Johnson asked.

"We're investigating a nicotine poisoning."

"That's unusual, isn't it?"

"First one I've ever had."

"The victim didn't eat any cigars or cigarettes, did he?"

"We have no indication of that."

"Because that'll do it, you know. Your lethal dose is what, forty or fifty milligrams?"

"In there."

"Well, that'd be something like three cigarettes or two cigars. If your victim ingested them. But you say he didn't."

"We don't think so."

"So what you want to know is how your man could've got his hands on something with nicotine in it, is that it?"

"Yes."

"Well, I ran a data-base printout before calling you, got it right here in front of me. The EPA—the Environmental Protection Agency—has twenty-four pesticides registered in which nicotine is one of the major active ingredients. They've also got four registered in which an active ingredient is nicotine sulfate. And another two, dating from the Forties, where the active ingredient is tobacco dust."

"These are all insecticides?"

"Some of them are animal repellents—like your Dexol Dog Repellent which contains six percent nicotine in a mixture of wood creosote, phenol, pine tar and soap. Or your Jinx Outdoor Dog and Cat Repellent, which has a very low percentage of nicotine mixed in with dried blood, Naphthalene and Thiram. Your nicotine content in any of the pesticides varies from a low of 1/700th of a percent to a high of ninety-eight percent. Some of the stuff is restricted, some of it's unclassified."

"Restricted how?"

"A pesticide company submits appropriate health and safety data to the EPA. The EPA studies the data, and then assigns a registration number. The company then has to register with the individual states before marketing a product in them. Some of the products are unclassified. This means the EPA hasn't yet determined whether they should be restricted or allowed for general use."

"Restricted to whom?"

"Certified applicators. Exterminators, lawn and turf people, forestry people . . . like that."

"How many of the products are *un*classified?"

"Most of them."

"Meaning?"

"Meaning you can buy them over the counter in your hardware store or garden center. No restrictions. You take something like your Black Leaf 40 Garden Spray, it's registered in twenty-seven states, your home owner can just pick it off the shelf. It's got a nicotine content of forty percent. For anything over that, you have to be a certified applicator. Is it possible your man's an exterminator?"

"We don't know what he is," Carella said.

"Well, let's say he isn't. And let's say he wanted to convert Black Leaf 40—or any other solution with a forty percent nicotine content—to a free alkaloid. He'd add sodium hydroxide to it . . . well, you may know all this."

"No, I don't."

"Well, what he'd do . . . let me see if I can explain this to you. He'd put a PH-meter on the solution, and that'd tell him how acidic it was. Then he'd set about making it more basic and less acidic. Once he . . ."

"How would he do that?"

"Well, by adding the caustic soda, you see. To remove the sulfate group. He might get a reading of, say, nine or ten to begin with, I really don't know for sure, and he might be going for a three or a four, again that's a guess. He's going for the free alkaloid, you see. The nicotine. Separating it from the sodium sulfate. Once he's got his nicotine and water, he'll mix that in a separating funnel . . ."

"Mix it with what?"

"Well, ether, for example. It'd be soluble in ether, and the ether layer would be lighter than water. He'd drain some of the water off, add more ether, shake the mixture again, separate it again, do the same thing over and over again till he got the purity of nicotine he was looking for."

"That's a long process, isn't it?"

"It wouldn't be easy, that's for sure, unless your man had access to laboratory equipment. I don't know *how* many grams of the solution he'd have to titrate to get a single gram of pure nicotine. Your fatal dose, forty milligrams, is just a *taste* of the stuff."

The exact word Blaney had used. A taste. Carella suddenly remembered all the cigarette ads that touted either "taste" or "flavor."

"All this is assuming he knows how to separate pure nicotine from a forty-percent solution."

"Well," Johnson said, "I suppose he could do what my daddy used to do when I was a kid in Kentucky."

Carella was suddenly all ears.

"What was that?" he said.

"Used to make his own bug-killer. Used to mix cigarette tobacco and water in a coffee can, let it soak for a week or so, then boiled it. Made a sort of a tea, you know? Mixed that with soap suds so it'd stick to the leaf. Worked real fine in his garden. I suppose your man could have gone through the same process. Mix cigars or cigarettes in a can of water, distill the mash, extract the poison." He paused a moment, and then said, "Have you got a police lab?"

"Yes," Carella said.

"Call your people there. Ask them about distillation."

"Thank you," Carella said. "You've been very helpful."

"No problem," Johnson said, and hung up.

Willis came into the squadroom just as Carella was dialing the lab. Both men looked up at the clock. Ten-fifteen.

"Captain Grossman, please," Carella said into the phone.

"Sorry I'm late," Willis said again, and went to his desk.

Meyer Meyer, who'd been waiting an hour and a half for Willis to relieve, said nothing. He went to the coat rack, took his hat from it, lighted a cigarette, and walked out.

"When do you expect him?" Carella said into the phone. "Well, would you ask him to call Detective Carella, please? Tell him it's urgent."

He put the receiver back on the cradle.

"Want to talk about this?" he asked Willis.

"Talk about what?"

"Moving in with a suspect."

Willis glanced across the room to where Andy Parker was hunched over a typewriter, laboriously pecking out a report. Parker was in shirtsleeves, the window behind his

desk open to a balmy breeze and the sounds of traffic
below on Grover Avenue. Parker was what Brown would
have called a ''burnout'' cop, a man who'd been coming
to work with a beard stubble long before the cops on
''Miami Vice'' considered it stylish, but only because he
thought the job was the pits and wouldn't dignify the work
by dressing up for it. It normally took Parker two hours
to type up a D.D. report, even if the perp had been caught
redhanded at the scene. Parker figured the best way to put
in a working day was to do as little work as possible. It
was not advisable to discuss anything sensitive within Parker's earshot. To Parker, sensitivity was for hairdressers
and interior decorators.

"Come on down the hall," Carella said.

"Sure," Willis said.

They walked through the slatted rail divider and down
the hall into the Interrogation Room. Carella closed the
door behind them. Both men sat on opposite sides of the
long table. Behind Willis, there was a two-way mirror
through which the room was visible from the room next
door.

"So?" Carella said.

"So it's none of your business," Willis said.

"I agree. But it *is* the Department's business."

"The hell with the Department," Willis said. "I can
live wherever I want to. *With* whoever I want to."

"I'm not sure that includes a suspect in a double homicide."

"Marilyn Hollis had nothing to do with either of those
murders!" Willis said heatedly.

"I'm not convinced of that. Neither is the lieutenant."

"You've got no reason to believe she . . ."

"I've got no reason to believe otherwise, either. What
the hell's wrong with you, Hal? You *know* she's a suspect!"

"Who says? In my book, if someone has an airtight
alibi for . . ."

"You know what you can do with airtight alibis, don't
you? Some of the best killers I've known had airtight . . ."

"She's *not* a killer!" Willis shouted.

The room went silent.

"What do we do here?" Carella said at last. "You're living with the woman, do we have to keep our thoughts on the case . . . ?"

"I don't care what you do," Willis said.

"If we've got a situation here where anything we say in the squadroom goes straight back to . . ."

"I haven't said or done anything to jeopardize this investigation!"

The room went silent again.

"I want to talk to her," Carella said. "Do I arrange an appointment through you?"

"No one's telling you how to run your case."

"I thought it was *our* case."

"It is," Willis said. "We just have different ideas on who's a suspect and who isn't."

"Is she home now?" Carella asked.

"She was when I left."

"Then if you don't mind, I'd like to go over there."

"I suggest you call first."

"Hal . . ." Carella started, and then merely shook his head.

He left Willis sitting at the long table in the Interrogation Room, the two-way mirror behind him.

"What is it you want to know?" she asked Carella.

She was wearing blue jeans and a man's shirt. Carella wondered if the shirt was Willis's. They were in the paneled living room. The house was silent at eleven o'clock in the morning, thick walls insulating the room from the sounds of traffic outside. It was difficult to remember she'd taken a fall for prostitution. She looked like a teenager. Flawless skin, alert blue eyes, no makeup on her face, not even lipstick. But you could apply the Multiple Mouse Rule here. If you saw one mouse in your barn, that meant you had a hundred. If a girl took one fall for hooking, you could bet she'd already turned a thousand tricks.

"About Basil Hollander," he said.

"What about him?"

"How'd you happen to know him?"

"Biblically," she said, and smiled.

Hooker's trick. Take the curse off intimacy by joking about it.

"So you told us," he said drily. "How'd you meet him?"

"Why do you want to know this, Mr. Carella?"

"He was a friend of yours," Carella said. "He's dead. Another friend of yours is also dead. I know you'll forgive our curiosity . . ."

"I don't appreciate sarcasm," she said. "Why don't you like me?"

"I neither like you nor dislike you, Miss Hollis, I'm a cop doing . . ."

"Oh, please, spare me the cop-doing-his-job routine, will you? I got enough of that from Hal."

Hal. Well, of course. What else would she call him? Detective Willis?

"Why don't you like me?" she said again. "Is it because we're living together?"

Straight to the point. Never mind the *other* point, the fact that he'd asked her how she'd met Hollander, and she still hadn't answered him.

"Hal's business is Hal's business," he said. Which wasn't what he'd told Willis less than an hour ago. "*My* business is . . ."

"I thought you and Hal were in the *same* business."

"I thought so, too," Carella said.

"But you don't think so anymore, huh? Because he's living with someone who may be a coldblooded killer, isn't that right?"

"You said it, not me."

"But that's what you think, isn't it? That I may have killed both Jerry *and* Baz?"

"I have no evidence to support . . ."

"We're not talking about *evidence* here," she said. "The *evidence* indicates that I was nowhere near *either* of them when they were killed. That's the *evidence*, Mr. Carella. We're taking about gut feeling, aren't we? What's your gut feeling? You think I may have killed them, don't you?"

"I think my job is to . . ."

"Yes, here we go with your *job* again."

"Which you're not making any easier," Carella said.

"Oh? How so? By living with your partner?"

"No, by not answering a question I asked you five minutes ago."

"Has it been five minutes already?" she said. "My, how the time flies when you're having a good time."

"Why don't you like *me?*" he asked.

"I've met you before, Mr. Carella. You're every cop I've ever met. With the exception of Hal. You think if a person's ever been in trouble with the law, he'll always be in trouble with the law. A leopard never changes its spots, right, Mr. Carella? Once a hooker, always a hooker."

"If that's what you want to believe about me, fine. Meanwhile, how'd you meet Basil Hollander?"

"At a concert," she said, and sighed.

"Where?"

"The Philharmonic."

"When?"

"Last June."

"Just met accidentally?"

"During intermission. We started talking about the program, and I discovered we shared the same tastes in music. We hit it off immediately."

"And began seeing each other when?"

"He called me the next week. He had tickets to the opera. I don't particularly care for opera, but I went with him, anyway, and we had a marvelous time." She smiled and said, "Though I *still* don't care for opera."

Very refined tastes, he thought. Hookers in Houston naturally went to the Philharmonic a lot, but not the opera. He squelched the thought. Maybe she was right about him. Maybe he'd been a cop too long and was jumping to conclusions based on knowledge he'd thought entirely empirical. But he'd never met either a reformed hooker or a reformed armed robber. He'd never met an armed robber who attended symphonies, either. *Or* operas.

Out of deference to Willis, he did not ask her when she'd started sleeping with Hollander. This bothered him. He was already compromising the investigation. Ordinarily, the intensity of a relationship between a man and a woman was of prime importance in a murder case, espe-

cially one of the Boy-Meets-Girl variety. Instead, he said,
"He was an accountant, is that right?"

"You know he was," she said.

"When did you learn this?"

"That he was an accountant?" she asked, looking surprised. "Of what possible interest . . . ?"

"Did he ever do any accounting work for you?"

"No. What? Basil?"

"You do have an accountant, don't you?"

"I do."

"Who is he?"

"A man named Marc Aronstein."

"How long has he been your accountant?"

"I hired him when I came here from Buenos Aires."

"Buenos Aires?"

"I thought Hal might have mentioned it."

"No."

"I was hooking in Buenos Aires."

"I see," he said. "How long were you doing that?"

"Five years."

"And in Houston."

"Only a year. I left shortly after I got busted."

Longer history than he'd thought. Willis had picked
himself a real winner.

"Went directly to Argentina from Houston?" he asked.

"No. I went to Mexico first."

"Were you hooking there, too?"

"No" she said and smiled. "Just sightseeing."

"For how long?"

"Six months or so."

"How old *are* you, Miss Hollis?"

"You're the detective, I'll let you figure it out. I left
home three months before my sixteenth birthday, went to
L.A. where I lived for a bit more than a year before heading for Houston."

"Why Houston?"

"I thought I might apply for admission to Rice."

"But you didn't."

"No. I met a sweet talker who turned me out."

"Joseph Seward?"

"No, Joe was later."

"How long were you in Houston?"

"I told you. A year. Are you adding all this up? Then to Mexico for about six months, then to Buenos Aires for five years, and I've been here for fifteen months. What do you get?"

"Sixteen when you left home . . ."

"Almost."

"I get twenty-four."

"I'll be twenty-five in August."

"You've led a busy life," he said.

"Busier than you know," she said.

"You told us your father had set you up here . . ."

"No, that was a lie. I'm sure you know that. Don't test me, Mr. Carella, I hate dishonest people."

"How *did* you come by this place?"

"Didn't Hal tell you? I came here with close to two million dollars. The place cost me seven-five. I invested the rest. That's why I needed an accountant."

"Marc Aronstein."

"Yes. Of Harvey Roth, Incorporated."

"Here in the city?"

"Yes. On Battery Street. Near the Old Seawall."

"Ever discuss financial matters with Mr. Hollander?"

"Never."

"Ever been audited by the IRS?"

"Once."

"Any problems?"

"Only the usual."

"Like what?"

"T & E deductions."

"What's that?"

"Travel and Entertainment."

"Oh," he said. In his line of work, you didn't take deductions for travel and entertainment. "Ever discuss that audit with Mr. Hollander?"

"I told you I never discussed financial matters with him."

"Even though you knew he was an accountant?"

"We had other things to discuss."

"Did he know you'd been a hooker?"

"No."

"Did any of your other friends?"

"No."

"McKennon?"

"No."

"Riley? Endicott?"

"None of them."

"The night McKennon was killed . . ."

"I was away skiing at Snowflake."

"With Nelson Riley."

"Yes."

"And the night Hollander was killed . . ."

"I was with Chip Endicott."

"Both good friends of yours."

"Past tense," she said.

"What do you mean?"

"Hal wants me to stop seeing them."

That serious, he thought.

"And will you?"

"I will." She paused, and then said, "I love him, you see."

11

A POLICE CAR WAS ANGLED INTO THE CURB IN front of Nelson Riley's building when Marilyn got there at ten o'clock on Saturday morning. She thought Uh-oh, and then hesitated a moment on the sidewalk outside, and then took a deep breath and went into the building.

During the week, a black man ran the elevator for the hat factory that still occupied the sixth floor of the building. The owners of the factory were not pleased that Riley had painted a huge bloated nude on the fourth-floor elevator doors, a lady who got divided in half—smack between the breasts and down through the belly button and crotch—whenever the doors were open. The hat factory was closed on Saturdays and Sundays, and the elevator was self-service on those days. This meant that you had to operate all by yourself the ancient lever-type, drum-contained mechanism that ran the elevator.

Marilyn had always had difficulty with it; she never seemed able to stop the elevator exactly on the mark identifying the fourth floor. She yanked the lever back and forth now, and finally maneuvered the floor of the car level with the fourth-floor corridor. She opened the inside gate, struggled the heavy nude-painted doors open, closed the gate and the doors behind her because that was what you had to do when the elevator was on self-service, and then walked down the corridor to Riley's loft.

The door to the loft was open.

Inside, she could see two uniformed policemen, one of them writing on a pad, the other one standing with his hands on his hips, listening. Riley was telling them he was certain someone had broken into the loft the night before.

"The minute they yank police protection, somebody breaks in," he said.

137

"What do you mean, police protection?" the cop with the pad asked.

"I've had a cop here with me twenty-four hours a day," Riley said.

"What for?"

"They felt I needed protection."

"Who felt?"

"The detectives investigating a case uptown."

"Where uptown?"

"The Eighty-seventh Precinct."

The cop with his hands on his hips said, "What kind of case?"

"A murder case," Riley said. "Hi, Marilyn, come on in."

"You hear this, Frank?" the cop with the pad said.

"I hear it, Charlie," the other cop said.

"Who's this?" Frank said, as Marilyn walked to where they were standing in the loft's work area.

"Friend of mine," Riley said, and kissed her on the cheek.

"What makes you think somebody broke in here?" Charlie asked.

"The window there in the living area was forced open," Riley laid. "Something, huh?" he said to Marilyn.

The cops moved into the living area. Riley and Marilyn followed them.

"You live here, that it?" Frank asked.

"I live here and I work here," Riley said.

"What kind of work you do?" Charlie asked.

"I'm a painter."

"You are?" Frank said. "Let me have your card, okay? My brother-in-law needs his house painted."

"I paint pictures," Riley said. "The ones out there." He indicated with a gesture of his head the paintings lining the walls of the loft.

"You done those, huh?" Frank said.

"Yes."

Frank looked past him and then nodded non-committally.

"So this is where you sleep, huh?" Charlie said. "This waterbed here?"

"Yes."

"How are they, these waterbeds?"

"Fine," Riley said. "Take a look at the window, you can see where it was forced."

Charlie moved to the window near the foot of the bed. He studied it carefully. Frank peered over his shoulder. Behind their backs, Marilyn rolled her eyes.

"These marks here, you mean?" Charlie said.

"Yes."

"They weren't here before?"

"No."

"They're new, huh?"

"Yes."

"What do you think, Frank?"

"Coulda been jimmied," Frank said, and shrugged.

"Anything missing?" Charlie said.

"No, I don't think so."

"So why'd you call us?" Frank said.

"If somebody broke in here, that's a reason to call the police, isn't it?"

"Why would somebody break in here and not *take* anything?" Charlie said.

"I don't see nothing worth taking," Frank said, looking around the living area.

"Mr. Riley gets upward of five thousand dollars a canvas" Marilyn said, bristling.

"A what?" Chariie said.

"A painting."

"No kidding?" Frank said. He looked into the loft's work area again, reappraising the paintings. "For those, huh?" he said.

"Any of these valuable paintings missing?" Charlie asked, stressing the word "valuable" so that it conveyed vast disbelief.

"No."

"So *nothing's* missing, right?"

"No, but . . ."

"So why'd you call us?"

"I called you because two people were murdered . . ."

"But not in this precinct, right?"

"What's that got . . . ?"

"You shoulda called the Eight-Seven," Charlie said. "They the ones working the homicides, they the ones you shoulda called."

"Thanks a lot," Riley said.

"Don't mention it," Charlie said. "I write up my report, I'll mention the Eight-Seven is already on this."

"You oughta put bars on that window," Frank said. "Fire escape out there, all these paintings the lady says are valuable . . ." He shrugged skeptically. "You get yourself bars on that window so nobody can get in."

"How do I get *out* if there's a fire?" Riley said.

"You gotta call the Fire Department," Charlie said.

"We done here?" Frank said.

"We're done here," Charlie said, and snapped his pad shut.

Riley sighed.

"See you," Charlie said, and both cops walked out.

The moment they were gone, Riley said, "The city's fucking finest, huh?"

"You should see the cops in Houston," she said.

"Somebody breaks in here, they stand around . . ."

"Are you sure somebody broke in?"

"Those marks weren't on the window when I went out last night."

"Maybe you *ought* to call . . ."

"What for? So they can tell me again why they can't spare any cops here? You should've heard them. The party line. Lots of crime in this city, men urgently needed elsewhere, sorry we can't continue the surveillance . . . that's a police word, surveillance. Surveillance of the premises and the subject. Those are police words, too. These are the premises and I'm the subject. Only I'm not a subject anymore, I'm back to being a possible *target!*"

Marilyn said nothing.

"So come give me a hug," he said, and grinned, and opened his arms wide.

"There's something we've got to talk about," Marilyn said.

"Later," Riley said. "Would you like a drink?"

"No, thanks."

"I've got a good bottle of scotch on the shelf there. Twelve years old."

"Not now, thanks."

"You look terrific, did I tell you you look terrific?"

"Thank you."

She was wearing a blue pleated skirt, pantyhose of the same color, high-heeled blue pumps, a shoulder bag to match, a pale blue blouse with a Peter Pan collar, and a navy blue cardigan sweater. Her long blonde hair was pulled back into a pony tall, held there with a barrette the color of the blouse.

"You really look terrific."

"Thank you."

"Something wrong?"

"No, no."

"Cops been hassling you?"

"Lots of questions, but not what I'd call hassling."

"Sure you don't want a drink?"

"Positive."

"How about some coffee?"

"I'll make some," she said.

"All I've got is instant."

"I know."

She walked familiarly to the cabinet under the sink, took out a kettle, and began filling it with water.

"You mind if I tidy up a bit out here?" he asked. "I quit late last night, and rushed out leaving a mess. I like to have things neat on the weekend. You never know who may drop in."

Marilyn carried the kettle to the hot plate, and turned it on. Riley walked into the loft's work area and picked up a broom.

"I've been meaning to call you," he said.

"I'm glad you didn't," she said, and went to the wall cupboard, and took two cups and a jar of instant coffee from it.

"How come?" he said. "You been busy?"

"Very."

She spooned instant coffee into the cups, and then looked at the kettle.

"Me, too," he said. "Which is why I *didn't* call, actually. You see this big one here?"

She walked into the work area.

"Recognize it?"

"Snowflake," she said.

"I had a hell of a time getting that white overlay," he said. "Looks like it's really snowing, though, doesn't it?"

"Regular blizzard," she said.

"Yeah," he said, grinning proudly. "Do you like it?"

"Yes."

"That's you there in the yellow parka."

"My parka isn't . . ."

"I know." He kept looking at the painting, grinning. "You really like it?" he asked.

"Yes. Very much."

She walked back into the other part of the loft, checked the kettle again.

"Watched pot," he said. "Shit, look at how I left these brushes!"

He began cleaning the brushes, sitting on a stool at his work table, his back to her. When he turned to look at her again, she was at the shelf beyond the divider-wall, the bottle of scotch in her hands.

"Twelve years old," he said. "Gift from the gallery owner."

She yanked the cork, sniffed at the lip of the bottle, wrinkled her nose.

"Sure you don't want some?"

"Too early for me. Anyway, I hate scotch."

He kept dipping brushes into turpentine, working the bristles.

"Amateur stunt," he said. "Leaving brushes overnight."

He kept working, his back to her. She was silent for a long time. He looked up when the kettle whistled.

"Coffee's ready," she said.

"There's milk in the fridge," he said. "Sugar in the . . ."

"I take it black," she said.

"Right, I should know that by now."

She carried the cups to where he was sitting at the work

table, and took the stool opposite him. There was the smell of turpentine. She fished into her shoulder bag, took out a package of cigarettes and a gold monogrammed lighter. She thumbed the lighter into flame, held it to the tip of the cigarette, let out a stream of smoke. She placed the package of cigarettes on the table, arranged the lighter neatly on top of them. He watched her hands. She looked up suddenly.

"Nelson," she said, "I want to end it."

He looked at her.

"Okay?" she said.

"What's the matter?"

"Let's just call it a day, okay?" she said.

"No, what is it? You mad I didn't call? I didn't think that kind of bullshit was important to our . . ."

"It's not that."

"Then what?"

"I've met someone."

"What do you mean?"

"Well, what do you *think* I mean, Nelson? I mean I'm involved with someone."

"Involved?"

"Yes, involved."

"You?"

"I don't see why that should . . ."

"I mean, *you?* Involved? I thought involvement . . ."

"I thought so, too."

"I mean, I thought *commitment* . . ."

"I've changed my mind, okay?"

"Look, don't get so damn impatient, okay? I mean, this is what you might call a bit of a shock, you know? You're the one who kept telling me what we had together was enough, isn't that what you kept telling me? The talking, the laughing, the sharing? Isn't that what you kept telling me, Marilyn?"

"It's what I said, yes."

"So all of a sudden . . ."

"Yes, all of a sudden."

"Who? One of these other guys you've been seeing?"

"No."

"Then who?"

"It doesn't matter who."

"It matters to me. Who's the guy?"

"His name is Hal Willis."

"Who?"

"Hal . . ."

"The *cop?* The one who was here asking me questions? You've got to be kidding."

"I'm not kidding, Nelson."

"I mean, there's no accounting for taste, but Jesus, Marilyn . . ."

"I *said* I wasn't kidding. Drop it, okay?"

The room went silent.

"Sure," he said.

The silence lengthened.

"So that's it, huh?" he said.

"That's it."

"Six, seven months of . . ."

"Nelson, we were good friends. Let's end it as good friends, okay?"

"Sure," he said.

"Okay?"

"Sure." He grinned suddenly. "Want to give the waterbed a last shot?"

"I don't think so," she said.

"Make a few waves?" he said, still grinning.

She smiled, rose, slung her shoulder bag, came around the work table, and kissed him on the cheek.

"Nelson . . ." she said. "Goodbye."

She looked at him a moment, seemed about to say something more, then simply shook her head, and walked out of the loft.

He listened to her high heels clicking along the corridor outside. He heard the elevator grinding its way up the shaft. He heard the big doors lumbering open. And then the sound of the elevator again, fading, fading.

And then there was only silence and the smell of turpentine.

Well, terrific, he thought.

Great way to start the weekend.

Guy breaks in last night, Marilyn breaks in this morning. Might as *well* have broken in, the news she brought. Sure, let's have some coffee, Nelson, and oh by the way I want to end it. Marilyn Hollis *involved?* Will wonders never! With a cop, no less. With a cop no bigger than my thumb.

He felt like crying.

Come on, he thought, this city is *full* of women. Swarm all over me at gallery openings, ooo, what lovely work. But none of them Marilyn, oh, what a lovely piece of work was Marilyn.

Past tense already.

Was.

Just like that.

Nelson, I want to end it.

Nelson . . . goodbye.

Yo te adoro, she'd told him once, the waterbed rippling beneath them, *yo te adoro,* I adore you in Spanish, which she'd picked up in South America. Spoke Spanish like a native, *yo te adoro.* Didn't mean it *seriously,* didn't mean she *really* adored him, *really* loved him, meant it within her own definition of their relationship, no commitments, no involvement, no strings.

He wondered now how deep his own involvement had been.

Out of his life for only ten minutes, and he felt like throwing himself out the window.

Yo te adoro.

Murmuring the words around his cock, talk about deep.

Come on, he thought, there are other women.

He rose from where he'd been sitting at the work table, the table stinking of turpentine, his hands stinking of turpentine, and he went into the living area, what she used to call the nook, their nook, nookie in the nook, he'd never had a woman like Marilyn in his life, never. He turned on the water tap, washed his hands over the sink, dried them on a dish towel.

He looked at the kitchen clock.

Twenty minutes to eleven.

Too early for a man to start drowning his sorrow?

Hell it was.

He went to the shelf near the bed, took down the bottle

of scotch and uncorked it. He took a glass from the cabinet, and poured three fingers into it. He raised the glass in a toast.

"Marilyn," he said out loud, "I think I was in love with you."

He tilted the glass to his mouth and took a deep swallow.

The clock on the kitchen wall read eighteen minutes to eleven.

His first reaction was an automatic one.

He spit out the vile-tasting scotch at once, *tried* to spit it out, but most of it had already gone down his throat and only a thin, brown, residual spray spattered onto the refrigerator door.

He felt fire burning the inside of his mouth, fire burning his throat and his insides. He clutched for his throat, dropping the glass, the glass shattering in a hundred brilliant shards on the kitchen floor, turned toward the sink, *water,* grabbed for another glass on the drainboard, reached for the water tap, and turned it open, his mouth filling with saliva. He spit into the sink, trying to clear his throat of whatever was burning it, burning his stomach now, saliva filling his mouth again, he spit again, and suddenly felt nauseous. He dropped the glass into the sink. It bounced but it did not break, he thought it remarkable that the glass didn't break and then he began vomiting into the sink, the stream of water splashing into the vomit as it spewed from his mouth, and clutched for his stomach when a sharp pain knifed his abdomen, causing him to bend over almost double.

He reeled away from the sink.

The phone.

A doctor.

He felt faint all at once. He fell forward onto the waterbed, the bed rippling beneath his weight as he reached for the telephone. His bowels let go in that moment, he felt a hot gush of liquid excrement in his pants, and this frightened him more than anything else had, letting go that way, but he had only seconds to consider his fear because all at once he was jerking spasmodically on the bed, arms and legs twitching, head snapping back, gasping for breath, he couldn't breathe, his lungs were closing, his throat was closing, his chest was caving in, oh Jesus, he thought, Marilyn, he thought, and then he didn't think anything else because he was dead.

The clock on the kitchen wall read sixteen minutes to eleven.

Due to the diligence of the Sixth Precinct, Carella and Willis were on the scene at ten minutes past twelve. A sculptor who lived down the hall from Riley had knocked on the door, eager to show him a new piece he'd just finished, tried the knob, found the door open, and discovered Riley lying dead on the waterbed. He'd run back to his own loft and immediately called the police. The responding patrolmen in Adam car were Charlie and Frank. They took one look, and then called back to their sergeant to say they had a stiff at 74 Carlson Street. They also told the sergeant that the Eight-Seven was working a pair of homicides the stiff had mentioned to them—when he was still alive, of course. The sergeant called the Eight-Seven at eleven forty-one. It took Willis and Carella less than a half-hour to get all the way downtown.

Charlie and Frank were still at the scene.

Their sergeant had arrived by then. A uniformed captain was also there; homicides sometimes brought out the brass.

"M.E.'s on the way," the captain said.

"Adam car responded to a previous complaint here at a little before ten this morning," the sergeant said. "Victim reporting a break-in last night."

"Nothing was stolen," Charlie said at once, eager to cover his ass. This damn thing had suddenly mushroomed into a homicide.

"We were gonna put in our report that the Eight-Seven had him covered," Frank said, which was stretching the truth a bit.

The captain looked at both men non-committally. Charlie and Frank knew that non-committal look. They both figured they were in deep shit.

"Bottle of scotch there on the cabinet, smells like a dozen politicians smoking in a backroom," the sergeant said.

Carella wondered if the sergeant had handled the bottle.

"Package of Virginia Slims and a woman's cigarette lighter on the table in the other room," the captain said. "Initials M.H. on it."

Carella looked at Willis.

"There was a lady came in around ten," Charlie said, figuring if he could solve this case on the spot, he was home free.

Carella said nothing.

"Tall blonde lady," Frank said.

"Good-looking broad," Charlie said.

"Dressed all in blue. To match her eyes."

"Victim said she was a friend of his."

"Did you get her name?" the sergeant asked.

"Carolyn, I think," Charlie said.

No, not Carolyn, Carella thought.

"Carolyn *what?*" the captain said.

"I don't know, sir," Charlie said.

"We were responding to a 10-21," Frank said. "The victim said the lady was a friend of his."

"Still, you shoulda got her full name."

We've already *got* her full name, Carella thought.

"Nothing was stolen," Charlie said again, and shrugged.

The M.E. came into the loft, breezing past the patrolman posted at the door.

"Did you see the naked lady on the elevator doors?" he said. "Where's the body?"

"There on the waterbed," the captain said.

"Oh my," the M.E. said, "it certainly does stink in here, doesn't it?"

He went directly to the waterbed, skirting the shards of glass on the floor.

"Puuu," he said, and knelt beside the body.

Carella walked into the working area of the loft. He looked down at the package of Virginia Slims on the table, the monogrammed gold lighter sitting squarely on top of it. M.H. You've come a long way, baby, he thought. He looked at the finished painting against the wall. Riley seemed to have worked out the problem of making it snow.

In the living area, Willis said, "We'll want that bottle tagged and sent to the lab. Anybody touch it?"

"Not me," Charlie said at once.

"Me, either," Frank said.

"I tented it," the sergeant said.

"Why?" the captain asked Willis. "You think something's in that scotch?"

"Nicotine," Willis said.

"You a doctor?" the M.E. said.

"No, but . . ."

"Then let *me* do the post-mortem, okay?"

Willis glared at him for a moment, and then walked over to where Carella was standing beside the work table. He looked down at the package of cigarettes and the lighter.

"Is it hers?" Carella asked.

Willis nodded.

"Did you know she was coming here?"

"Yes."

"Okay, who talks to her?"

"I do," Willis said.

12

HE SAT ALONE IN THE LIVING ROOM.

When he'd left for work this morning, she told him she'd be going first to Riley's loft—"To end it," she'd said— and then uptown to do some shopping. She said she'd be back at about one o'clock and she promised to call him at the squadroom then, to let him know how it had gone.

The clock on the mantel over the fireplace ticked noisily.

It was now a minute to one.

He kept thinking someone had ended it for Riley, all right, someone had laced his scotch with nicotine and sent him to join McKennon and Hollander. Three of her close buddies dead and gone now. Only Endicott left and she planned to meet him for a drink sometime next week, break the news to him. "End it" with him, too.

The clock chimed.

A single chime.

Ding.

Into the silence of the living room.

He kept waiting.

He heard her key in the latch at a quarter past one. She came in, put her shoulder bag on the table just inside the door and was starting for the stairs leading to the upper stories when she saw him sitting there.

"Hey, hi!" she said, surprised. "What are you doing home?"

"Riley's dead," he said.

Flat out, shoot from the hip and shoot to kill.

"What!"

"You heard me."

"Dead?"

"Dead. Tell me everything that happened there, Marilyn."

150

"Why? You don't think . . ."

"If you don't tell *me*, you'll have to tell Carella. He knows you were there. You left your cigarette lighter behind, and two blues have already described you."

"So now I'm a suspect again, is that it?"

"You never *quit* being one. Not on Carella's block."

"I didn't kill Nelson. For Christ's sake, I was only there a few minutes!"

"Who said he was killed?"

"You said he was dead, I'm assuming it wasn't a goddamn heart attack!"

"Tell me everything that happened. From the time you got there till the time you left."

Marilyn sighed.

"I'm listening," Willis said.

"I got there at a little past ten, it must have been."

"And left when?"

"Around . . . I don't know exactly. Ten-thirty?"

"That's a half-hour, not a few minutes."

"Yes, about a half-hour."

"All right, what happened in that half-hour?"

"He offered me a drink, we had some coffee, I told him . . ."

"What did he offer you to drink?"

"Scotch."

"Did you drink any of it?"

"No. It smelled awful."

"You smelled it?"

"Yes."

"You handled the bottle?"

"Yes. I took the cork off the bottle and smelled it."

"What'd it smell like?"

"Awful."

"What *kind* of a smell, Marilyn?"

"How do I know? How do you describe a *smell*? It smelled like scotch. Awful."

"Only like scotch?"

"Yes. I think so. Why? Was something in it?"

"What'd you do then?"

"I put the cork back on the bottle, and I put the bottle

back on the shelf. Was Nelson poisoned? Was something
in that bottle?''

"Then what?''

"Answer me, damn it!''

"He was poisoned, yes.''

"Christ! My fingerprints are on that bottle! That gives
your partner everything he needs, doesn't it?''

"If your fingerprints are in fact on the bottle . . .''

"Of course they are!''

"And if the contents test out poison . . .''

"You know they will!''

"Then the police will want to know a lot more about
what you did with that bottle.''

"All I did was . . . what do you mean the *police?* Your
partner, do you mean? Or you, too?''

"I'm still listening,'' Willis said.

"I didn't put anything in that bottle!''

"You just picked it off the shelf . . .''

"Yes.''

". . . and took out the cork . . .''

"Yes, damn it!''

". . . and sniffed the scotch.''

"Yes!''

"Why?''

"Because Nelson said it was very good stuff. Twelve
years old, he said. So I . . . wanted to . . . I was curious.
I've never liked scotch, I thought maybe twelve-year-old
stuff might smell better than what I'd had before. It always
smells like medicine to me.''

"But this didn't smell like medicine.''

"I don't know *what* it smelled like! I told you! It smelled
awful.''

"Did it smell like tobacco?''

"I don't know.''

"Think!''

"If I say it smelled like tobacco, then I'm clean, right?
He was poisoned with nicotine, isn't that it? The same as
Jerry. So if I say I smelled tobacco, then the nicotine was
already in the bottle when I picked it up. But I'm telling
you the *truth!* I don't *know* what it smelled like! I took a
quick sniff and then put the cork . . .''

"Okay," Willis said, and sighed. "Then what?"

"We drank some coffee, I told him I wanted to end it."

"How did he react?"

"He didn't like the idea."

"You told him about us?"

"Yes."

Willis nodded.

"Then what?"

"He wanted me to go to bed with him."

"Did you?"

"No!"

"What *did* you do?"

"I kissed him on the cheek and left."

"Uh-huh."

"I said goodbye and left."

"And ten minutes later, twenty minutes later, he was dead."

"*I* didn't kill him!"

"How much time did you spend with that bottle?"

"A minute. *Less* than a minute. All I did was . . ."

"Get your bag."

"What?"

"Your bag. There on the table."

"Why?"

"I want to see what's in it."

"There isn't *nicotine* in it, if that's what you . . ."

"Get it."

She went to where she'd put the bag when she came in, carried it to where he was sitting and unceremoniously turned it upside down, dumping its contents on the floor near his feet.

"Have a good time," she said. "*I'm* going to have a drink."

She went to the bar and poured a hefty portion of gin onto three ice cubes. She took a good swallow and then walked back to where he was sifting through the stuff at his feet. Lipstick, eye liner, makeup brush, tissues, chewing gum, a red wallet, a checkbook, keys, some loose change . . .

"Find a vial of poison?" she asked.

He began putting the stuff back into the bag.

"Where'd you go when you left Riley's loft?"

"Uptown."

"To do what?"

"I told you I had some shopping to do."

"What'd you buy?"

"Nothing. I was looking for a pair of earrings, but I didn't see anything I liked."

"You shopped from ten-thirty till . . ."

"I shopped till about noon. Then I had a sandwich . . ."

"Where?"

"In a luncheonette off Jefferson."

"Then what?"

"I took a taxi and came home."

"Got here at a quarter past one."

"I didn't look at the clock. Do you want a drink?"

"No."

"It won't have poison in it, you don't have to worry."

Willis was silent for a long time, hands clasped, head bent. "Carella's gonna want a motive," he said at last, almost to himself. "Three of your close friends killed, he'll want to know . . ." He looked up suddenly. "Do *I* know everything there is to know, Marilyn?"

"From the minute I got there to the minute I . . ."

"I'm not talking about the time you spent with Riley. I'm talking about *you.*"

She looked at him, puzzled.

"Did any of these three men know something about you that . . ."

"No."

". . . you haven't told me?"

"I've told you everything. None of them knew anything about my past."

"How about Endicott? Does *he* know you used to be a hooker?"

"No."

"What *does* he know?"

"Only what I told the others. I lived in L.A., I lived in Houston, I traveled in Mexico, I lived in Buenos . . ."

"You never told me about Mexico."

"I'm sure I mentioned Mexico."

"No. What did they think you were *doing* in all those . . . ?"

"I told them I had a rich father."

"Same as you told me."

"Yes. In the beginning. But then I told you everything. You *know* I did, Hal!"

"Are you sure?"

"Yes."

"Because if you left anything out . . ."

"I didn't."

". . . and it has some bearing on what happened to these . . ."

"No."

". . . Carella's going to find out. He's damn good, Marilyn, and he'll find out."

"I told you everything," she said.

The room went silent.

"Everything you need to know," she said.

"What *don't* I know, Marilyn?"

She said nothing.

"What else, Marilyn? What about Mexico?"

She walked to the bar. She put more ice cubes in her glass, poured gin over them, and came back to where he was sitting.

"Why don't we go upstairs to bed?" she said.

"No," he said.

They kept looking at each other.

"Tell me," he said.

In Houston, the first job she got was dancing topless in a joint on Telephone Road. Part of the job was sitting with customers when you weren't onstage, getting them to buy you cheap champagne marked up high. You got a commission on each bottle. Occasionally, you let them cop a feel. Your thigh, your breast, keep them buying the champagne. When she'd been there a while, she learned that some of the other girls were doing handjobs in the back booths, ten bucks a throw. She started doing that, too.

There was a piano in the place, and this guy used to come in, sit down and play jazz every now and then. Nice guy, never took any of the girls to the back booths, just

watched them dancing, played piano, had a few drinks at
the bar, went on his way. Came in two, three times a
week, she finally realized he had his eye on her. He got
to talking to her one night, real shy guy, told her he used
to play jazz in Kansas City, finally asked if she'd like to
go out with him sometime. She dated him the next Sunday
night, her night off. They had a real nice time.

She started going to bed with him, oh, it must've been
on their third date. When they'd been seeing each other
for three months or so, he told her she was losing a lot of
money giving it away, said there were big bucks to be
made in Houston, conventions coming in all the time, oil
men, did she think she might like to try it sometime? Try
what? she said. Try getting paid for it, he said, a hundred
bucks a shot.

She thought it over.

She was making like two-fifty a week tossing her tits
and her ass on the stage, maybe another hundred in com-
missions on the champagne, and another hundred doing
the handjobs. The piano player told her she could make
that much money in a single night, even after he took his
commission for setting her up with guys who might be
interested, he knew plenty of guys who might be interested.

So six months after she hit Houston, she got turned out
by a sweet-talking piano player.

A month later, he got stabbed in a barroom brawl, and
she hooked up with Joe Seward, who had a small stable,
three girls, he wasn't a bad sort for a pimp. Never beat
any of his girls, some pimps thought the way you got girls
to behave was to knock them around like the beach bum
in L.A. used to do to her.

The first time she got busted, she was scared to death.

In Texas, prostitution—if it's a first offense—is only a
Class B misdemeanor, punishable by a fine not to exceed
a thousand bucks, confinement in jail for a period not to
exceed 180 days, or *both*. She was terrified she'd have to
spend six months in jail. But the judge was a lenient one,
who took her tender age into consideration—she was only
seventeen—and Seward paid the five-hundred-dollar fine

without a whimper, and she was free as a lark again. But still very scared.

She told Seward she needed a vacation.

He looked her dead in the eye—any other pimp would've beat the shit out of her—and he said, "Sure, Mary Ann, you take your vacation," but she could see in his eyes that he knew she was about to split and he'd never see her again.

She didn't know where she'd be going when she left Houston, didn't know where she might end up, so she applied for a passport in case she decided to go any place where she might need one, that was her biggest mistake, getting the passport. But she didn't know that at the time, got her passport in spite of the single 43.02 arrest, Mary Ann Hollis, black-and-white picture of a pretty seventeen-year-old blonde girl smiling at the camera. In the space where you were supposed to list your occupation, she wrote "Teacher."

Crossed the border from Eagle Pass to Piedras Negras, driving a car she'd rented in Houston. She'd put away some money, figured she'd spend a little while in Mexico, just driving around, taking it easy, Mary Ann Hollis, teacher. Didn't know where she'd go after Mexico, or what she'd do when her money ran out. She had something like a thousand dollars with her, she didn't know how far that would take her. She had it in her mind that she'd quit hooking. She had a passport, she could go anywhere in the world. She'd be eighteen years old in August, she had her whole life ahead of her.

Coming out of the Sierra Madre mountains, in the state of Guerrero, near the town of Iguala, she ran across a man who looked like a farmer but who was selling very good marijuana, what they called gold, selling at the time for twenty-two dollars a kilo in Mexico, something like three hundred, three-fifty a pound back in the States. She bought a kilo from the man, what the hell, only twenty-two bucks. Kept driving along, stopping here and there along the way, this or that motel, wherever she happened to be at sunset, drank tequila, smoked pot in her room, got a good suntan.

Life was good.

She felt terrific.

She was carrying only a big leather tote bag. In the tote, she packed her passport case with her passport and her money, and a plastic container with her diaphragm inside it, and a tube of jelly, and some panties and jeans and blouses and toilet articles, and buried under it all the steadily diminishing kilo of gold.

At the end of a blistering hot August, shortly after her eighteenth birthday, she decided she'd had enough of Mexico. She drove back toward the American border one day, wearing sandals and panties and a white caftan she'd bought in a little shop in one of the towns, came through Saltillo, came some ten kilometers later to a little village called Ramos Arizpe, and had just passed through there when up ahead she saw a long line of cars stopped at a roadblock manned by uniformed Mexicans.

She didn't speak or understand a word of Spanish at the time but an American kid in the car ahead of hers told her they were checking for guns since there'd been rumors of some kind of trouble brewing, some revolutionary group, she never did get it straight because all at once she was scared to death again.

Not because she was carrying a gun in the car, which she wasn't.

But because what was left of the kilo of gold was in her tote bag.

They found the dope in three minutes flat, and then they—

"Do you really want to hear the rest of this?" she asked Willis.

"Yes," he said.

13

THEY TOLD HER THEY HAD INFORMED THE American Consulate in Monterrey of her arrest. She did not believe them. In Mexico back then—and for all she knew, it was the same now—a narcotics violation was a felony and any felony suspect could be held and interrogated for a maximum of seventy-two hours without access to a lawyer. Within six days, if a magistrate found that a trial was indicated by the evidence, and if the offense was punishable by a term of more than two years (which Marilyn's alleged offense was) the prisoner could be held for as long as a year before his case was brought to trial. Mexican law was—and is—premised on the Napoleonic Code. In simple terms, you were guilty until you proved yourself innocent. When Marilyn demanded that she be allowed to make a personal telephone call, the local police officer told her this was something to be discussed with the District Attorney; he would either allow it or he would not.

Eight days after she'd been arrested, a consular officer came to see her at the *Comisaría*. He told her she was being charged with possession of marijuana. He told her that if she was convicted, she could expect a prison sentence of from five years and three months to twelve years. He promised he would call the people she listed for him on a sheet of American Embassy stationery: her mother, Joseph Seward, and the beach bum she used to live with in Los Angeles. The consul later told her he'd been unable to contact any of these people. She did not know who else she could ask him to call.

On the twelfth day of September, she stood trial in Saltillo, represented by a Mexican lawyer whose name had been supplied by the consular officer. She was sentenced to six years' imprisonment for possession of what turned out to be eight ounces of marijuana, all that was left of the kilo she had bought in Iguala. The consul told her an American Embassy official would report the arrest, trial, and sentence in detail to the State Department, which would in turn notify relatives or friends in the States. But she did not know where her mother was, and most of her friends were transient hookers.

On the morning of September fifteenth, she was transported by van to *La Fortaleza*, a centuries-old prison in the state of Tamaulipas, some two hundred miles southwest of Brownsville, Texas. In the van with her were a woman she later learned had killed her husband with a grubbing hoe, and a man who had stolen a typewriter from the offices of an air-conditioning firm in Monterrey. Marilyn was still wearing the white cotton caftan and thonged sandals she'd had on when they arrested her. Her tote bag had been requisitioned in Ramos Arizpe, presumably because it contained evidence of a crime. Her makeup, her diaphragm, her passport, and her underwear were in that bag, together with several pieces of silver jewelry she could have used to good advantage at *La Fortaleza*.

She learned there on the day she arrived, and only through deductive reasoning, that the only thing you could get in that place was what you paid for. She discovered this after the internal search, when she and a dozen female prisoners from towns all over Coahuila, Nuevo León and Tamaulipas were standing in a line that led to a long table upon which were piled blankets and clothing and woven straw mats and thin mattresses covered with striped ticking. The grubbing-hoe murderess— a short, hefty dark woman with curly black hair, solemn brown eyes, pendulous breasts and wide buttocks—took from a black leather purse on a chain around her thick neck a wad of pesos which she handed to the matron, a stern-faced woman with hair dyed a flaming red. The matron then passed over the table a mattress, a blanket, two pairs of cotton panties, and several tentlike faded grey smocks.

When the woman protested in voluble Spanish, the matron generously added another pair of panties to the pile she now held on her extended arms. She protested again. The matron shook her head and waved her on. Marilyn's money had disappeared somewhere between the Ramos Arizpe roadblock and the local jail; she had nothing with which to engage in prison commerce. She had only the caftan folded over her arm, the long flowing cotton robe somewhat less than pristine after almost three unwashed weeks in Ramos Arizpe. The matron said something to her in Spanish. Marilyn did not understand. She repeated it. Marilyn shook her head. The matron waved her on, naked.

La Fortaleza had been built by the Spaniards back in the sixteenth century as a second-line coastal defense. Some two thousand feet above sea level, it dominated the countryside and afforded a distant view of the Guff of Mexico, some twenty-five miles to the east. The prisoners never saw anything but the walls. In the late 1820's, when the new Mexican government took over the fortress and turned it into a prison, only a hundred and ten convicts were transferred there. Now there were four hundred and eighty of them, sixty-seven in the women's compound alone. Because this area had once been used for the solitary confinement of male prisoners—at a time when *female* murderers, armed robbers, extortionists and kidnapers were virtually unheard of in Mexico—it was in effect a prison within a prison, a square within a square, its walls twenty feet high, the higher walls of the prison proper visible beyond them. The thickness of the compound walls was dictated by the width of the cells into which the women were locked each night at ten and released into the courtyard each morning at six, when the cells were hosed down. Marilyn visualized the whole as a sort of labyrinth in the puzzle books she used to buy when she was a little girl.

The walls surrounding the entire prison were eight feet thick, a conglomerate of boulders, bricks and concrete. The only gate into the prison was at the front, where the bars were four inches in diameter, and this opened onto a cobbled, arched passageway—a holdover from when the prison was a fortress—to a second gate beyond that opened onto the warden's office on the left and the search

room on the right, where the monied prisoners had purchased the clothing and other articles they needed for
survival here. Immediately beyond these two rooms, and
opening onto the courtyard lined with the men's cells and
the various prison workshops, was a third barred gate.
Marilyn and the other women were marched through this
gate and past the watchful eyes of the male guards and
prisoners idling in the courtyard—some of them squatting
in the dirt playing cards, others smoking or talking, some
playing guitars—to the smaller inner prison where first
there was a barred gate and then a massive wooden door
that shielded the women from the further prying eyes of
the male population, but not from the eyes of the ma-
chine-gun guards in the four watchtowers, who could look
down from their vantage points directly into the enclo-
sure.

There were seven women, including herself, in Marilyn's cell.

The cell was six feet wide by eight feet long.

On either side of the cell, there was a double-decker
wooden bunk. There was a three-foot space between the
bunks. Immediately inside the bars, there was a space of
perhaps two feet between them and the footboards of the
bunks. In this space, in one corner of the cell, was the
toilet hole over which the women squatted to relieve
themselves in full view of the guards in the towers. For
the first three days of her confinement, Marilyn did not
move her bowels. Neither did she eat the foul-smelling
food prepared in the prison kitchen and distributed twice
daily, at eight in the morning and at six P.M. She learned
later that the male prisoners operated a small *cocina* in
the outside compound and that edible food could be purchased there—but in the beginning, she had no money,
anyway.

The four bunks were occupied by prisoners who'd been
there when the others arrived. Marilyn and one of the
other newcomers slept as best they could on the stone
floor of the cell. Teresa Delarosa, the grubbing-hoe murderess, slept on the floor, too, on the mattress she had
purchased, but only for the first two weeks of her confinement. After that, and after it was learned that she had

viciously struck her husband twenty-six times on the face,
head and neck with the hoe—almost decapitating the poor
man before finally severing his jugular with one powerful
swipe—Teresa was afforded the respect to which she was
entitled, and the woman occupying the bottom bunk on
the lefthand side of the cell moved to a deferential sleeping spot on the floor. Marilyn slept sitting up, her back
to the wall, in the two feet of space just inside the cell
bars, opposite the toilet hole where all night long the
women pissed.

There was a shower in the courtyard, and the women
would use it once a week; here in prison, cleanliness was
neither next to godliness nor next to necessary. The
guards in the watchtowers would study the single shower
stall through binoculars, the sunlight glinting off the
lenses. For the first two weeks of her incarceration, Marilyn did not shower. She never took off the caftan. It was
perhaps this that called her to the closer personal attention of the warden. She did not know that the prison
guards had already nicknamed her—because of the flowing white garment and her long blonde hair—*"La Árabe
Dorada":* The Golden Arab.

The first time she ate prison food, she vomited it all
back into the shit-reeking toilet hole in the corner of the
cell. Panchita, one of the other women, apparently in-
censed by Marilyn's breach of dining etiquette, began
kicking her violently while she was crouched over the
hole retching up her guts. Teresa said something about
it, and Panchita whirled on her and shoved her back
against the far wall of the cell and both women began
screaming at each other while a bright green lizard examined the food Marilyn had just thrown up. Teresa, it
turned out, had purchased from one of the male prisoners
who ran the *cocina* outside, a spoon honed to razor-blade
sharpness, and she brandished this now, and—whispering in Spanish that was incomprehensible to Marilyn but
nonetheless hair-raising—said something to Panchita that
caused her to retreat muttering to the top bunk she occupied on the righthand side of the cell. The lizard
scampered away into the sunlight.

She learned the names of the other women only because she heard them repeated so often, but she could not speak the language and therefore said nothing to any of them. She received no visitors. She could buy neither writing paper nor postage stamps because she had no money, and so she wrote no letters. She was lonelier inside that prison than any of the other inmates, lonelier than she'd ever been in her life. And then, all at once, the language came to her. One moment it was unfathomable, the next it was crystal clear.

"I can remember," Panchita said, "in Veracruz where I was born, the fiesta for Our Lady of the Rosary. In the second week of October."

"I have never been to Veracruz," Beatriz said.

"It is a beautiful town," Teresa said. "My husband took me there once."

"They would march in costumes . . ."

"To the church in the Plaza Zamora," Engracia said, and sighed wistfully.

"And later there would be dancing in the town."

"There is no dancing here at the Fortress," Beatriz said.

"But in Veracruz, ah," Panchita said. *"En Veracruz, todos los días eran dorados, y todas las noches violetas."* In Veracruz, all the days were golden, and all the nights were purple.

Panchita was serving a lifetime sentence for drowning both her children in the Rio de la Babia. Belita and Engracia were lesbians. They shared the bottom bunk below Panchita's. Wrapped in each other's arms each night, they would whisper themselves to discreet orgasm. Another of the women had been in prison for close to twenty years. She never said a word. She stood against the wall at the far end of the cell, staring out past the bars and into the sunlit inner courtyard. The other women called her *"La Sordomuda."* Beatriz, who was here because she had attempted armed robbery at the Hertz rental office in Matehuala, suffered from asthma. She paid for the medication supplied to her on a weekly basis by the prison's hospital staff, a single nurse who was herself a prisoner working in a bare stone room called *"La Enfermería."* More often than not, Beatriz would gasp for breath in the middle of the night, her mouth open, lying on the stone floor, moaning, *"Quiero morir, quiero morir,"* occasionally calling to the matron at the end of the corridor, *"Qué hora es?"'* to which the matron invariably replied, *"Es tarde, cállate!"*

Whenever anyone was wanted in the warden's office, a messenger from the outer prison would be let in through the barred inner gate, and then would knock on the wooden door beyond to shout the prisoner's name, and the dreaded word *"Alcaide!"* which meant "Warden!" *El carcelero*, the turnkey, would then unlock the inner door, and the prisoner would be led through the courtyard with its watchful male prisoners, and through the innermost of the prison's front gates to wait on a wooden bench outside the warden's office till he was ready to grant an audience.

On the tenth day of October, Marilyn heard her name called, and then the word *"Alcaide!"* and the door was unlocked, and she walked through the courtyard behind the messenger, sunlight streaming through the caftan as the men watched her long legs in silhouette.

She sat on the wooden bench and waited.

Lizards scampered about the open area before the office and the search room across the way. The warden called from behind his closed door, and the messenger— a trustee named Luis, who also brought food from the *cocina* to those women prisoners who could afford it— opened the door, ushered Marilyn inside, and then left, closing the door behind him.

The warden's name was on his desk, on a small wooden plaque made in the prison's woodworking shop: HERI-BERTO DOMINGUEZ. He was a short, dark-skinned man with a pencil-line mustache under his nose. He was wearing the olive-green uniform all of the prison guards wore, but on the collar of his tunic were several red and green stripes, obviously the markings of his rank. A riding crop was on his desktop, close to his right hand. A framed picture of a woman and two children was on the other end of the desk.

"Sit down," he said in Spanish.

She sat.

"I have some valuables that belong to you," he said.

She did not answer.

"Your passport—that is valuable, eh?"

"Yes," she answered in Spanish. "My passport is valuable."

"And some jewelry as well. We do not steal from the prisoners here at the Fortress. It is different elsewhere in Mexico. The prison at Saltillo is the worst. Not here. I have been keeping these safe for you."

"Mil gracias," Marilyn said.

"Tu hablas Español muy bien," he said.

"Solo un poco," she replied.

"No, no, you speak it very well," he said. "This jewelry," he said. "It could help you here in the Fortress. I understand you sleep on the floor and possess only the single garment on your back."

"Es verdad," she said. "That is true."

"Would you like the jewelry?" he asked.

"Yes, I would like it."

"I will let you have it then," he said, and smiled. "But for another jewel."

She did not understand him at first.

"Tu mejor tesoro," he said. "Your greatest treasure."

"Thank you, no," she said, and rose, and started for the door.

"Un momento," he said. "I did not yet give you permission to leave."

"I wish to go back to my cell," she said.

"You will go back when I allow you to go back."

"I wish to telephone the American consul."

"Ah, yes, we once allowed prisoners to telephone outside. But the privilege was abused, an escape was arranged via telephone." He shrugged. "We do not permit it any longer."

"When the consul comes to visit . . ."

"Yes, he is supposed to come once a month. But Monterrey is so very far away, eh? Has he been here yet?"

"When he comes . . ."

"We had another American here once, a man. The consul came to see him three, four times a year."

"When he comes, I'll tell him you have my passport."

"Ah, but he already knows this. A prisoner's personal belongings are always turned over to the authorities for safekeeping. I am keeping your passport safe for you, *querida*. I could burn it, you know, and then it would be very difficult for you to obtain another one when finally you are released from here. But, in any event, that is a long time in the future. For now, I will keep the passport safe for you. And I will give you your jewelry, if you want it. The jewelry can make things easier for you here. It is not such a terrible life here if one has the wherewithal. The jewelry can make things easier. *I* can make things easier."

He picked up the riding crop, and rose, and came around the desk. He was at least six inches shorter than she was, a squat little man wearing jodhpurs and high, brown leather boots. Smiling, he walked to where she was standing.

"Raise your gown for me," he said.

"No," she answered, and turned, and walked swiftly to the door.

It was locked from the outside.

He came up behind her and struck her without warning, bringing the short whip down hard on her shoulder. She was turning toward him, her hands instinctively curled in defense, when he struck her again with the crop, just above the collar bone, and then once more across the breasts. She punched out at him, and then dodged away from him and around him, running from the door to the small shuttered window, and throwing the shutters open—the window was barred.

She ran back to the door again, twisting the unresponsive knob again, the riding crop striking her back, shouting "Help!" in English and then *"Socorro!"* in Spanish, and then whirling on him and flailing helplessly at the hissing whip, feeling its sting on the palms of her hands, backing away from it, wincing with each rhythmic slash, covering her face at last, and crumbling beneath the blows he rained on her withering shoulders, finally collapsing on her knees before him, her face still covered.

He would not stop hitting her.

He whipped her till she was whimpering, her hands

streaked with blood, blood seeping through the shoulders of the white caftan. "Help me, someone, please," she moaned, and still he hit her, his grunts accompanying the swishing of the crop, whipped her flat to the floor, whipped her prone at his feet, her bleeding hands clasped behind her neck. He rolled her over then, and lifted the hem of the caftan with the tip of the riding crop.

"You have splendid legs," he said. *"Tienes hermosas piernas."*

With both hands he yanked the blood-spattered caftan above her waist and then brought back the whip as if to strike her across her exposed crotch. She cowered in terror, but he did not hit her again. He began laughing instead and then slowly unbuttoned the flap of his trousers.

He paid for her services later.

With a gold bracelet she had bought in Los Angeles.

She sold the bracelet for sixteen hundred pesos, the equivalent back then of two hundred U.S. dollars. She had paid four hundred dollars for it in L.A. With the money, Marilyn bought clothing, blankets, and a mattress, and was able to keester the remainder for the purchase of food. It was Belita who taught her to put the money inside a condom (which Marilyn purchased from Luis) and slide it up into her rectum; Belita had been in and out of prisons and jails from the time she was fourteen. The Spanish words for asshole keestering were *"metertelo en el culo."*

With part of the money, she bought writing paper, envelopes and postage stamps, and paid Luis two hundred pesos besides to mail a dozen letters to people she had known in Los Angeles and Houston. She learned later that all correspondence passed through Dominguez's office, and when she received no answers, she realized he had not permitted her letters to leave the prison, for fear of spoiling the very good arrangement he had with her. *"Nuestro pacto secreto,"* he called it.

Every day at three o'clock, Luis would knock on the door leading to the cell block, and he would call out her name, and then shout *"Alcaide!"* and she would be led again to the warden's office where the entire prison population knew Dominguez would take his pleasure with "*La Árabe Dorada,*" the nickname sticking because Dominguez insisted she wear to their daily meetings not the grey smock she now wore in the cell block, but instead what he called her "*vestido de novia*"—her wedding dress. He no longer used the riding crop on her, except to raise the hem of the caftan as she stood before him, the tented cotton hanging on the tip of the whip as he examined her blonde pubic hair in seemingly amazed discovery each time.

He took to calling her Mariucha, the Spanish diminutive for Mary. Tenderly, he would caress her burnished mound, hoping for a response from her. She stood before him glacially; he might have been her gynecologist. He would ask her then to hold the robe above her waist while he unbuttoned his fly as he had done the first time, slowly and deliberately, lingeringly, as if threatening an awesomely massive exposure that would cause her to gasp in wonder. The mountain labored and brought forth a mouse. In minuscule erection, he would lead her to the battered leather sofa against the wall, there to achieve within minutes the climax he had been hungering for since breakfast.

Afterward he would shout vituperation, blaming her for the corruption of his religious beliefs and his moral values, heaping upon her obscenities he dredged from the reeking swamp of his mind. He would then angrily knock on the door and bellow to Luis to unlock it. He told her once that he did not trust a key anywhere within her reach. "You are a treacherous *cunt*, Mariucha," he said to her, the Spanish word "*concha*"—despite its literal translation as "shell"—just as stinging as its English counterpart.

She still feared the whip.

He had stopped beating her, yes, but the whip was always in his untrusting hand, even as he mounted her. She suffered his weight upon her, suffered the worm of his manhood inside her, suffered his daily ejaculations because she dreaded the whip and was afraid he might use it again if she provoked his displeasure. Better the words of scorn and anger following his pitiful spasms.

Better the endearment "Mariucha." And then, quite suddenly, it occurred to her that she might become pregnant by him, spawning an evil little monster in his own image, and this frightened her more than the whip did.

When one day at the beginning of November he generously offered her another piece of her own jewelry as recompense for her imagined ardor, she asked if she might have her diaphragm instead. He had never seen such a contraption before, and did not know what it was. He suspected it was more valuable than the jewelry, perhaps, but he could not fathom how. He examined it closely, turning it over and over in his hands, searching for the hidden clue to its worth. Shrugging, he gave it to her at last, together with the mysterious tube of jelly.

Late in November, his interest seemed to dissipate. Prison rumor had it that his wife, a formidable battle-ax named Margarita, had learned of his post-meridiem activities and had called an abrupt halt to them by threatening to have her brother teach him the meaning of honor. Margarita's brother, or so the prison grapevine maintained, was a prize fighter who had recently won a huge purse in Mexico City, or Acapulco, or perhaps Tampico—the grapevine was often vague. But whatever the reason, the daily summonings ceased, and by the end of the month, Marilyn was convinced she had heard the last of Dominguez.

And then one day, the knock came on the thick wooden door, and she heard Luis calling for the Golden Arab, heard the word *"Alcaide!"* and exchanged a frightened glance with Teresa.

The weather had turned uncommonly cold and damp. There was no heat in the cell block, and only the matrons enjoyed the comfort of a coal brazier set up in the stone corridor open to the wind that raged in off the hills. *"Ponte el vestido de novia,"* Luis told her, and she took the caftan from where it was folded under the mattress, and removed first the threadbare overcoat she had purchased with the last of her keestered money, and then her grey smock and cotton panties, and quickly slipped the caftan over her head, and put on the coat again. Squatting, she inserted the diaphragm while Luis watched from the corridor outside. *"Puerco de mierda!"* she yelled at him, and he laughed. Before she left the cell, Teresa took her hands between both her own, and whispered, *"Coraje"*—Courage.

The men called to her as she crossed the windy courtyard.

"Hola, Árabe!"

"Quieras acostarti con migo, Árabe?"

"Mira, Árabe! Mira mi pija!"

This time, there was a stranger in the office with Dominguez.

He was perhaps forty years old, a horse-faced man wearing the uniform of a prison guard. He was smiling somewhat foolishly, shifting his weight from one foot to the other, occasionally stroking the sparse mustache under his bulbous nose.

"Mariucha," Dominguez said, smiling, "I would like you to meet Señor Perez. He has expressed an interest in you."

She said nothing. She stood just inside the door Luis had again locked from the outside. The barred window across the room was shuttered. She waited.

"Señor Perez and I have made an arrangement," Dominguez said.

"What arrangement?" she asked at once.

"A satisfactory arrangement, do not worry."

"What arrangement?" she asked again. She was beginning to tremble. She thrust her hands into the pockets of the coat, hoping they would not see that she was trembling.

"Take off your coat," Dominguez said. "Raise your gown."

"No," she said. "Ask Luis to unlock the door, please." Her voice was shaking. "I wish to go back to the cell."

"Your wishes are of no concern to me," Dominguez said. "Señor Perez is willing to pay for your company, now let the man see what he is buying! Do as I tell you!"

"No," she said, and took her hands from her pockets, the fists clenched.

Dominguez was already coming around the desk, slapping the riding crop against the open palm of his hand.

"Keep away from me, you son of a bitch," she said in English. "I'll kill you," she said, *"Te mataré!"* she said, hurling the threat in Spanish, her eyes searching the room for something she could use to smash his face.

He lashed out at her with the whip, and when she tried to grab it from his hands, he pulled it back and struck her again, and then kept striking her while the grinning guard looked on, battered her to her knees, and then to the floor, and forced her kicking onto her back. She fought him as he tried to unbutton the coat, clutched his hand by the wrist and bit the fleshy part of his palm near the pinky, fought the whip and then the punches he threw at her breasts and her face.

Her nose began bleeding, she was certain he had broken her nose, but she fought him still, fought him till there was no strength left in her, and even then she tried to roll away from him as he clawed at her buttons, straddling her. She spit into his face, and then shrieked as he slapped her with his open hand, continued slapping her, back and forth, the square hard hand incessant, blood spattering in a fine red mist as he hit her backhanded, forehanded, slapped her into near insensibility, and still she struggled. And finally he ripped the buttons off the coat, and forced the coat open, and pulled the caftan above her waist, her back arched, kicking, twisting, still trying to free herself from him. In a frenzy, swearing, he whipped her across her naked thighs until they were bleeding, and then he moved away from where she lay sobbing and trembling and broken on the stone floor, and said to Perez, *"Lleva la puta!"*—Take the whore!

The next time he sent for her, Marilyn was carrying in her coat pocket the razor-honed spoon Teresa had purchased from the kitchen entrepreneur. There was a new man in Dominguez's office this time, a squat and burly brute, also wearing the uniform of a prison guard. A knife scar ran across one of his bushy eyebrows. He studied her appraisingly as she came into the office. In the righthand pocket of the coat, her hand was curled around the sharpened spoon.

"Show him," Dominguez said.

She shook her head.

Smiling, Dominguez came around the desk, the riding crop in his hand.

"Another taste, yes?" he said, and raised the crop and saw the glittering metal clutched in her fist an instant before she stabbed at him.

He turned sideways to avoid the blow aimed at his heart, caught the blade on the flesh of his biceps instead, and backed away from her in terror as she came at him once again, her blue eyes slitted, her lips skinned back over her teeth. The other man sidestepped gingerly around her and behind her. With both hands clenched together, he swung them at the back of her neck. She stumbled forward with the force of the blow, and then turned on him with the spoon still clenched in her fist. He swung his interlocked hands as though wielding an imaginary baseball bat, and this time the blow caught her on the temple, and she staggered, she, the room, the spoon fell clattering to the stone floor, she dropped dizzily to her knees, and the whip lashed at her back, Dominguez shouting invective and striking her again and again until the guard took gentle hold of his arm and whispered that the Arab was unconscious.

She regained consciousness hours later in what the prisoners called "El Pozo," a dark dungeon set into the stone floor and covered with a barred grate, a three-foot cubicle in which it was impossible to stretch full-length, impossible to sit upright, impossible even to curl into a fetal position on one's side. She crouched there naked, her lips swollen and crusted with blood, shivering in the cold evening air, crying out in rage to whoever might hear, shouting for the American consul, screaming for justice. She was continent for as long as she could bear it, and then she soiled the narrow space, and became ill on the stench of her own filth, and vomited up the food she had eaten the day before. No one came to feed her. No one brought her water. She crouched on the cold stone floor, her back aching, her limbs beginning to stiffen, her mouth throbbing with pain.

She called to the matrons, who did not answer.

She shouted for Teresa until she was hoarse, but though Teresa could hear her from the cell block, they would not allow her to go to the sunken cage.

Sobbing, she called upon the President of the United States to please intercede on her behalf.

She beseeched the Pope, remembering all the prayers she had learned at St. Ignatius, reciting them aloud and then begging His Holiness to come here to the prison to see for himself the injustice being done.

She called her mother's name again and again, weeping, choking, "Mama, please help me, Mama, tell them I'm a good girl."

On the fifth day, she became feverish, and in her delirium she imagined that she was standing on an elevated train platform in a nameless city, waiting for the train to come in, holding only an umbrella in her hand and watching a horde of rats swarm up out of the ghetto gutters to climb the steel supporting pillars and scurry across the tracks.

Hundreds of them.

Thousands of them.

Swarming across the tracks.

She was standing on the platform, it was broad daylight there on the platform, and there were millions of rats coming at her. The rats were grey and brown and black, they had long tails that switched in the sunlight, they had long teeth that glinted in the sunlight, they seemed to glide in the sunlight. She tried to tell them who she was. She held up the umbrella. It wasn't raining, there was bright sunlight, but she held up the umbrella.

They were nibbling at her feet now, they were climbing up her legs, she tried to hit them with the umbrella. They chewed the umbrella, they chewed the black silk, they chewed the ribs, they ate the wooden handle. They were climbing up her chest, her chest burned, her chest was on fire. Stop, please, she said, where's my umbrella, what did you do with my umbrella? They were all over her now, they were attacking her face. She couldn't breathe. She clawed at them. They were chewing her face. They were ripping open her face, blood was gushing from her mouth. Stop, she yelled, *stop!* and awakened to discover the nightmare was reality, the dungeon was swarming with rats the size of alley cats, nibbling at her dried feces, crawling over her naked body, licking at the blood caked on her lips.

She screamed.

She screamed.

She screamed.

On the morning of the sixth day, Dominguez sent a matron to uncage her. The matron unlocked the grate and slid it back, and then grimaced and pinched her nostrils against the stench from below. She held out her hand to Marilyn and helped her to climb out of the hole. Marilyn tried to stand, and collapsed to her knees. She tried again, and again fell. "Wow," she said, and blinked at the courtyard sun.

Impatiently, the matron began walking toward the shower stall, Marilyn staggering along behind her. The temperature that morning was in the low fifties. There was only cold water in the shower, but Marilyn stood beneath the icy spray, washing from her body the blood and the filth, cleansing herself and feeling oddly victorious. Her lips were still swollen, her right eye had been blackened and was closed to a narrow slit, every bone in her body ached—but she had won.

When Luis came to her with the white caftan folded over his arm, she refused to put it on. She insisted instead that she wear the grey smock, like all the other women. Luis shrugged. On the way to Dominguez's office, he tried to put his hand on her behind, and she knocked it away, and the men in the courtyard hooted and laughed. Before he rapped on Dominguez's door, he tried to touch her breast, but she backed away from him and crouched as if ready to spring for his throat, and his face went white. Timidly, he knocked on the door.

"Yes, come in!" Dominguez called.

There were a dozen prison guards in the office.

She fainted before the fifth man was finished with her.

He would have to kill her next time.

She would force him to kill her. She would force him to beat her to death with the crop or with his hands. She had been a whore in Houston, but this was not being a whore. This was being owned, and she would not be owned by him or any other man.

He did not summon her to his office again until shortly before Christmas. Again, she would not wear the caftan even though Luis told her it was the warden's specific desire that she look particularly beautiful today. She said in English, "Fuck the warden," and then followed Luis across the courtyard, wearing the blue overcoat over the faded grey smock, the buttons gone from the coat, clutching the coat closed against the wind, her arms folded across her waist. The courtyard was silent. The men knew what had happened to her, and there was no more sport in taunting her with sexual jibes or innuendo.

A man was sitting in the wooden chair beside Dominguez's desk. The man was wearing a dark blue business suit, a grey tie on a striped silk shirt, highly polished black shoes. A grey hat was perched on his lap. He seemed to be in his late sixties, a dapper little man with a neat mustache under his nose, glittering brown eyes surveying her as she came into the room and stood before the desk.

"This is the woman," Dominguez said.

"Does she speak Spanish?" the man asked.

His voice was very low. Marilyn suspected he had never had to raise it in his life. He was watching her steadily. He had directed his words to Dominguez, but he kept staring at her. She thought If he tries to lay a finger on me, I'll rip the eyes from his head. She thought *This* time, they'll have to kill me.

"You heard the question, Mariucha," Dominguez said. She still said nothing. Dominguez shrugged. "She speaks Spanish, yes," he said.

"Will you not speak then, Miss?" the man said.

"Who are you?" she asked him in Spanish.

"Ah, very good," he said. "I am Alberto Hidalgo."

"*Don* Alberto," Dominguez corrected.

"You do me great honor," Hidalgo said, "but no, I am not what you say. No, no," he said, shaking his head and smiling.

"What do you think of her?" Dominguez asked.

"She appears thin."

"The closer the bone," Dominguez said, and chuckled. "Don Alberto is here from South America," he said. "We are trying to arrange your release from the Fortress."

"Sure," she said in English.

"Cómo?" Hidalgo asked.

"How are you going to manage that?" she asked in Spanish.

"Don Alberto has many friends here in Mexico," Dominguez said. "It may be possible for you to be released in his custody. To serve out the remainder of your sentence in his custody. The authorities may permit that."

"We are not certain, of course," Hidalgo said. "We are talking now about Argentina. There may be difficulties."

"Not for a man with your friends," Dominguez said.

"Well, perhaps. We shall see."

"But *if* it can be arranged . . ."

"Yes, I am interested," Hidalgo said. "But, of course, the young lady may prefer staying here."

"I do not think she would prefer staying here," Dominguez said, and smiled.

"Señorita?"

"What are you, a pimp?" she asked in Spanish.

"No, no, no, no, no," he said, smiling. "No, no, a pimp, what gives you that idea?"

"Just came to me out of the blue," she said in English.

"Cómo?"

"What are you then?"

"A businessman," he said, and shrugged. "A humanitarian perhaps. I would not like to see someone as beautiful as you languishing in prison." The words were particularly sonorous in Spanish, they rolled off his tongue mellifluously, *"languideciendo en la cárcel."* He smiled again. "Does she have a passport?" he asked Dominguez.

"Yes, I've been keeping it safe for her," Dominguez said.

"Well, that should make things easier," Hidalgo said. He turned to her again. "So," he said, "it's up to you, after all. If it can be arranged, would you be interested?"

She weighed her decision for only an instant. She did not for a moment believe he was anything but what she'd labeled him; he was a pimp and he was buying her. But if he could take her out of here, if she could accompany him out of this place into broad daylight and open streets, then there was a chance for eventual escape.

"Yes, fine," she said. *"Muy bien."*

"Si es así, está hecho," Hidalgo said. "In that case, it is done."

"She will give you no trouble," Dominguez said, and then added something Marilyn didn't fully understand. *"Ya está domesticada."*

He had told Hidalgo she was already housebroken.

14

"THEN WHAT?" WILLIS ASKED.

"A happy ending," she said. "I was with Hidalgo for a little more than a year. He called me in one day, handed me my passport, and told me I was free to go whenever I wanted to."

"How come?"

Marilyn shrugged. "Maybe I'd already earned what he'd paid to get me out of prison, I don't know. Or maybe he really *was* a humanitarian."

"I've never met a humanitarian pimp," Willis said.

"In any case, I went out on my own, stayed in B.A. for another four years, saved every nickel, and came here with a nice bundle."

"Two million bucks, you told me."

"More or less."

"Divide that by four years, that's five hundred thousand a year."

"Lots of big spenders in B.A. I was averaging three hundred a trick. You multiply that by four, five tricks a night, that comes to a lot of money."

Willis nodded. If she'd earned five hundred grand a year, at an average three hundred bucks a trick, then she'd been to bed with close to seventeen hundred men a year. Something like thirty, thirty-five men a week. Say five tricks each and every night of the week. For a full four years.

"Talk about damaged goods, huh?" she said, as if reading his mind.

Willis said nothing.

"Listen, that's what the girl in *From Here to Eternity* did, isn't it? The book? The girl in Hawaii?"

"I didn't read that book," Willis said.

"Didn't you see the movie?"

"No."

179

"Well . . ." She shrugged and lowered her eyes. "That's what she did."

He was thinking seventeen hundred men a year. Times four years is six thousand eight hundred men. Add the year she'd been working for Hidalgo, you could figure maybe eight, nine thousand. Marilyn Hollis had been to bed with what could be considered the entire male population of a fair-sized town. *If* all of them were men. Had there been a few hundred *women* in the total? Half a dozen police dogs? An Arabian stallion? Christ!

He shook his head.

"So now you walk," she said.

He didn't answer for a moment. Then he said, "None of them knew this, huh?"

"If you mean . . ."

"I mean McKennon, Hollander and Riley."

"None of them knew it," she said softly.

"How about Endicott? Did you tell him?"

"You're the only one I've ever told."

"Lucky me," he said.

The room went silent.

She kept looking at him.

"What are you going to tell your partner?" she asked at last.

"Not *this* that's for sure."

"I meant . . . about my handling that bottle."

"I'll tell him what you told me."

"Do you *believe* what I told you?"

He hesitated for what seemed a long time.

Then he said, "Yes," and took her in his arms.

The handcuffed man sitting with Meyer and Hawes in the Interrogation Room was perhaps fifty years old, a dignified-looking gentleman wearing a brown sports jacket and tan trousers, a cream-colored sports shirt, brown socks and brown loafers. His hair was greying at the temples. His mustache was greying, too. The gun on the desk was a .38 Smith & Wesson.

"I've read you your rights," Meyer said, "and I've informed you that you may have an attorney present if you request one, and I've also informed you that you may refuse entirely to answer any questions, and may at any time during the questioning refuse to answer any further . . ."

"I don't want an attorney," the man said. "I'll answer any questions you ask me."

"And you know that this is a tape-recorder here on the table, and that whatever you say will be recorded and . . ."

"Yes, I understand that."

"And are you now willing to answer any questions Detective Hawes or I may put to you?"

"I told you yes."

"You *do* understand that you're entitled to an attorney if you . . ."

"I understand. I do not want an attorney."

Meyer looked at Hawes. Hawes nodded.

"May I have your full name, please?" Meyer asked. "Peter Jannings."

"Would you spell the last name, please?"

"Jannings. J-A-N-N-I-N-G-S."

"Peter Jannings, is that correct? No middle name?"

"No middle name."

"And your address Mr. Jannings?"

"5318 South Knowlton Drive."

"Any apartment number?"

"3-C."

"How old are you, Mr. Jannings?"

"Fifty-nine."

"You look younger," Meyer said, and smiled.

Jannings nodded. Meyer figured he'd been told this many times before.

"Is this your gun?" Meyer asked. "I'm indicating a .38-caliber Smith & Wesson, Model 32, commonly known as a Terrier Double Action."

"It's my gun."

"Do you have a permit for it?"

"I do."

"Carry or Premises?"

"Carry. I'm in the diamond business."

"Were you in possession of this gun . . . I refer again to the Smith & Wesson, Model 32 . . . were you in possession of this gun when the officers arrested you?"

"I was."

"Was that at three forty-five this afternoon?"

"I didn't look at my watch."

"The time given on the arresting officers' report . . ."

"If they say it was three forty-five, then I'm sure that's what it was."

"And were you arrested, sir, in a motion-picture theater complex called Twin Plaza . . ."

"Yes."

"At 3748 Knightsbridge Road?"

"I don't know the address."

"Where there are two theaters, sir. Twin Plaza One, and Twin Plaza Two. Am I correctly identifying the theater complex where you were arrested?"

"Yes."

"And you were in the theater called Twin Plaza One, is that correct?"

"Yes."

"Were you holding this Smith & Wesson, Model 32, in your hand when you were arrested?"

"I was."

"Had you recently fired the pistol?"

"Yes."

"How many times did you fire the pistol?"

"Four."

"Did you fire the pistol at a person?"

"I did."

"At whom did you fire the pistol?"

"A woman."

"Do you know her name?"

"I do not."

"Are you aware, Mr. Jannings, that a woman sitting in the seat directly behind yours . . . behind the seat you were occupying when the officers arrested you . . . was shot four times in the chest and head . . ."

"Yes, I'm aware of that. I'm the one who shot her."

"You shot the woman sitting behind you, is that correct?"

"I did."

"Do you know that the woman died on the way to the hospital?"

"I didn't know that, but I'm glad," Jannings said.

Meyer looked at Hawes again. On the tabletop, the tape kept unreeling relentlessly.

"Mr. Jannings," Hawes said, "can you tell us why you shot her?"

"She was talking," Jannings said.

"Sir?"

"All through the movie."

"Talking?"

"Talking."

"Sir?"

"She was *talking* behind me all during the movie. Identifying the characters. Oh, look, there's the husband! Oh, look, here comes the boyfriend! Uh-oh, there's a lion! Uh-oh, *two* of them! Explaining the locale. That's her farm. Now they're in the jungle. That's a doctor's office. He's the doctor. Second-guessing the plot. I'll bet she goes to bed with him. I'll bet the husband finds out. At one point, when the doctor says, 'You have syphilis,' the woman behind me said, 'She has *what?*' I turned to her and said, 'She has *syphilis,* madam!' She said, 'Mind your own business, I was talking to my husband.' I went back to watching the movie, *trying to* watch it. The woman said, 'Whatever it is, I think she caught it from the husband.' I controlled myself all through the movie, all through the incessant chatter behind me. Then, toward the end of the film, I couldn't bear it any longer. There was a long graveside speech, Meryl Streep reads this lovely poem, and then she walks off toward the edge of the cemetery and looks out into the distance and we know everything she's feeling in that moment, and the woman behind me said, 'That girl with the husband is the rich one he married.' I turned around and said, 'Madam, if you want to talk, why don't you stay home and watch television?' She said, 'I thought I told you to mind your own business.' I said, 'This *is* my business. I paid for this seat.' She said, 'Then sit in it and shut up.' That was when I shot her."

Hawes looked at Meyer.

"My only regret is that I waited too long," Jannings said. "I should have shot her sooner. Then I could have enjoyed the movie."

Meyer wondered if he could get off with a plea of justifiable homicide.

Captain Samuel Isaac Grossman was hunched over a microscope when Carella got to the Police Laboratory at a little before five that Saturday afternoon. The days were getting longer. The sky beyond the huge windows fronting High Street was only now beginning to show the first faint pinkish tint of dusk, the windows in the surrounding buildings glaring sun-reflected light. Grossman was totally absorbed. A tall, rangy man who would have seemed more at home on a New England farm than in the sterile orderliness of a laboratory, he sat on a high stool, adjusted a knob, peered again into the microscope's eyepiece. Carella waited.

"I know you're there, whoever you are," Grossman said, and turned on the stool, and lowered his glasses from their perch on his forehead back to the bridge of his nose. "Well, well," he said, "long time no see," and got off the stool and walked toward Carella, his hand extended. The men shook hands.

"Did you hear the one about the man who goes to see his urologist?" Grossman asked.

"Tell me," Carella said, already smiling.

"The urologist says, 'What seems to be the trouble?' The man says, 'I can't pee.' The urologist says, 'How old are you?' The man says, 'Ninety-two.' The urologist says, 'So you peed enough already.' "

Carella burst out laughing.

"Another man goes to see the same urologist," Grossman said. "The urologist says, 'What seems to be the trouble?' The man says, "I lost my penis in an automobile accident.' The urologist says, 'No problem, we'll give you a penis transplant.' The man says, 'I didn't know you could do that.' The urologist says, 'Sure, I'll show you some samples.' He brings out a sample penis, shows it to the man. The man says, 'It's too short.' The urologist brings out another penis. The man looks at it and says, 'I was really hoping for something with more authority.' The urologist brings out this magnificent penis. The man looks at it. 'Now that's more like it,' he says. 'Does it come in white?'"

Laughing, Carella said, "I'll have to tell that one to Artie."

"I love urologist jokes," Grossman said. "What brings you here?"

"I called you yesterday," Carella said.

"I never got the message. What about?"

"How do I get pure nicotine from cigarette butts?"

Grossman blinked.

"I'm working a nicotine poisoning," Carella said. "Maybe two of them."

"That's rare nowadays," Grossman said, "nicotine poisoning."

"That's why I want to know how to make the poison from scratch. I'm assuming my man wouldn't know how to refine it from an insecticide."

"So you want to know how to make it from cigarette butts. You want to know how to *distill* it."

"Cigar butts, pipe tobacco, whatever."

"Mmm," Grossman said.

"Can it be done?"

"Sure," Grossman said.

"So how do I do it?"

"Do you know how to make whiskey?"

"No. My father makes wine."

"Fermentation. Close but no cigar. We're talking about distillation."

"Which is?"

"You got an hour?"

"That complicated, huh?"

"For me, it's easy. For you . . ." Grossman shrugged.

"What do I need?"

"Are you assuming your man has access to laboratory equipment? Well, I guess not. Otherwise titration would be an option."

"That's right."

"Then what you need is a relative in Georgia who knows how to make moonshine booze."

"Lacking such connections . . ."

"You'd have to make your own still."

"How do I do that?"

"You don't know anything at all about distillation, huh?"

"Nothing."

"Terrific. They sent me the class dunce. Okay. Distillation is transferring a liquid or a solid in its gaseous state to another place where it is *again* liquified or solidified."

"Why?"

"To purify it."

"What do you mean by another place? New Jersey? Kansas?"

"Ha-ha," Grossman said mirthlessly. "They *did* send me the class dunce. Pay attention."

"I am paying attention," Carella said.

"Booze is made by distilling a fermented mash of grain—rye, barley, wheat, corn, you pays your money and you takes your choice. You heat up the mash, carry off the vapor—the steam, if you will—and then condense it. When vapor condenses, you get liquid. *Voilá!* Booze!"

"How about poison?"

"Same animal. Let's say you use tobacco in whatever form. You make a mash from, let's say, a dozen cigars. Your average cigar has a nicotine content of somewhere between fifteen and forty milligrams. This doesn't mean that if you *smoke* a cigar, you're going to keel over dead, even though the fatal dose of nicotine is considered to be around forty milligrams. If you chewed it up and ate it, though, you'd get pretty damn sick. And if you distilled the *alkaloid* from that cigar . . ."

"Here we go again," Carella said.

"Okay, step by step. Step one: you make a mash of a dozen cigars, two dozen, a hundred, however many. Step two: you heat up the mash. At atmospheric pressure, nicotine'll boil without decomposition at two hundred and forty degrees."

"Is that important?"

"Merely a scientific observation. Step three: you carry off the steam in a tube. You've seen pictures of bootlegger's stills, haven't you? All those tubes and coils? The tubes are to carry off the steam, the coils are to condense it. That's step four, the condensation."

"How does that work?"

"A natural process. It cools, it condenses. So now you've got a colorless liquid that's your alkaloid, more or less, the toxic nicotine you're going for."

"What do you mean, more or less."

"More or less *pure*. Step five: you take this liquid and distill it again. Step six: you distill it yet another time. And then you keep distilling it until you get your pure alkaloid. Whammo. You drop it in somebody's drink and he drops dead."

"I thought you said it was complicated," Carella said, grinning. "Do me a favor, will you?"

"Name it."

"Make me a sketch of a still."

Early Monday morning, Carella went downtown again, not to the lab on High Street, but to the courthouse several doors down, where he presented to a superior court magistrate two written requests for search warrants. The first request looked like this:

1. I am a detective of the Police Department assigned to the 87th Squad.
2. I have information based upon autopsy reports from the Medical Examiner's Office that nicotine was used as a poison in two homicides I am investigating.
3. I have further information based upon a conversation with Captain Samuel Grossman of the Police Laboratory that toxic nicotine can be distilled from ordinary cigarette, cigar or pipe tobacco.
4. I have further information based upon my personal knowledge and belief that such distilling apparatus, commonly known as "a still" (drawing attached), may be on the premises of Miss Marilyn Hollis, who resides at 1211 Harborside Lane in Isola.
5. Based upon the foregoing reliable information and upon my personal knowledge and belief, there is probable cause to believe that a still in possession of Marilyn Hollis would constitute evidence in the crime of murder.

Wherefore, I respectfully request that the court issue

a warrant in the form annexed hereto, authorizing a
search of the premises at 1211 Harborside Lane.
No previous application in this matter has been made
in this or any other court or to any other judge, justice or magistrate.

The second request was identical in every way except
for the name and address. For Marilyn Hollis, Carella had
written in Charles Endicott, Jr. For 1211 Harborside Lane,
he had written in 493 Burton Street. Each request was
accompanied by a photocopy of Grossman's sketch of a
still:

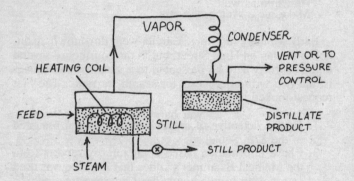

The magistrate carefully read the first request, started
reading the second one, and then looked up and said,
"These are identical, aren't they?"

"Yes, Your Honor," Carella said. "Except for the
names and addresses."

"And there have been two nicotine poisonings, is that
correct?"

"Yes, Your Honor. In addition to a fatal stabbing that
is not relevant to the search-warrant requests."

"Where's your reasonable cause, Detective Carella?"

"Your Honor, two people were poisoned by . . ."

"Yes, yes, where's your cause?"

"The three victims were all close friends of Miss Hollis. Mr. Endicott is also a close friend of . . ."

"I'm looking for a reason to allow you to walk into a private citizen's home and conduct a search."

"I recognize, Your Honor, that I may be short on cause . . ."

"I'm happy you recognize that."

"But if someone manufactured that poison . . ."

"That's exactly the point. *Someone* may have. But why should you believe the *someone* was either Miss Hollis or Mr. Endicott?"

"Your Honor, Miss Hollis was intimately linked with all three of the victims."

"And Mr. Endicott?"

"With him as well."

"Did *he* know the victims?"

"No, Your Honor. Not according to . . ."

"Then what are you suggesting? That they acted in concert?"

"I have no evidence to support such a theory."

"Do you have evidence for an arrest?"

"No, Your Honor."

"What evidence do you have that would lead you to believe a still may be on either of these premises?"

"None, Your Honor. Except that distillation is a means of . . ."

"This is not Russia, Detective Carella."

"No, sir, it's America. And three people have been killed. If I can find a still . . ."

"I'm denying both requests," the magistrate said.

That was the way Monday morning started.

It was also raining.

Carella was soaking wet when he got to the squadroom. A soggy manila envelope was sitting on his desk. Seal of the Medical Examiner's Office in the lefthand corner. Carella glanced at it cursorily and then went to the sink in the corner of the room, yanked some paper towels from the rack there and tried to dry his hair. Andy Parker was sitting at his own desk, reading through a sheaf of D.D. reports on a burglary.

"I heard a good joke the other day," Carella said.

"Yeah?" Parker said.

Carella told him Grossman's joke about the black penis.

"I don't get it," Parker said. "M.E.'s office delivered an envelope for you."

"I saw it," Carella said, and went to his desk and ripped open the flap on the envelope. The envelope contained Blaney's typewritten report on the McKennon murder.

Carella looked at the calendar on his desk.

April 14.

McKennon had been murdered on the twenty-fourth of March.

Three weeks to get the paperwork, not bad for this city. He leafed through the pages. Most of the report detailed what Blaney had already told him on the phone. There was a dental chart, though, and he looked at that now:

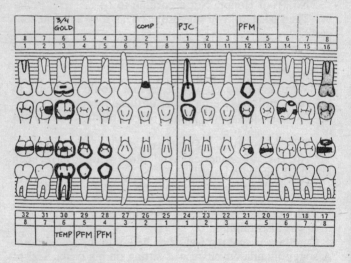

He read Blaney's notes on what the markings for the variously numbered teeth meant—

1. Tooth missing.
3. ¾ crown, gold.
7. Composite filling.
9. Root canal, porcelain jacket crown.
12. Full crown, porcelain fused to metal.
14. Silver fillings, cavity.

16. Tooth missing.
17. Silver filling, cavity.
20. Silver filling.
21. Silver filling.
25. Full crown, porcelain fused to metal.
29. Full crown, porcelain fused to metal.
30. Root canal, temporary crown, cavity.
31. Silver filling.
32. Silver filling.

—leafed through the rest of the report, put it back into the envelope and then carried it to the M-Z filing cabinet, where he put it into the manila folder marked Mc-KENNON. He looked up at the clock. Twenty minutes past nine.

"The lieutenant in yet?" he asked Brown.

"Got here at nine."

"Willis is due in, isn't he?"

"Should be."

Carella debated calling him at the Hollis house.

He looked at his own watch.

Twenty-one minutes past nine.

He went to the lieutenant's door, and knocked on it.

"Come!" Byrnes shouted.

The lieutenant was sitting in a shaft of sunlight that streamed through his open windows. He looked like a religious miracle.

"How'd you make out?" he asked.

"Denied."

"I knew it."

"So did I. But it was worth a shot."

"What now?"

"I want round-the-clocks on Hollis and Endicott."

"Protection?"

"No. Surveillance."

Byrnes nodded. "Granted," he said.

There was something about Marilyn's story that bothered Willis.

He had immediately asked "How come?" when she told him that Hidalgo had cut her loose after a bit more than a year. He still wondered how come. He didn't know what it had cost Hidalgo to spring her from that Mexican prison but from what he understood about Mexican justice, *la mordida* came high. In that meeting in the warden's office, Hidalgo had told her he was a businessman. Oh, yes, a humanitarian as well, but *first* a businessman. It seemed odd to Willis that any businessman—especially if he happened to be a pimp—would be willing to give up an asset for which he had laid out cold cash. Even assuming she'd more than earned her keep in the year or so she'd worked for him, why would he have turned over her passport and given her her walking papers? Pimps didn't operate that way, not any pimps Willis knew. Pimps were on the gravy train. Pimps were users and takers. Hidalgo's act of generosity simply didn't ring true. Willis wanted to believe her, but he didn't.

He was not in the squadroom that morning because he was busy doing some detective work *outside* the squadroom. She had left the house at ten-thirty, heading downtown for an appointment with her hairdresser. It was now a quarter to eleven, and Willis was in the wing of the house that served as a storeroom, rummaging through the cartons of junk Marilyn had saved. He was looking for something that would shed some light on those years she had spent in Buenos Aires. A year and a bit more with Hidalgo, another four years on her own.

He found no letters.

Well, that was understandable. She'd lost touch with her friends in Los Angeles and Houston and her mother's whereabouts were unknown at the time. Besides, she'd been busy fucking her brains out, and that didn't leave much time for letter-writing.

He found no bankbooks or bank statements, either, no receipts, no copies of paid bills, odd for a woman who'd been on her own for four years, "an independent," as she'd put it, a woman amassing two million bucks. Where'd she keep all that money? Under her mattress?

Well, maybe she was the kind of person who threw out a bankbook when an account was closed, a bill as soon as it was paid, a bank statement the moment next month's statement arrived. There were people like that; the clutter of paperwork simply overwhelmed them. But then why had she saved these mountains of clippings? A saver saves, a pack rat is a pack rat. Why not a scrap from those years in Argentina?

He began going through the clippings.

The collection was encyclopedic, she seemed to have saved anything and everything that captured her momentary fancy. There was an article on something called labonotation which was a system for recording ballet positions, another article on cha-no-yu, the Japanese tea ceremony originated in China and later practiced by Zen priests in Japan. There were articles on Marie Curie and Ancient Egyptian furniture and massage techniques and Robert Burns and data processing. There were articles on English art and architecture, Wolfgang Amadeus Mozart, the Punic Wars, motorcycles, color photography, and Geronimo the Indian. And then, lying on top of a stack of articles in one of the cartons, Willis found:

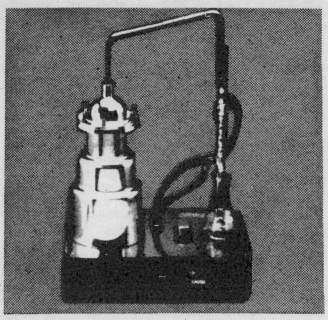

THE GAGGIA ELECTRIC DISTILLER. With this distiller from Milan, Italy, you can extract flavors, oils and scents from flowers, fruits, herbs or any organic material to make your own fresh cooking ingredients, perfumes, health or beauty oils at home. The electrical element heats up to 1¼ liters of the liquid or solid organic material of your choice at gradually rising temperatures, slowly extracting the desired flavor or scent as vapor. The vapor passes through a Pyrex® condenser cooled by three liters of water (continuously circulated by a 6-watt pump), and the distillate is collected in a Pyrex® flask. Purity of distillate is assured by use of copper and glass tubing and brass fittings. An 18-watt fan cools circulating water. Mercury thermometer (included) inserts in top of distiller to help you determine temperatures at which particular flavors will vaporize. ABS plastic base. Water level indicator. On/off switch. Plugs into household outlet. Height: 25¼ inches. Width: 16¾ inches. Length: 11 inches. Weight: 31 pounds 11 ounces.
20659R $395.00
Postpaid and Unconditionally Guaranteed

15

MEYER FIGURED IT WAS BORING TO TAIL A lawyer because lawyers were essentially boring. He had met only three interesting lawyers in his entire life. The rest of them were as dull as the telephone book. And more often than not, they were his adversaries. Tell me, Detective Meyer, when you made this arrest, were you aware of the fact that . . . ?

But Meyer had not yet met every lawyer in the world, and the possibility existed that one day he might run across yet another interesting one: Hope is the thing with feathers. Meanwhile, he did not like lawyers. And Charles Endicott, Jr., was a lawyer.

Moreover, he was a lawyer who may or may not have poisoned two people and stabbed a third. Which, if such proved to be the case, made him a bit more interesting but far more dangerous than your usual learned adversary. Meyer did not appreciate tailing him, and he wished the lieutenant had chosen someone else for the job.

Besides, it was raining cats and dogs.

Meyer had started his surveillance two hours earlier by reading all the D.D. reports Willis and Carella had filed. He then called Endicott's office, identified himself as Lieutenant Charles Wilson, in charge of public relations, and asked if the police officers assigned to his earlier protection had been courteous and respectful. Endicott said they had been, and wanted to know why they had been pulled off the case. Meyer said he didn't know anything about that, but he was glad the assigned men had done their jobs properly.

He had called only to ascertain that Endicott was in his office.

That was at seven minutes past eleven, five minutes after he'd finished reading the D.D. reports. He wanted to get downtown before the lunch hour, start the actual tailing. The lieutenant had told him that Hawes would relieve on post at four o'clock. Hawes, in turn, would be relieved by O'Brien at midnight. Wall to wall coverage.

At a quarter to twelve, Meyer called Endicott again, this time from a phone booth across the street from his office on Jefferson Avenue. Lowering his voice to a deep growl, he asked if Endicott handled divorce cases, and when he was assured that the firm of Hackett, Rawlings, Pearson, Endicott, Lipstein and Marsh did indeed handle such cases, he gave his name as Martin Milstein and made an appointment to see Endicott at four-thirty on Friday. He would call sometime later in the week to cancel the appointment; in the meantime, he knew that Endicott was still in his office, and he hoped he would be going out for lunch sometime between twelve and one, when most people did.

The only detective on the squad who knew what Endicott looked like was Hal Willis. For reasons not divulged to Meyer, it was thought best that he not be assigned to the surveillance. That was why a patrolman in plainclothes was waiting for Meyer when he came out of the phone booth. The patrolman was one of the six men earlier assigned to protect Endicott. He was with Meyer only for purposes of initial identification. The moment he pointed out Endicott, he was expected to go back to his duties uptown.

For now, both men stood in the rain outside the office building.

The patrolman complained bitterly about the lousy weather.

Meyer kept watching the front door of the building. Only one way in or out. If Endicott left, he would have to come through those revolving doors.

"Keep your eye on the doors," he told the patrolman.

"Don't I know that?" the patrolman said.

Meyer wondered if he did.

At ten after twelve, the patrolman nudged Meyer.

The man coming through the revolving doors was tall and slender, with brown eyes and white hair. Endicott's description in the D.D. reports. The patrolman nodded, and Meyer took off. Endicott was wearing a Burberry raincoat, not a good thing for somebody following him. In this city, when it rained, Burberry raincoats sprouted like mushrooms.

He was a fast walker, Endicott was, and apparently he enjoyed the rain. Hatless, he bounded through it like Gene Kelly, mindlessly stepping in puddles, dashing across streets against the lights, a man in one hell of a hurry. Meyer did not like surveillances involving fast walkers. Meyer preferred stakeouts that took place in cozy liquor stores.

The man walked eight goddamn blocks in the pouring rain. Meyer could swear he was whistling.

He turned off Jefferson Avenue at last, into a side street where the rain was blowing in sheets from north to south off the River Harb. Endicott plunged into the rain like a galleon under full sail, went halfway up the block, turned in under a red, white and green awning, opened a brass-studded wooden door, and disappeared from sight. The lettering on the awning identified the place as Ristorante Bonatti. Feeling very much like Popeye Doyle in *The French Connection,* Meyer hunched his shoulders against the wind and the rain and hoped Endicott's lunch would not be a long one.

The trouble with tailing your partner's girlfriend was that it made you feel like some kind of a shit. Carella had picked up Marilyn Hollis outside the building on Harborside Lane at ten-thirty this morning, had followed her to her hairdressing salon, was waiting outside for her when she emerged at twenty after twelve, and followed her on foot crosstown to the Stem where she hailed a taxi. He'd immediately flagged another taxi, identified himself to the driver, and told him not to lose that taxi up ahead. The cabbie did not appreciate driving a cop. Visions of getting stiffed danced through his head.

Marilyn's cab proceeded downtown, first on the Stem, then on Culver, then around Van Buren Circle and southward on Grover Park West, continuing southward to Hall Avenue, hanging a right, driving three blocks farther downtown, then hanging a left and pulling up in front of

a building with a red, white and green awning. Marilyn
got out of the cab, paid the driver, and walked swiftly
toward a brass-studded door. Carella's cab pulled into the
curb some two cars back. To the driver's enormous surprise, Carella tipped him generously and then stepped
out into the rain.

The lettering on the awning read Ristorante Bonatti.

Meyer Meyer was standing outside the restaurant,
peering through the plate glass window, his hands cupped
to the sides of his face.

Carella came up beside him, and tapped him on the
shoulder.

Meyer turned, surprised. "Well, well," he said.

"Enjoying the rain?" Carella asked.

"Oh, yes, very much, thank you."

"Is Endicott in there?"

"With a blonde who just joined him," Meyer said.

At four-fifteen that Monday afternoon, Arthur Brown
relieved Carella on post outside the Hollis house. Carella
told him the joke about the black penis, and Brown burst
out laughing and then immediately wondered if it was a
racist joke. He knew his customer well, though, and just
as quickly decided it wasn't. Still laughing, he said, "Got
to tell that to Caroline when I get home. Who's relieving
me?"

"Delgado."

"Hope he's on time. I don't like standing around in
the rain."

Carella had been standing around in the rain since ten
this morning, give or take an hour or so for taxi rides
around town, following Marilyn hither and yon and finally back here to the house.

"Fill me in," Brown said.

"Blonde white woman, twenty-four years old, five
eight, weighing about a hundred and twenty, more or
less. Her name's Marilyn Hollis."

"What are you looking for specifically?"

"She may be a killer. Maybe she'll make another
move."

"Very nice," Brown said.

"I'll talk to you in the morning," Carella said, and walked off through the rain.

The first surprise Brown got was at four-thirty, when a car pulled up across the street from where he was standing under a tree in the park, and a man got out of the car, and locked it, and began walking toward 1211 Harborside Lane. The man was either Hal Willis or his double. The man climbed the low, flat steps to the front door, took a key from his pocket, inserted it into the latch, and let himself into the building.

Brown blinked.

Had that *really* been Willis?

It sure as hell *looked* like Willis.

But Carella hadn't mentioned Willis being in on the stakeout. Was that a skeleton key he'd let himself in with? He hadn't looked like a man messing with a ringful of skeleton keys. He'd looked like a man who had the key to the front door of a house occupied by a lady Carella thought might be a killer.

The second surprise Brown got was at twenty minutes past seven when the front door opened again and first out came the blonde Marilyn Hollis girl Carella had described, and next out came Willis, who pulled the door shut behind him, and then the girl took Willis's arm and they walked off up the street together, making a right turn on the corner, heading crosstown toward the Stem.

Brown wondered what the hell was going on here.

He followed them to the Stem, and then downtown on the Stem, the neon lights filtered by a fine, soft drizzle now, the sound of automobile tires swishing on the black asphalt, keeping a decent interval behind them because if Willis *wasn't* in on the stakeout, Brown didn't want to be made by an experienced cop. But if he *wasn't* in on this, then what the hell was he doing with a broad who maybe killed somebody?

Up ahead was a Chinese restaurant named Buddha's Feast.

Willis opened the door for the girl, and the girl went in, and Willis went in behind her.

Brown peeked in through the plate glass window, and that was when he got his third surprise.

Because sitting there in one of the booths was a person who looked very much like Bert Kling, who was in *fact* Bert Kling, and sitting with Kling was his girlfriend, Eileen Burke, who was *also* a working cop, and Willis and the Marilyn Hollis girl came over to the booth, and it looked as if Willis was introducing her to them, and then Willis and the girl sat down and Willis signaled to the waiter.

Man, Brown thought, this is a bigger stakeout than I figured! The whole damn *police* department is in on it!

Eileen Burke kept trying to hide her left cheek. The plastic surgery looked very good to Willis, you could hardly tell she'd been slashed not too long ago, even if you were looking for a scar. But Willis noticed that she kept bringing up her left hand to cover her cheek.

"Eileen does a lot of work with the Rape Squad," he told Marilyn.

"Really?" Marilyn said.

"As a decoy," Willis said.

"I'm not sure I'd like that kind of work," Marilyn said, and rolled her eyes.

Willis was sitting beside Kling on one side of the booth, Marilyn and Eileen opposite them on the other. Willis thought the two women looked very beautiful together, Eileen with her red hair and green eyes, Marilyn blonde and blue-eyed, one a big-boned, full-breasted woman, the other slender and pale and somehow fragile-looking. A nice combination.

He wanted tonight to be a very special one. Marilyn's coming-out party, so to speak. Her introduction to two people he liked and admired, both of them working detectives. And, perhaps more important, *their* introduction to her. He knew Carella well enough to be certain he hadn't revealed to the other cops on the squad anything about Marilyn's past. The lieutenant, yes, Carella would have felt duty-bound to tell him that Willis had moved in with a former hooker whom Carella considered a murder suspect. But beyond the lieutenant, no. Carella was a working cop, not a gossip. Carella was a friend.

There were secrets at this table.

Marilyn's secret was that she'd been a hooker.

Eileen's secret was that she'd been raped and slashed in the line of duty.

There were also mysteries at this table.

Willis wondered if two experienced, eagle-eyed detectives would take one look at Marilyn and know what she'd been.

Kling wondered if Marilyn would ask questions that would again trigger memories of what had been the most horrible night in Eileen's life. He wished Willis hadn't mentioned her work as a decoy.

Willis wished nobody would ask Marilyn what sort of work *she* did.

"What sort of work do *you* do?" Eileen asked.

"I'm independently wealthy," Marilyn said breezily, and then said, "How about the orange chicken?"

Eileen looked at Kling.

"How does a person get to be independently wealthy?" Kling asked.

"I have a rich father," Marilyn said, and smiled.

Kling was thinking he'd once been married to a woman who earned a hell of a lot more money than he did. He wondered if Willis was serious about this girl. If so, did she know how much a Detective/Third earned?

"What do they do?" Marilyn asked. "Just turn you out on the street?"

"Sort of," Eileen said. "Would anyone like the crispy fish?"

"I'd be terrified," Marilyn said.

I *am* terrified, Eileen thought. Ever since that night, I've been scared to death.

"You get used to it," she said, and again brought her hand up to her cheek.

"Why don't we just order the special dinner?" Kling said. "Do you think that'd be too much to eat?"

"I'm starved," Marilyn said.

"Sure, let's do that," Willis said, and signaled to the waiter.

The waiter padded to the table.

"The special dinner for four," Willis said. "And another round of drinks, please."

"I go on at midnight," Kling said. "No more for me."

"Oh, come on," Eileen said.

"No, really," Kling said, and covered the top of his glass with his palm.

"The night shift's a good time for cooping," Eileen said. "Have another drink."

"What's cooping?" Marilyn asked.

"Sleeping on the job," Willis said.

"Special dinner for four," the waiter said. "More drinks." And walked off.

"Why do Chinese waiters always sound surly?" Marilyn asked. "Have you noticed that?"

"Because they *are* surly," Kling said.

"Racist remark," Eileen said.

"Who me? I have nothing against Chinks," Kling said.

"Compounding the felony," Eileen said.

Marilyn wondered if they were going to use police jargon all night long.

Eileen wondered if Marilyn knew Kling had used the word "Chinks" deliberately, as a reverse joke.

"That was deliberate," she said.

"What was?" Marilyn asked.

"Him saying 'Chinks.' "

"Actually, I like Chinks," Kling said. "Japs, too. We have a Jap on the squad."

"That, too," Eileen said. "Deliberate. His sense of humor."

"I have no sense of humor," Kling said, dead-panned.

"Have you ever wondered why there are no blue-eyed Chinese?" Willis said.

"Mendel's Law," Marilyn said. "If you mate a black cat and a white cat, you get one white kitten, one black kitten, and two grey kittens."

"What's that got to do with blue-eyed Chinese?" Willis asked.

"Brown eyes are dominant, blue eyes are recessive. If everybody in a country has brown eyes, then everybody's children will also have brown eyes. Well, that isn't quite true. It doesn't *always* work with people the way it works with fruit flies or cats, unless everybody's got dominant genes to begin with. For example, my father had brown

eyes and my mother had blue eyes, but there must have
been some recessive blues in previous generations. When
two recessives get together, you get another recessive,
which is what I am, a recessive blue."

"How do you happen to know that?" Willis asked.

"I saved a clipping on it," Marilyn said.

He wondered why she had saved a clipping for an electric distiller. He had not yet asked her. She had told him
the moment he walked into the house this afternoon that
she'd broken the news to Endicott. Met him for lunch,
told him she didn't want to see him again. So he'd put
off asking her about the distiller, even though Carella's
last report had mentioned that one way to make home-
made nicotine was by distilling tobacco.

"Are both your parents dead?" Kling said.

Uh-oh, Willis thought. Cop catching a discrepancy.
She'd used the present tense in talking about her father
earlier: I *have* a rich father. And just now she'd switched
to past tense: My father *had* brown eyes.

Kling was waiting for an answer. Not probing, not a
cop on the job, no suspicion here, just puzzlement. Waiting for clarification.

"Yes," Marilyn said.

"Because earlier," Eileen said, "I got the impression
your father was still alive."

Another county heard from, Willis thought.

"No, he died several years ago. He left me quite a bit
of money," Marilyn said, and lowered her eyes.

"I thought that was only in fairy tales," Eileen said.

"Sometimes in real life, too," Marilyn said.

"I used to love reading Grimm's fairy tales," Eileen
said, somewhat wistfully, as if talking about an uncom-
plicated time long ago.

"Did you know that Jakob Grimm . . . the one who
wrote the fairy tales . . . is the same Grimm who for-
mulated Grimm's Law?"

Fancy footwork, Willis thought. Reverse the field,
change the subject. Nice work, Marilyn.

"What's Grimm's Law?" Kling asked.

"Section 314.76," Eileen said. "Consorting with fairies."

"Sexist remark," Kling said.

"Something to do with p's becoming b's, and v's becoming w's or vice-versa, I forget which," Marilyn said. "It was in a clipping I saved. In German, of course, the German language."

"The clipping was in German?" Eileen said.

"No, no, the law. Grimm's Law. It pertained to the German language. He was German, you know."

"What's taking him so long with those drinks?" Willis said, and signaled to the waiter.

"Drinks coming," the waiter said, and went into the kitchen.

"See?" Kling said. "Surly as a boil."

"Maybe he doesn't understand English," Eileen said.

"Does anybody here speak Chinese?" Kling said.

"Marilyn speaks fluent Spanish," Willis said, and then immediately thought *Jackass! You're opening the wrong can of peas!*

"I wish *I* spoke fluent Spanish," Kling said. "Come in handy around the precinct."

"Well, you know a few words," Eileen said.

"Oh, sure, you pick them up, but that's not *fluent*. Where'd you learn it?" he asked Marilyn. "In school?"

"Yes," she said at once.

"Here in the city?" Eileen asked.

"No. In Los Angeles."

Getting in deeper and deeper, Willis thought.

"Did you go to college out there?"

"No. I learned it in high school."

Deeper and deeper and deeper.

"It's a much simpler language than English, actually," Marilyn said, sidestepping again. "I'd hate to be a foreigner learning English, wouldn't you? All those words that sound alike and are spelled differently? Like joke and oak and folk. Or all the words that have the same spelling but are pronounced differently? Like bough and though and rough. I'd go crazy."

"Say something in Spanish," Willis said.

"Yo te adoro," she said, and grinned.

"Talk about English," Eileen said, "I know a girl

who when she knocks on the door and you ask, 'Who is it?' she answers, 'It is I.' "

"Well, that's proper English," Kling said. "Isn't it?"

"Oh, sure, but who ever uses it? Most people say 'It's *me*.' "

"Even when it's somebody else?" Kling said.

The second round of drinks arrived at the same time the dinner did.

"Terrific," Willis said sourly.

But he was happy for the intrusion. He'd felt back there a few minutes ago that Marilyn's diversionary tactic had become a bit obvious, so eager was she to get off the topic of where and how she'd learned Spanish. Were two experienced cops, both adept at detecting nuances of speech and behavior, really buying everything she told them? He wondered.

But only once during the meal was there an open clash, cop versus civilian, police mentality versus—hooker mentality? Kling was talking about a recent case he'd handled where this guy was regularly and repeatedly raping the woman who lived next door to him and the victim never told her husband about it because she was afraid the husband would beat her up if she did.

"I'd have killed them both," Marilyn said, with such sudden vehemence that all conversation stopped.

Eileen looked at her.

Kling said, "Actually, that's what almost happened. She took a cleaver to the guy next door. A neighbor heard all the ruckus and called 911. Before they got there, though, the husband came home. She'd already hacked off the neighbor's hand and was going for his head when all at once there's the husband. So she turns on him, goes at *him* with the cleaver. That was when 911 walked in. It took four cops to get her off him."

"The husband?" Eileen asked.

"Oh, sure. The other guy was passed out cold on the kitchen floor."

"So what happens to her now?" Marilyn asked.

"We charged her with two counts of attempted murder."

"Her lawyer'll plea-bargain it down to assault," Willis said.

"No, I'll bet he tries for self-defense," Eileen said.

"With the neighbor maybe," Kling said. "The husband didn't do anything but walk in there."

"Either way, she goes to jail, right?" Marilyn said.

"Well, she *did* chop both of them up a little," Kling said.

"They had her terrified," Marilyn said. "They *deserved* to be chopped up."

"There are laws against chopping up people," Eileen said.

"Go tell that to Lizzie Borden," Kling said. "*She* got away with it."

"Which makes the song wrong," Eileen said.

"What song?"

"About chopping up your Mama in Massachusetts."

"I really don't see anything funny about it," Marilyn said, and the table went silent again.

Willis cracked open his fortune cookie.

" 'You will have new clothes,' " he read out loud.

"Maybe that means you'll get a promotion," Kling said. He had turned his eyes away from Marilyn, who shook a cigarette loose from her package of Virginia Slims, held a flaming match to it, her hand trembling, and then let out a furious stream of smoke.

Eileen looked at her watch.

"Have you really got the Graveyard?" she asked Kling.

"Would I kid about the Graveyard?" Kling said.

"Come on," Eileen said, "I'll treat you to a taxi."

In the taxi, Kling said, "What'd you think of her?"

"Who, the Encyclopedia Britannica?" Eileen said, and then fell into a fairly good imitation of Marilyn. "Are you familiar with Mendel's Law? Black cats and white cats, brown eyes and blue, dominant and recessive? Do you know that a great may words in the English language sound the same but are spelled differently? Like pause and paws and sent and scent. Or vice versa, like bass the fish and bass the fiddle? Did you know that Grimm's Law changes blue fairies to pink fairies? Did you know that

Yo te adoro means 'I adore you' in Spanish? Did you . . . ?''

"Is that what it means?"

"No, it means 'Would you like to play with my yo-yo?' This is one tough customer, Bert, I'm telling you, hard as nails. Did you catch the murderous intent in those baby blues when she said she'd have *killed* those two guys? Man, I believed her. Last time I saw eyes like that was on a guy who'd just used a Sten gun on his whole family."

"Maybe that's how you get when you're independently wealthy," Kling said.

"And, yeah, what about *that?*" Eileen said. "Was I dreaming, or did I hear her say, 'I *have* a rich father'?"

"That's what you heard."

"So how come five minutes later she's an orphan?"

"Slip of the tongue."

"Sure, because the English language is so *contrary*, right? Is Hal serious about her?"

"I think he's living with her."

"I hope he's not asking for more trouble than he needs," Eileen said.

"I gather you didn't like her much."

"Not much," Eileen said.

"I didn't think she was so bad," Kling said.

"Well," Eileen said, and shrugged. "One man's mead . . .''

"What'd you think of them?" Willis asked.

"They were okay," Marilyn said.

They were walking up toward Harborside Lane. It had stopped raining, but the night had turned very cold; you couldn't trust April in this city. She was clinging to his arm, her head bent against the wind that blew in off the river.

"Only okay?"

"Limited," she said. "Why'd Eileen take the side of those two bums?"

"She wasn't taking their side. She was taking the *law's* side. She's a cop. The woman *did* use a meat cleaver on . . .''

''So Eileen's ready to throw her in jail, never mind the circumstances. She ought to try spending a little time in jail herself. Then maybe she wouldn't make jokes about chopping up your Mama in . . .''

''She's got a heavy load to carry,'' Willis said. ''I don't deny her any jokes she cares to make.''

''Yeah, life is tough all over,'' Marilyn said.

''Tougher for her maybe,'' Willis said. ''She was raped a while back, messed up pretty bad in the process.''

''What do you mean?''

''A case she was working. Guy cut her and raped her. It takes a while to get over something like that. Especially if your job throws you on the street as a decoy.''

Marilyn was silent for several seconds.

Then she said, ''I wish you'd told me that.''

''Well . . . it's sort of family,'' Willis said.

''I thought I was sort of family, too.''

''I meant . . . well . . . what happened to Eileen isn't something we talk about.''

''We,'' Marilyn said.

''The squad,'' he said.

She nodded. They walked in silence, turned the corner.

''I'm sorry I said that about her.''

''That's okay don't worry about it.''

''Really, I'm sorry.''

''That's okay.''

They were approaching the house. He was thinking he had to ask her about that electric distiller, that clipping she'd saved. Had she gone out to *buy* that thing? Was it somewhere in the house? Had she already used it? Too many questions. He sighed deeply.

''What is it?'' she said.

''I have to move the car.''

''What?''

''Alternate side of the street parking. Got to move it before midnight.''

''Don't you have some sort of identification on it?''

''Yes, but . . .''

''Some kind of cop thing?''

"I don't like breaking the law," Willis said, and smiled. "I'll just be a minute, you go on in."

"Hurry," she said, and went to the front door to unlock it.

Willis started walking up the street to where he'd parked his car.

Brown had followed them from the Chinese restaurant, keeping back a good distance, no danger of losing them, the streets were virtually empty at this time of night. Eleven-thirty, he'd tuck the girl in, wait for Delgado to relieve him fifteen minutes from now. He wondered if Willis planned to spend the night here. Was he shacking up with the Hollis woman? Was that part of the stakeout?

He was just coming around the corner when he saw Willis walking up the street toward him. He backpedaled away, ducked into the nearest doorway. What now? he wondered, and then saw Willis unlocking the door to his car. Well, well, he thought, the man *ain't* making it with her, after all, the man's going home to his own little—

Two shots cracked the brittle night air.

Two shots in a row, coming from somewhere in the small park across the street from the building.

Willis threw himself flat to the ground.

Brown came out of the doorway, pistol already in his hand, and started running for the park.

Another shot, and then another, bullets ricocheting off the car door above Willis's head.

"I'm with you, Hal!" Brown shouted over his shoulder. "Artie Brown!"

Insurance against Willis pumping a few slugs into his back.

Willis was off the ground now, yanking his pistol from its hoister, running across the street toward the footpath Brown had already entered. He heard Brown pounding along up ahead there, heard other footfalls in the distance, someone running up the path and then thrashing into the bushes. What the hell is *Brown* doing here? he wondered. And realized in a instant that they'd put a tail on Marilyn.

"Police officer!" he heard Brown shout. "Stop or I'll shoot!"

Two shots in the blackness up ahead, muzzle flashes on the night. He came running up to where Brown was standing on the edge of the path, gun in hand, breathing hard, peering into the bushes.

"Did you get him?" he asked.

"No."

"He still in there?"

"I don't think so," Brown said. "Let's check it out."

They fanned out into the bushes, moving in a slow, steady, flushing pattern some twenty feet apart from each other, until finally they reached the edge of the Park closest to the river.

"Gone with the wind," Brown said.

"Did you get a look at him?"

"No. Man was trying to shoot you, though."

"Tell me about it."

They began walking back through the bushes, up toward the path again.

"You on a stakeout?" Willis asked.

"Yeah," Brown said. "You on it, too?"

"No. Who set it up?"

"The Loot."

Meaning Carella had requested it.

"Better see we can find any spent cartridge cases," Brown said.

"We'll need lights," Willis said. "I'll call in."

He went out of the park and was walking toward his car when the front door of the house opened. Marilyn was standing there in a robe.

"Were those shots?" she asked.

"Yes," he said.

"Who?"

"I don't know. He got away."

"Was he trying for you?"

"Yes."

She came over to the car. Light from the open doorway of the house spilled onto the sidewalk. Willis thumbed open the glove compartment and took out the walkie-talkie.

"Eight-Seven," he said into it. "This is Willis."

"Go ahead, Hal."

"Who's this?"

"Murchison."

"Dave, I'm here at 1211 Harborside Lane. Somebody just tried to blow me away, Brown and I need lights at the scene."

"You got 'em," Murchison said.

"Who's catching upstairs?"

"Kling and Fujiwara just relieved."

"Ask them to check on Charles Endicott, Jr., his address is in the files, they can look in the McKennon folder. I want to know if he's home. If he's not home, I want them to wait there till he *gets* home."

"I'll tell 'em," Murchison said.

"Thanks," Willis said. He took a flashlight from the glove compartment, came out of the car, clipped the walkie-talkie to his belt, and then closed and locked the door. "I guess I won't have to move it, after all," he said.

"You think it was Chip, don't you?" Marilyn said.

"I don't know who it was," Willis said.

"Then why are you sending policemen there?"

"Because he's the one you kissed off this afternoon."

"Why do you need lights?"

"If he was using an automatic, there'll be spent cartridge cases. You'd better go back inside, this may take a while."

He turned on the flashlight, played it on the car door.

"Son of a bitch put two holes in it," he said. "Right above where my head was."

Marilyn looked at the holes in the car door. One was about sixteen inches above the pavement. Another was two inches above that. He saw the puzzled look on her face.

"*That* short I'm not," he said, and smiled. "I was lying flat on my belly." He began playing the flashlight on the pavement at his feet.

"What are you looking for?" she asked.

"Bullets," he said.

"What'll they tell you?"

"The kind of gun he used."

She came into his arms and held him close. "See?" she said. "I'm trying to be family."

The lights in the park were on until two in the morning. A lot of neighbors gathered to watch the policemen milling around over there. None of them knew what was going on. If any of them had heard the earlier shots, they'd dismissed them as backfires. When the police finally turned off the lights, the neighbors went back to their houses. They figured something had happened, but they still didn't know what. The police van carrying the portable equipment drove off. One by one, the patrol cars angled into the curb, backed out and moved off into the night. Willis went to the house across the street, and let himself in with his key.

Marilyn was already in bed. He undressed silently, and climbed into bed beside her. She moved instantly into his arms.

"Did you find anything?" she asked.

"Three bullets and four spent cartridge cases."

"That's good, isn't it?"

"If we ever come up with a gun that matches them."

"Your feet are cold," she said, and snuggled closer to him. "Do you want to make love?"

"No, I want to talk," he said.

"About what happened tonight?"

"No. About what happened this afternoon. While you were having lunch with Endicott."

"I already told you. He was very nice about it . . . well, he's a very nice man. Wished me the best of . . ."

"Marilyn," he said, "I found a clipping in the storeroom. An ad for an electric distiller. Costs three hundred and ninety-five bucks."

"Want to buy it for me?" she said.

"No. I want to know if *you* bought it."

"Why would I buy something like that?"

"You tell me. Why'd you save the clipping?"

"I thought it might be fun to make my own perfume."

"Or your own poison," Willis said.

She was silent for a moment.

"I see," she said at last. "So what do you want to do? Search the house?"

"Do I have to?" he said.

"If you think I've been making *poison* here . . ."

"Have you?"

"Let's search the fucking house."

"Just tell me you didn't buy that distiller."

"I didn't."

He nodded.

"Is that enough for you?" she asked.

"Yes," he said, and kissed her fiercely.

They talked the night away, they loved the night away, as they had that first time here in this house, only now there was the scent of woodsmoke on the air from someone's fireplace up the street, wafting through the open window, and when Marilyn screamed in orgasm, she tried to muffle it because she didn't want cops knocking on the door wanting to know who was being murdered. Nobody was being murdered. Little deaths aside, nobody was getting killed.

But if theories of conspiracy take into account the moment when hands are irrevocably clasped and allegiances permanently sworn, then yes, they were witch-whispered Macbeth and his ambitious lady, confirming to each other in the crucible of dawn that this metal and this metal had been fused into this alloy, and that come what might they were locked into each other as immutably as iron and carbon into steel.

"I love you," he said, "oh, Jesus, how I love you!"

"I love you, too," she said.

She was crying.

16

ON TUESDAY MORNING, APRIL 15, WILLIS AND
Carella met with Byrnes in his office. Elsewhere in the
city, a great many citizens were mailing off their federal
income tax returns. But death is as certain as taxes, and
the men were there to discuss three corpses. Plus an attempt on Willis that could have made *him* a corpse.

"Anything from Ballistics yet?" Byrnes asked.

"Supposed to hear from them sometime today," Willis
said.

"Four shots fired?"

"Recovered three of the bullets and the four spent cartridge cases."

"If it's the same man, he's versatile," Byrnes said
drily.

"Or desperate," Carella said.

"Where was Endicott at the time?" Byrnes asked.

"Home in his beddie," Willis said. "Kling beeped
Hawes—who, by the way, I didn't know was tailing Endicott—and Hawes rapped on his door five minutes after
the shooting. It would've been impossible for Endicott to
get all the way downtown in that time. He was in his
pajamas when he answered the door."

"So we can scratch Endicott," Byrnes said. "How
about the woman?"

"Home," Willis said.

"Across the street?"

"Yes."

"Firing came from the park?"

"Yes."

"So that lets her out," Byrnes said.

"Unless either of them hired the shooter," Carella said.

"Come on, Steve," Willis said, flaring immediately.

"It's a possibility," Byrnes said. "But an extremely remote one. What it looks like to me, we just lost two suspects.''

"I hope we don't lose them for *keeps,*" Willis said.

"What do you mean?"

"I'd like to recommend renewed protective surveillance."

"I'll talk to Frick."

"The sooner the better," Willis said.

"I understand you're living with this woman," Byrnes said.

"Yes, sir. And I've got to tell you it pisses me off that I wasn't informed about the tails on her and Endicott."

"Be that as it may . . .''

"No, sir, I'd like to make this a formal complaint. As far as I know, I'm still working this case, and withholding information from me . . .''

"All right, your point is well taken. We thought, however . . .''

"Who's we?"

"Me and Steve."

"Well, next time let *me* know what you're thinking, okay? And *doing.*"

"I *said* your point was well taken," Byrnes said. "Meanwhile, what've we got now?"

"We should have a make on the gun sometime today," Carella said. "The stabbing instrument is anybody's guess. As for the nicotine, it could've been titrated from a pesticide, or distilled from tobacco mash."

"That takes equipment."

"Yes, sir."

"Which could be anywhere in the city."

"Yes, sir."

"In anybody's possession."

"Yes, sir."

"So where the hell do we start? This case is three weeks old and we're for Christ's sake just *starting!*"

"Sir," Carella said, "what happened last night . . .''

"And I wish to hell you'd both stop sirring me to death. Whenever a cop starts sirring me, I begin thinking he isn't doing his goddamn job."

"Sorry," Carella said, and squelched the "sir" on the tip of his tongue.

"What *about* last night?"

"Until last night, we were working two possibillties. Boy-Meets-Girl or Smokescreen. Somebody knocking off Marilyn Hollis's close friends—some jealous guy, a spurned lover, somebody's girlfriend, whatever. Or the lady *herself* doing them in for whatever reason, and trying to make it *look* like a Boy-Meets-Girl. Okay, last night somebody tried to get Hal. The lady didn't fire those shots, and neither did Endicott. So unless we go with the Hired Gun premise . . ."

"I think we can safely dismiss that," Byrnes said.

"Well, it's still a possibility," Carella said: "And so's the Boy-Meets-Girl. The only problem now . . ."

"I *know* the problem," Byrnes said. "The problem is we've run out of suspects."

"Or maybe we've got too *many* suspects," Carella said. "That depends on the lady."

"How so?" Willis said, bristling again.

"On how active she's been."

Byrnes looked from Carella to Willis.

"How long has she been in this city?" he asked.

"Bit more than a year," Willis said.

"I want a list of everyone she knows here," Byrnes said, "men and women both. People she's dated, people she's socialized with . . ."

"More than that, Pete," Carella sald. "I'd like the names of anyone and everyone she's ever dealt with, even casually—her hairdresser, her doctor, her shoemaker, her grocer, the whole orbit. If this is a grudge-type thing . . ."

"I agree," Byrnes said, and turned to Willis. "Can you get that from her?"

"I'll try," Willis said.

"Never mind *trying*, just *get* it. Meanwhile, I'll talk to Frick about renewing the round-the-clocks on her and Endicott. Do you want protection, too?"

"Is that a rhetorical question?" Willis said.

"I don't know what that means," Byrnes said. "Yes or no?"

"No."

"Good," Byrnes said, and nodded briefly. "Get going."

"Everybody I know?" Marilyn said. "That's ridiculous."

"Everybody," Willis said. "I don't care how insignificant you think . . ."

"I know my goddamn dry *cleaning* man isn't killing anybody!"

"Did you ever have an argument with him?"

"Never."

"Never complained about a spot that wouldn't come out? Never . . ?"

"Well, maybe. But . . ."

"That's exactly the point," Willis said. "If we're dealing with a nut here . . ."

"A spot on a skirt isn't a reason to *kill* somebody."

"For *you* it isn't a reason, for *me* it isn't a reason, but for a *nut* it could be a reason."

"That makes everybody in this *city* a suspect!"

"Do you know everybody in this city?"

"No, but everybody in this city is a nut."

"I only want the people you know. Start with all the men you dated since you came here. Then give me all your girlfriends. Then I want the names of all your professional people—your internist, your gynecologist, your dentist . . ."

"The old one or the new one?"

"Both. Your periodontist . . ."

"I don't have one."

"Your dermatologist, your . . ."

"I don't have a dermatologist, either."

"Your chiropractor, your lawyer, your stockbroker . . ."

"You already have his name."

"List it again. Your accountant . . ."

"You have his, too."

"The real estate broker who sold you this house . . ."

"I bought it from the owner."

"Put his name on the list."

"Her name."

"Your banker, your plumber, your electrician, your butcher, your baker . . ."

"My candlestick maker . . ."

"Are you beginning to get the idea?"

"I'm beginning to get a headache."

"Nothing compared to the one *we'll* have."

Marilyn sighed.

"Okay?" he said.

"I'll need a ream of paper," she said.

The man from Ballistics called at three that Tuesday afternoon.

He reported that an examination of the recovered bullets and cartridge cases indicated they had been fired from a Colt Super .38 automatic pistol.

He explained to Carella—which Carella already knew, but he was always willing to give an expert his time in the sun—that the action of an automatic pistol was what made it possible to identify shells fired from such a pistol. Since the automatic action involved a number of movable parts, and since those parts were made of steel whereas shell casings were made of softer metals like copper or brass, the gun's parts always left marks on the cartridges. And since no two guns were exactly alike, no two guns would mark a cartridge in the same way. Similarly, a bullet could be examined for direction of rifling twists and number of lands and grooves which—together with the cartridge data—would yield a weapon's model and make. Was there anything else Carella needed at the moment? Carella said he did not need anything else at the moment.

He looked at the wall clock.

What the hell was taking Willis so long to get that list?

"That's all of them," Marilyn said, and tossed down the pencil. "I have writer's cramp."

Willis glanced cursorily at the list.

"What would you say? Sixty, more or less."

"It felt like a *hundred* and sixty."

He went to her, kissed the top of her head.

"Thank you," he said.

"De nada," she said.

"I want to get back to the squadroom. I'll call you later, we can figure out what we want to do tonight, okay? We'll have company. They're putting you back on protective."

"Oh, great," she said, and rolled her eyes.

He was starting for the door when she said, "Hal?"

"Yes?"

"Do you really think this could be someone with a grudge?"

"It could be." He looked at her and then said, "Why?"

"No reason," she said, and shrugged.

He came back to where she was sitting.

"Can you think of such a person?" he asked.

"Not really. I mean, it could be anyone, right? The spot on the blouse, right?"

"Or something more important than a spot."

He kept watching her.

Her eyes met his.

"Hal," she said, "suppose . . . suppose a long time ago, I did something that . . . that maybe somebody now is . . . trying to revenge."

"What'd you do?" he asked at once.

"I'm only saying suppose."

"All right, *suppose* you did something. Like what?"

"Like something if . . . if somebody found out about it, maybe they'd want to . . . you know . . . *get* me for it. Or maybe get my *friends* for it. Maybe as a sort of warning, you know? That they were coming for *me*, you know?"

"Who, Marilyn? Who'd be coming for you?"

"I used to know a lot of bad people, Hal."

"Pimps, are you talking about? You think Seward may be coming after you? For running out on him in Houston?"

"No, he let me go with his blessings. I told you that."

"Then who? Your Los Angeles beach bum? That was ancient . . ."

"No, not him. But . . . maybe someone from Buenos Aires."

"Hidalgo? The guy who bought you out of that Mexican prison?"

"No, not him, either. But maybe . . . if somebody in Buenos Aires thought I'd *done* something . . ."

"What'd you do, Marilyn?"

"Nothing. I'm only saying maybe somebody down there got the *idea* I'd done something . . ."

"Who? And how'd he get this idea?"

"People get ideas."

"What people?"

"You know, people. You meet a lot of people in the life. Hidalgo had a lot of friends."

"Hidalgo let you go. He gave you your passport and let you go. Why would any of his friends . . . ?"

"Well, people get ideas, you know."

"What kind of ideas?"

"You know how Spanish men are."

"No, I don't know how they are. Tell me how they are."

"All that *macho* bullshit. You know. Blood brothers. Revenge. You know."

"Revenge for what?"

"For something they think a person might have done."

"Marilyn, what the hell did you *do?*"

She was silent for a long time.

Then she said, "I'll lose you."

"No, you won't. Tell me."

"I'll lose you, I know it."

"Damn it, if somebody's after you . . ."

"Hidalgo didn't *give* me my passport," Marilyn said. "I *took* it."

"You . . ."

"I stole it."

"Is that all you did?" Willis said, relieved. "Honey, honey . . ."

"That's not all I did."

He sat down beside her.

"All right," he said, "let me hear it."

Hidalgo was a man of means, an ambitious pimp with a large clientele serviced by a modest stable. Born in Caracas, he lived in Buenos Aires by choice, and was as paranoid as only someone with a great deal to lose can be. Even recognizing the hold he had over Marilyn, he rarely let her out of his sight, fearful she would either run away or go to the American Embassy. She could have done either, had she realized her true circumstances. The American woman named Mary Ann Hollis was already lost to the Mexican and American authorities; monies had changed hands, records had been destroyed, she had in effect been *sold* to Hidalgo.

But she believed that if she disobeyed him, her parole (or whatever it was) would be revoked, and she would be sent back to *La Fortaleza*. Hidalgo nurtured this misunderstanding from the very beginning, telling her immediately that he was in possession of her passport, which was the truth, and that if she went to the American Embassy to apply for a new one on the grounds that it had been lost or stolen, they would discover at once that she was a convicted felon on parole and in the custody of one Alberto Hidalgo, who was not without influence in Argentina.

"Influence, certainly," she said. "You're a pimp."

"Yes," he said, "that may be true, but the Mexican authorities have nonetheless seen fit to place you in my custody for the remainder of your prison term. As you well know, you will be free to go wherever you wish or do whatever you choose once you have served your full sentence. But, Mariucha, my dear"—all this in his soft, persuasive voice—"you had only served four months of it when you were released in my custody, and you must still serve another five years and eight months until the authorities will consider your debt paid. At which time, of course, they will inform your State Department. But for now, Mariucha, you are not a free woman. You must remember that."

There were six other whores in Hidalgo's stable, all of them very high-priced horseflesh, racehorses as they were known in the trade, bringing prices of upward of a hundred an hour. Most of them had been ransomed from prisons, as Marilyn had been, or else openly abducted into white slavery, as a buxom blonde from Munich claimed she'd been. Each of the girls—Hidalgo called them *"las muchachitas,"* the little girls—felt he had absolute control over their lives and their destinies. If one or another of them ever complained about an indignity to which she'd been submitted, or a future indignity she was being asked to endure, always there was the threat, the reminder that she was not a free agent.

"I won't go," Marilyn told him.

"Yes, you will," Hidalgo said.

"No. You don't own me."

"For certain, I do not own you. The Mexican *prison* system owns you. I am only your legally appointed custodian. But, Mariucha, I must tell you that if you become too troublesome, it would be simpler for me to wash my hands of you completely."

"You wouldn't do that," she said. "You paid them good money. You wouldn't send me back."

"I would merely consider it a bad business investment," Hidalgo said, and shrugged. "I would tell the authorities that you are incorrigible."

"You're a pimp. They wouldn't believe you."

"They would believe *you,* of course," Hidalgo said. "A woman convicted of trafficking in narcotics."

"I wasn't trafficking!"

"A cheap whore," Hidalgo said.

"I'm not a cheap whore," Marilyn said, and began weeping.

He took her in his arms. "There, there, little girl," he said, "why must we argue this way? Do you think it pleases me to have to threaten you?"

"Yes," she said, sobbing.

"No, no, little girl. Please now, no more tears, eh? Go to meet this gentleman, do whatever it is he desires of you. He will be good to you, Mariucha, I promise."

"No," she said. "I'll run away. You'll never find me. I'll go all the way to Santa Cruz, I'll . . ."

"But you do not have a passport," he said gently.

"I don't need a passport to travel inside Argentina. I speak Spanish, everyone will think . . ."

"Oh, yes, with your blonde hair, they will certainly believe you're a native."

"I'll dye my hair black."

"And your eyes? Will you dye them black as well? Mariucha, Mariucha, the police will know in an instant that you are American. They will ask for your passport.''

"I don't care. You can't keep me here."

"Do you know what will happen to you if you run away? Let us say you succeed in getting to any other city in Argentina. Let us say—although it is impossible—that you even managed to cross the border into Chile or Bolivia or Paraguay, let us say that. Do you know what will happen to you? A woman without funds of her own? A woman without a passport? You will become a common street-walker beckoning to tourists. Is that what you want?''

"Yes."

"Mariucha, Mariucha."

"You don't own me," she said.

But she knew that he did.

She never had a cent of her own. She took taxis to and from her various assignations, but the money came from Hidalgo's pocket before she left the apartment she shared with him and the other girls. She paid for all her meals with money Hidalgo provided, and usually ate with the other girls in a small restaurant around the corner from the apartment. Hidalgo bought all her clothing, garments he felt were elegant, but which were only provocative. If ever she wanted to go to a movie, Hidalgo gave her the price of admission beforehand and often asked her for change when she got back to the apartment. If ever she sulked or seemed in any way rebellious, he forced her into alliances he knew she detested, the better to maintain his stubborn rule.

"But why are you *objecting* to this?" he asked. "I know what happened at the Fortress, do you think I'm unaware of what they did to you there?"

"I'm afraid," she said.

"I would not let anyone harm you, you know that. But those men at the Fortress were brutes, and these men are gentlemen who . . ."

"Oh, yes."

"They are, truly. And they asked specifically for you."

"Send one of the other girls."

"No, no, I can't do that."

"Please, Alberto. If you cared for me . . ."

"I do, Mariucha, you know that."

"Then send one of the others. Please, Alberto, please, *querido,* do that for me."

"You are making me impatient," he said. "You are supposed to be there at four o'clock, and it is already three-thirty. Go to them at once, and do what they ask, and do it graciously or—I promise you—you will have reason to regret your impoliteness."

"One of these days," she said, "I'm going to call your bluff."

But she never did.

And the iron grip tightened.

"Mariucha, what is it *now?* What do you object to *now?* I do not understand you, I sometimes think you are taking leave of your senses. What is the matter *this* time?"

"Papa," she said—she had taken to calling him Papa, as did all the other girls—"I'm not going. Send me back to prison, okay? Call whoever it is you have to call. Tell them to come get me."

"I will call the Mexican Embassy at once," he said, and went to the telephone. "As you wish. But will you not at least tell me . . . ?"

"Yes, I'll tell you," she said, "I'll tell you, all right. If you're going to keep sending me to these *creeps*"—the word in Spanish was *patanes*—"then I'd rather go back to prison, I mean it, make your phone call, go ahead."

"Who is this person you're talking about?" Hidalgo asked.

"I'm talking about the man Arabella went to see last week, the man you're sending *me* to right now, I'm talking about the *creep* who . . ."

"He is a gentleman," Hidalgo said.

"Oh, yes, Arabella *told* me what a gentleman he is."

"He comes from a very good family."

"Maybe that's why he likes to shit on people's faces."

"I do not enjoy it when you're crude," Hidalgo said.

"And *I* do not enjoy . . ."

"Forgive me, Mariucha, but I suspect in your heart of hearts that you truly miss the Fortress. I will make the call. I will telephone."

"Good. Do it."

"I will."

"Because you don't *give* a damn, Papa. You just don't give a *damn* about a person's feelings."

"I care for you deeply, Mariucha. I care deeply for all my little girls. But, please, I have had enough of you. Please, no more. Enough." He picked up the telephone receiver.

"Why don't you send Constantia?" she said, naming the girl from Munich. "She'll do anything."

"Yes, she is not an ingrate. I *will* send her perhaps, but only after you are already on your way. I will call for them to come take you. Do you have any personal belongings you wish to pack? You know what it is like in prison. Take whatever you think will help you there. I will not begrudge you the many gifts I've lavished on you."

"Papa, please," she said. "Please don't send me to this man, Papa, I beg of you."

"But I am *not* sending you to him. I am sending you back to prison," he said, and began dialng.

"Por favor," she said. *"Por favor."*

He slammed down the telephone receiver. "Then will there be an *end* to this?" he shouted. "Or must I listen to it day and night forever?"

"I'll . . ."

She shook her head.

"Yes, what is it?"

"Nothing," she said. "Give me the address."

"You will need money for the taxi," he said.

"Yes," she said, and turned away from him because she did not want him to see that she was weeping.

In the fifth year of her indenture to him, and despite all her precautions, she became pregnant by one of Hidalgo's "gentlemen." Hidalgo generously offered to pay for the abortion, but he did not tell her what else he had arranged with *"el médico"* who performed the operation in the dingy back room of a hardware store in one of the worst sections of the city. Marilyn fainted while he was working on her. When she regained consciousness hours later, she was bleeding severely. It was then that Hidalgo told her the doctor—he insisted on calling the man a doctor—had also scalpeled out her uterus.

She struck out with her fists at Hidalgo and the butcher both, and then ran to the bathroom and vomited into the filthy toilet bowl where the fetus still floated. She fainted again, and woke up in the apartment hours later, remembering the horror of her ordeal and screaming as she had in Mexico when she'd been covered with rats, screaming until one of the other girls slapped her and told her to shut up. Before she was fully recuperated, Hidalgo put her back to work again.

That was when she decided she had to kill him.

"No," Willis said. "You didn't. Please, Marilyn, you . . ."

"I did. I killed him."

"I don't want to hear it. Please, I don't want to hear it."

"I thought you wanted the truth!"

"I'm a cop!" he shouted. "If you *killed* a man . . ."

"I didn't kill a *man*, I killed a *monster!* He ripped out my insides, I can't have babies, do you understand that? He stole my . . ."

"Please, please," he said, shaking his head, "please, Marilyn . . ."

"I'd kill him again," she said. "In a minute."

He sat shaking his head, unable to stop shaking his head. He was afraid he would begin crying. He covered his face with his hands.

"I poisoned him," Marilyn said.

He kept shaking his head.

"Cyanide," she said. "For rats."

Shaking his head. Breathing in great gulps of air.

"And then I went into his bedroom and searched for the combination to the safe because I knew that was where my passport had to be. I found the combination. I opened the safe. My passport was in it. And close to two million dollars in Argentine currency."

Willis sighed deeply. He took his hands from his face.

"So what now?" she said. "Do you turn me in?"

The tears came. He took the handkerchief from his hip pocket and wiped at his eyes. He began shaking his head again, sobbing, wiping away the tears.

He did not know what to say.

He was a cop.

He loved her.

He was a cop.

He loved her.

Still sobbing, he went to the front door, and fumbled for the knob, and opened the door—

''Hal?''

—and went out into an afternoon smelling of springtime.

17

HIS EYES WERE SWOLLEN AND RED. CARELLA knew he'd been crying, but he did not ask him why. They were sitting at Carella's desk, side by side, Willis in a chair he'd pulled over, both men studying the list of names Marilyn had provided. Under any circumstances, this would have been a part of police work they found tedious. But there was about Willis a melancholy listlessness that exaggerated the normal boredom of paper legwork, hovering over the desk like a cloud threatening an imminent storm. Carella was tempted to ask, "What is it, Hal?" tempted to say, "Tell me." Instead he went about the work as if it were merely routine, when he knew with every fiber of his being that it was not.

They looked together at the first page, which listed the men Marilyn had dated since her arrival in the city last year. The list was not extraordinarily long. Some twenty-five names on it, Carella guessed.

"Not many addresses," he said.

"Only the ones she knew," Willis said. His voice was toneless. He did not raise his eyes to Carella's. They stayed lowered to the sheet of paper with the names scrawled in her handwriting. Carella could not even guess at what pictures were behind those eyes.

"Means we'll be hitting the phone books," he said.

"Yeah." Same dead voice.

"Did she tell you anything about these people?"

"Everything she could remember. Some of them she only saw once or twice."

"Anybody jump out at you?"

"Nobody I could see."

"Okay," Carella said, and sighed. "Let's get started."

They took her list down the hall to the Clerical Office and ran off a copy on the Xerox machine, her handwriting

228

duplicated now, the names seeming to multiply although the list was still only as long as it had been. Carella started with the Isola directory, Willis with the one for Calm's Point. They might have been accountants hunched over ledgers. They worked in silence, side by side, Willis's gloom almost sentient, jotting down addresses and telephone numbers wherever they found them, putting a check mark beside any name for which no number was published, intending to get those numbers later from the telephone company. It took them almost an hour to match the list of men's names with a partial list of addresses and telephone numbers from all five city directories. The list of women's names was shorter; it took them only forty minutes to come up with a second partial matching of names with addresses and telephone numbers.

It was almost six o'clock when they tackled the list of professionals.

They had come halfway down it when Carella said, "We did this one, didn't we?"

"What?" Willis said. Preoccupied, going down his own list like an automaton, eyes blank.

"This one."

"Which one?"

"Right here."

Willis looked at the name. "Oh," he said and nodded. "Her dentist."

"Are you sure? Isn't he on the other . . . ?"

"Used to be, anyway. She . . ."

"But didn't I see his name on the other list?" Carella said, and turned back to the first page, and began running his finger down it. "Sure," he said, "here it is, Ronald Ellsworth. One of the guys she dated." He looked at the name again. "Ellsworth," he said, and frowned. "Didn't we . . . ?" He frowned again. "Wasn't he . . . ?" And suddenly he looked up sharply, and turned to Willis, and said, "Hal . . ."

"What've you got?" Willis said at once.

"He was McKennon's dentist," Carella said, and immediately shoved back his chair and got to his feet. "Where the hell's that file?" he said, coming around the desk and moving swiftly toward the filing cabinets. "Did she really date him? Or is that a mistake? His name on the other list?''

''No, she dated him for a month or so.''

Carella threw open the file drawer, yanked the McKennon folder, came back to the desk, and began leafing through it. ''Here,'' he said. ''I talked to Ellsworth after we caught the Hollander case. Here's the report. April second. I talked to him in his apartment, here's the address.''

The two men looked at each other.

''Get on the phone to Marilyn,'' Carella said, ''find out *when* she dated him, when she *stopped* dating him, and *why* she stopped. Where's that dental chart Blaney sent over?''

Willis was already dialing Marilyn's number. Carella took a quick look at McKennon's dental chart, and then began dialing the Medical Examiner's Office.

''Marilyn,'' Willis said into the phone, ''it's me. Tell me about this guy Ellsworth.''

''Hello, yes,'' Carella said into his phone. ''Paul Blaney, please.''

''When was that?'' Willis said. ''Uh-huh. For how long? Uh-huh. And why'd you stop seeing him?''

''Paul,'' Carella said, ''this is Steve Carella. I've got some questions on the McKennon dental chart.''

They did not get to Ellsworth's apartment on Front Street until seven-thirty that night. That was because they had to go all the way downtown first. Ellsworth and his wife were having dinner when they arrived. Mrs. Ellsworth—he introduced her as Claire—was a pleasant-looking woman in her late thirties, Carella guessed, with remarkably beautiful dark brown eyes.

''We were just about to have coffee,'' she said. ''Won't you join us?''

''Thanks, no,'' Carella said, ''there are just a few questions we'd like to ask your husband.''

''Well, sit down anyway,'' she said.

''Privately,'' Carella said, watching Ellsworth's face. Not a flicker there. Mrs. Ellsworth seemed puzzled for a moment. She looked at her husband, looked back at Carella, and then said, "Well, I'll leave you then." She looked at her husband yet another time, and then went into a room Carella guessed was the bedroom. A moment later, he heard a television set going.

"So," Ellsworth said, "are you making any progress?"

He was wearing blue jeans and a loose-fitting sweater, the sleeves shoved up on his forearms. The sweater matched his blue eyes. Those eyes were smiling behind his dark-rimmed glasses. There was a smile on the mouth below his sandy brown mustache. He could have been announcing to a patient that he'd found no cavities.

"Dr. Ellsworth," Carella said, opening his notebook, "when I was here on the second of April, I asked you some questions . . ."

"Yes?" Ellsworth said.

"I asked you if Mr. McKennon had ever mentioned any of the following names to you: Marilyn Hollis, Nelson Riley, Charles Endicott and Basil Hollander. You told me he had not."

"That's right," Ellsworth said.

"That *is* what you told me, isn't it?"

"If that's what you have in your notes . . ."

"Yes, that's what I have in my notes," Carella said, and snapped the book shut. "Dr. Ellsworth, was Marilyn Hollis ever a patient of yours?"

"Marilyn . . . what was the last name again?"

"Hollis. H-O-L-L-I-S."

"No, I don't believe so."

"Wasn't she a patient of yours from December of last year through the early part of February *this* year?"

"Not to my recollection."

"Wasn't she, in fact, the person who recommended you to Jerome McKennon?"

"I don't believe Mr. McKennon came to me on anyone's recommendation," Ellsworth said.

Toughing it out, Carella thought. We've got him cold, and he's toughing it out.

"Dr. Ellsworth," Willis said, "isn't it true that in December of last year, while Marilyn Hollis was still your patient, you asked her out . . ."

"No, that's not true," Ellsworth said sharply and glanced toward the bedroom door.

". . . and saw her a total of six times before she . . ."

"I didn't see her at *all!* What is this?" Ellsworth asked indignantly.

They always said the same thing, Carella thought. The indignant *What is this?*

"Dr. Ellsworth," Willis said, "we have very good reason to believe that you were seeing Marilyn Hollis socially, that in fact you were intimate with Miss Hollis, and that she ended her relationship with you in February when she learned . . ."

"I think I've heard just about enough of this," Ellsworth said.

Carella had also heard *that* one before.

"Dr. Ellsworth," he said, "I have here a search warrant granted earlier this evening by a supreme court magistrate, empowering us to search your person and the premises here as well as the premises at 257 Carrington Street, where your dental office is. Would you care to look at this warrant, Dr. Ellsworth?"

"Search? A search warrant? For what?"

"Specifically for a Colt Super .38 automatic pistol. Do you own such a gun?"

"It's in the top drawer of his dresser," Mrs. Ellsworth said.

The detectives turned at once. She was standing in the open door to the bedroom.

"You bastard," she said.

And Ellsworth broke for the front door.

Willis's gun came out of its holster.

"Freeze!" he shouted.

Ellsworth kept running.

"Stop or I'll shoot!" Willis shouted. The gun was trembling in his hand. The muzzle was leveled on the center of Ellsworth's back.

"Don't force me!" he shouted.

Ellsworth stopped dead.

He turned.

He looked past the detectives to where his wife was still

standing in the bedroom door, a sitcom laugh track blaring
from the television set behind her.

"I'm sorry," he said to her.

Which line, too, Carella had heard a hundred times before.

The Q & A took place in Lieutenant Byrnes's office at
nine forty-five that night. Present were Detective/Lieuten-
ant Peter R. Byrnes, Detective/Second Grade Stephen L.
Carella, Detective/Third Grade Harold O. Willis, an assistant district attorney named Martin J. Liebowitz, and
the man they had charged with three counts of murder and
one count of attempted murder, Dr. Ronald B. Ellsworth.

Because Willis had spoken to Marilyn Hollis about her
relationship with Ellsworth, he handled the early part of
the questioning. Because Carella had spoken to Paul Blaney about McKennon's dental chart, he picked up where
Willis left off.

Q: Can you tell us when Marilyn Hollis first came to
   your office?

A: In December sometime. Last year in December.

Q: Miss Hollis says it was on December fourth, a
   Wednesday according to her appointment calendar.

A: I don't recall the exact date. If that's what her appointment calendar . . .

Q: Yes, that's the date in her calendar. Did you continue
   to see her regularly as a patient after that date?

A: I did. She needed extensive treatment. Her teeth were
   in very bad condition, I don't know why she'd let
   them go so long without adequate dental care.

Q: According to Miss Hollis, shortly before Christmas,
   you asked her out. Is that correct?

A: It is.

Q: And continued seeing her on a more or less regular
   basis . . .

A: I saw her six times.

Q: A total of six times during December, January and
   February—when she ended the relationship.

A: Yes. Six times.

Q: Were you at any time intimate with Miss Hollis?

A: I was.

Q: Can you tell us now why Miss Hollis ended the relationship? Excuse me, I'd like to ask first if she
   terminated your *professional* services at the same
   time.

A: She did.

Q: And this was early in February, was it not?

A: It was.

Q: Why did she stop seeing you, Dr. Ellsworth?

A: I made a mistake.

Q: Sir?

A: She was always talking about total honesty, I made
   the mistake of being honest with her.

Q: In what way?

A: I told her I was married.

Q: What was her reaction to this?

A: She told me she never wanted to see me again. She said she didn't date married men.

Q: What was your reaction to that?

A: Well, what do you think it was? I was furious.

Q: But your anger had no effect on her, isn't that right? She did, in fact, stop seeing you.

A: She did.

Q: Now, Dr. Ellsworth, when did Mr. McKennon start coming to you as a patient?

A: Late in January.

Q: And he came on Miss Hollis's recommendation, did he?

A: Yes. She told him I was a good dentist. That was before we broke up, of course. Then I *wasn't* such a good dentist anymore. Then she stopped coming to me.

Q: He said she had recommended you as a good dentist?

A: He said a friend of his had recommended me. I'm not sure whether he told me at the time that the friend was Marilyn. I may have learned that later.

Q: He did not mention her name on his first visit?

A: He may have, I don't remember. I guess he did. But at the time, I didn't know what his relationship with Marilyn actually was. He only said a friend. I didn't know they were sleeping together.

Q: When did you discover that?

A: In February sometime.

Q: How did that come about?

A: I had seen him several times by then. I did an extraction, as I recall, and several fillings. I also recommended that a root canal be done on the lower
right first molar. We'd become quite friendly—within
the context of a professional relationship, of course.
I believe it was during one of those visits that he
mentioned Marilyn.

Q: Said he was intimate with her?

A: Well, you know the way men talk.

Q: What did he say, exactly, Dr. Ellsworth?

A: He said he was fucking this terrific woman, said he'd
never had a woman like her in his life.

Q: He was referring to Marilyn Hollis, of course.

A: Yes. Well, I didn't know that at first. It wasn't until
later that he told me her . . .

Q: Later during that same visit?

A: Yes. He was rinsing, I believe. He said Well, you
remember the girl who sent me here, don't you?
She's the one I'm fucking.

Q: And what was your reaction to that?

A: Anger.

Q: Why?

A: Because she'd thrown *me* overboard—a professional
man—and she'd taken up with this idiot who worked
for a *burglar*-alarm company!

Q: Did you mention to him that you'd been dating Miss Hollis?

A: Of course not! I'm a married man!

Q: Then he didn't know that you'd also shared a personal relationship with her?

A: He did not know.

Q: This anger you experienced . . .

A: *Rage!*

Q: Was it transmitted to Mr. McKennon? Was he aware . . . ?

A: No, no, of course not. He never once suspected.

Q: Suspected what, Dr. Ellsworth?

A: Why, that I was going to kill him.

Q: Did you, in fact, kill him?

A: I did.

Q: Did you also kill Basil Hollander?

A: I did.

Q: Why?

A: For the same reason. An accountant, for Christ's sake! Because, you see, after McKennon was out of the way, I began to wonder if there were any *others*. So I began following her. And, of course, there *were* others, plenty of others, oh, a fine little slut *she* is, I can tell you!

Q: Did you kill Mr. Hollander with a knife?

A: A scalpel. From my office.

Q: Did you also kill Nelson Riley?

A: I did. He was another one, you see. She was seeing
   four men altogether. I was going to kill Endicott
   next, the lawyer. But then . . .

Q: Yes.

A: This is nothing personal.

Q: What is it, Dr. Ellsworth?

A: Well, she started seeing *you*. So I . . . it was going
   to take some planning to get to Endicott, the way it
   had with Riley. Getting into that loft was no picnic,
   believe me. So I needed time to get to Endicott.
   And you were handy. You were living with her,
   weren't you? I assumed you were. Which made it
   simple to track you. I've had that gun for a long
   time, by the way, I even have a Carry permit for it.
   I told them I sometimes transport gold, for fillings,
   you know, which was stretching the truth a bit, but
   they gave me the Carry permit.

Q: You tried to kill me—I identify myself for the tape,
   Detective Harold O. Willis, Detective/Third Grade,
   Eighty-seventh Squad—with this gun, is that correct? I show you a Colt Super .38 automatic pistol
   with the serial number 3478-842-106.

A: That's correct, that's my gun.

Q: How did you kill Nelson Riley?

A: I put nicotine in a bottle of scotch I found on a shelf
   in his loft.

Q: How did you kill Jerome McKennon?

A: Nicotine. I would have used nicotine on Hollander, too, but there was no way I could get to him. So I just went in there with the scalpel.

Q: How'd you get into the apartment?

A: I just walked in.

Q: He let you into the apartment?

A: No, no. I tried the knob, and the door was *open!* I couldn't believe it! This city? A man leaves his door unlocked? So I walked in, and he was sitting in the living room, reading, and I stabbed him.

Q: If the door had been locked, what would you have done?

A: Knocked. And stabbed him when he opened it.

Q: Because you were angry with him as well, is that correct?

A: Oh, all of them.

Q: Because Miss Hollis had stopped seeing you . . .

A: Yes.

Q: And was continuing to see them.

A: I loved her.

Q: Steve?

Q: Dr. Ellsworth, I show you this dental chart prepared by Dr. Paul Blaney of the Medical Examiner's Office. It is a chart of the condition of Jerome McKennon's teeth at the time of autopsy. By looking at this chart, can you tell me whether it appears to be an accurate representation?

A: Well, yes, I would say so. There's the extraction I performed, the number sixteen tooth, and there are the several fillings I did, yes, that's his mouth. The other work had already been done before he came to me.

Q: And the root canal?

A: Yes, on the number thirty tooth. The lower right first molar.

Q: You performed that root canal, did you not?

A: I did.

Q: Removed the nerve, I believe you told me, when Mr. McKennon visited you in February . . .

A: If that's when it was, yes.

Q: And obtunded the root canal, sealed it . . .

A: Yes.

Q: And on March eighth, you fitted it with a temporary cap . . .

A: Yes. A temporary plastic cap.

Q: And when he came back a week later, you took an impression of the tooth for a permanent cap, and—as you also told me—cemented the temporary cap back on.

A: Yes.

Q: Dr. Blaney of the Medical Examiner's Office suggested that you may have done something *else* during that visit. Did you?

A: Yes.

Q: What did you do, Dr. Ellsworth?

A: I hollowed out the middle of the tooth, down to the floor of the pulp chamber.

Q: Did you do anything else?

A: Yes. I inserted a number five gelatin capsule into the tooth. That's the biggest tooth in the mouth, you know, that molar, and the number five is the smallest capsule there is, only ten millimeters long and four millimeters wide. But even then I had to shave the capsule down a bit—where the two ends slip into each other—to get it inside the tooth.

Q: What did you do then?

A: I cemented the temporary cap back on.

Q: With the capsule inside the tooth?

A: Yes.

Q: And covered by the temporary cap.

A: Yes.

Q: What was in that capsule, Dr. Ellsworth?

A: A fatal dose of nicotine.

Q: Dr. Blaney at the Medical Examiner's Office indicated on the chart—here's the mark, Dr. Ellsworth, this small circle on the number thirty tooth—that there was a cavity in the temporary cap. He had a theory as to how that cavity got there, but I'd like to hear your explanation of it.

A: Well, you see, I had thinned out the underside of the chewing surface. Of the temporary cap. Before I cemented it back into place. And I told Jerry—Mr.

McKennon—that he could chew and brush normally
until the next visit . . .

Q: Which would have been on March twenty-ninth, two
weeks after the March fifteenth visit.

A: Yes.

Q: What did you expect to happen, Dr. Ellsworth?

A: I expected the normal grinding motion of the upper
and lower molars would erode the temporary cap.

Q: And then what?

A: Then the gelatin capsule would dissolve and the poison would be released.

Q: Killing Mr. McKennon within minutes.

A: The number five capsule holds from sixty-five to a
hundred and thirty milligrams, depending on the
chemical. I didn't need quite that much.

Q: Forty milligrams of nicotine is the fatal dose, isn't
that right?

A: Yes.

Q: How did you come by nicotine in toxic strength, Dr.
Ellsworth? Did you distill it from tobacco?

A: No. I used an insecticide called Spot Forty. I bought
it over the counter in the next state. It has a nicotine
content of forty percent.

Q: How did you get nicotine in toxic strength from . . .

A: I'm a dentist. I had access to laboratory equipment.

Q: In your office?

A: No, at a research lab. I told them I was conducting an experiment on the effectiveness of fluoride in removing nicotine stains from teeth. They even allowed me to use chromatographic instruments.

Q: As I understand it then, you took a can of this insecticide called Spot Forty into the lab . . .

A: No. It was *several* cans. And I emptied them first into glass containers.

Q: And kept titrating the solution until you had the purity of nicotine you were looking for.

A: Yes.

Q: How long did it take you to do this?

A: Not long. My college grades in chemistry were very high, straight A's, as I recall. I decided to kill Jerry the day he told me about him and Marilyn. I was ready to kill him by the eighth of March when I did the root canal. I had the poison ready by then.

Q: Hal?

A: Nothing else.

Q: Mr. Liebowitz?

A: Nothing.

Q: Is there anything you'd like to add to what you've said, Dr. Ellsworth? Anything you'd like to change?

A: Nothing. Except . . .

Q: Yes?

A. You see I figured she'd come back to me. If the

others were gone, I figured there was a chance of getting her back.

Q: I see.

A: Yes. That was it, you see.

Q: Anything else, Dr. Ellsworth?

A: No. Well . . .

Q: Yes?

A: No, nothing.

Q: Then thank you, Dr. Ellsworth.

A: Just . . . would you play the tape back for me, please?

They went out of the precinct and into the fenced lot behind it, where they had parked their cars. The night was balmy; spring was truly here.

"I was wrong," Carella said.

"We were both wrong," Willis said. "We were zeroing in on too narrow a range. We should have been looking wider."

"That's not what I meant, Hal." He said it again. "I was wrong."

"Okay," Willis said.

Carella extended his hand. "Good night, huh?" he said.

Willis took the hand. "Good night, Steve."

They got into their cars, and drove out of the parking lot, and then off in opposite directions, Carella to his house in Riverhead, Willis to the house on Harborside Lane.

It was a little before midnight when he got there. She was sitting in the living room, a brandy snifter on the endtable near her chair. She was wearing a white caftan. He did not know if it was the one she'd worn so many years ago, when she was known as the Golden Arab in a prison called the Fortress. She wore no makeup. Her eyes looked puffy and swollen. He went to the bar unit and poured himself a cognac.

He told her about Ellsworth, told her they had a signed confession.

The clock on the mantel chimed midnight.

Twelve soft chimes into the silence of the room.

He went to where she was sitting.

"You've been crying," he said.

"Yes."

"Why?"

"Because I know I've lost you."

"Marilyn . . ."

"Oh, shit, here it comes."

"Marilyn, I'm a short, little ugly guy . . ."

"You're beautiful."

"And you're tall and gorgeous . . ."

"Sure, with my eyes all red and my nose dripping."

"I've been to bed with maybe six girls in my entire life . . ."

"The rest of the women in the world are missing something."

"And you've known ten thousand men . . ."

"You're the only man I've ever really known."

"Marilyn, you're a hooker . . ."

"Was."

"And a thief . . ."

"True."

"And a murderer."

"Yes, I killed the son of a bitch who was destroying me."

"Marilyn . . ."

"And I *enjoyed* it! The way you enjoyed killing that kid with the .357 Magnum in his fist. Only I had a better reason."

"Marilyn . . ."

"What are you going to tell me? You're a cop? Okay, you're a cop. So turn me in."

"Do they know you killed him?"

"Who? The Argentine cops? Why would they even *give* a damn about a dead pimp? But, yes, I'm the only one who split from the stable, yes, and the safe was open, and a lot of bread was gone, so yes, they probably figured I was the perpetrator, is that the word you use?''

''Is there a warrant out for your arrest?''

''I don't know,'' she said.

Silence.

''So what are you going to do?'' she said. ''Phone Argentina? Ask them if there's a warrant out on Mary Ann Hollis, a person I don't even *know* anymore? *What*, Hal? For Christ's sake, I love you, I want to live with you forever, I love you, Jesus, I *love* you, what are you going to *do?*''

''I don't know,'' he said.